Into the

Chapter 1

L*ACHLAN*
Kingdom of Rohn, Emuria

The stench of horse and sweat is thick in the air, but at least up here, high above the plains, we are free of the flies and mosquitoes that arrive every summer. My soldiers are pleased to be returning to the mountains; I would delay this return if I could. But a King can only spend so long away from his throne. We've been on patrol for six weeks, and my soldiers are tired and eager to see their families. As for me, I have no wish to resume my pacing of the empty corridors with nothing but thoughts of my wife to keep me company. Wife! What a joke that is.

Sara is not my wife. Not in any true sense. *She could have been*, that voice in my head taunts me. I know that voice too well and silence it quickly. The soldiers are boisterous, laughing and jostling each other along the narrow paths. I wish I could share their excitement at returning to Rohn. My dark moods are impossible to hide lately, and needing to put some distance between myself and the rest of the group, I give my horse reign, nudging its flank with my heel. Less than five minutes pass, and I hear another horse closing the

1

distance and falling in alongside me. I don't need to look to know that it's Izod. That Fae never lets me out of his sight.

"You know I'm not letting you ride on alone, your majesty." He offers my title with a sardonic twist of his lips, which makes me laugh. He's the only one of my soldiers who would dare address me this way.

"I wasn't going far." But he only shakes his head, and I give him up trying to make my escape.

"Have you heard from her?" His quiet question startles me, and I'm too shocked to answer for a minute. While I'm aware that Izod knows everything about me, he doesn't usually voice his concerns. To do so now means he's as anxious about her as I am... or worried about me and my worsening temper.

"Sara?" I ask, just to be clear, and he nods sharply. His dark eyes scan my face and then move past me, checking the mountains. Izod can find danger in a small bunch of daisies. Although to give him his due, he has foiled at least three assassination attempts in the last year.

"No word from Sara... or Arlen," I add. Thinking about my brother hurts nearly as much as thinking about my wife.

"Do you think she followed him to Soraya?" The blunt way Izod asks that question hurts. As though it's obvious, as though it's the only possible explanation for her disappearance.

I don't want to answer his question. I don't want to think about my wife.

Liar.

When I growl out my frustration, I feel Izod's eyes on me again. I know he's worried about me. I'm worried about me.

Winter has finally released its grip on Rohn. The snow has melted, sending torrential waterfalls cascading down the cliffs. The mountains are green and wild, and the fjords an icy blue far below us. This is the Rohn that I love, this is the Rohn that I wanted to show Sara, but she left just as the snow was starting to melt. As if she was a part of that icy landscape. Now this beauty around me only makes me feel bitter and old.

My eyes snag on the outline of the city walls, and a heavy weight presses down on my shoulders; the thought of returning to that dark castle depresses me more each day. No matter what I do, I can't shake the menace from its stones.

Because the darkness behind those stone walls is the same darkness that lives inside you.

Is that why Sara left? I don't know. My wife is a mystery to me. A beautiful, alluring mystery.

After six months of marriage, she finally let me kiss her. One kiss. That was all it took for her to break through my magic and get inside my head. *Inside me.* And then she ran. Disappeared in the middle of the night. I can't even think of that night without fear clasping at my throat. Why would she do something so reckless? She knows how dangerous Emuria can be. I don't understand, and knowing she's safe doesn't help the panic from waking me most nights.

It's not just the panic that wakes you, the voice again, snide this time, and I huff out a tired breath as I acknowledge that he's right about that.

It's been six weeks since I kissed Sara, and I can't even think of that kiss without wanting to drag her back to Rohn. With my Tracker magic, I could have her at my side within a day, and as her King, I could force her to live here with me. Force her to be a real wife to me. Real in every sense. A growl rumbles in my chest; *I want my wife.* That whispering voice startles me. I don't want to force Sara to stay with me. That was never what I wanted.

But the beast in me is restless and demanding. Sara woke him, and she did it with just one kiss. If I let her have more of me, I might not survive it. My beast will push me to the background and take over completely, destroying everything I am. That kiss lasted mere minutes— minutes that are tattooed onto my skin. Her soft sigh against my lips made me yearn and ache for more. When her fingers tangled in my hair, holding me to her, I finally let my lips touch hers, softly at first and then more firmly, demanding, needy. I couldn't get close enough.

And then the recoil.

The shock.

Her hands on my chest, shoving me away from her. She didn't say a word, no explanation. She turned and ran out of the room, her magic shields shored up so tight around her even my magic couldn't understand; I couldn't get a read on her. Not that I tried. I know what sent her running. My wife had finally met the beast inside me.

This beast is the curse of the Rohn Kings— in our blood lives a dark, angry creature that prowls beneath our skin, waiting to feast on the weak. I have spent my whole life keeping it in check, controlling every impulse, every desire. But with Sara, I'm weak, and the beast knows it. After that kiss, he wanted her even more than I did. For months I managed to keep Sara at a polite distance. It was an arranged marriage, and she had made it clear from the beginning that she didn't want anything real from me. That suited me fine—my beast was unhappy, but I was okay with that too. I didn't want him anywhere near Sara. He was not entitled to a say in this. But then that kiss—

The castle gateway looms over me, and I realize we're home. The last three miles have passed in a blur, my thoughts too full of Sara to see anything else. A darkness that has nothing to do with my beast brushes against my magic, and the rumbling in my chest grows louder.

Leading my horse to one side of the courtyard, away from my soldiers, I try to calm the beast. He's close to the surface today, ready to break free. I sense him sniffing the air, tracking Sara, searching for her scent. *She's gone*, I try to convince him but fail... he doesn't believe me.

A movement from above catches my eye, and tilting my head back, I hold one hand to my eyes to block the glare of the sun. The white hawk, larger than our native red-tailed hawks, is as rare as the unicorn and dragon in our realm. This mythical white hawk is the reason I married Sara. The hawk's sudden appearance on the morning of Luneda's missive was a sign that I should agree to her treaty. The Queen of Soraya suggested a marriage alliance to heal the rift between our two kingdoms. She offered me her niece as a bride in exchange for my support in her war against the Ruark. Of course, I knew who Sara was. Like all royal families in Emuria, I have my spies in the other kingdoms.

I couldn't have cared less about Luneda, her alliance, or her niece, but... the white hawk was a sign. It was a sign I would gladly have ignored, but my magic whispered at me with such insistence that I knew I had no choice but to accept Luneda's treaty. My council was unhappy, and the Rohn Fae were unhappy. In truth, I was unhappy. What did I want with a wife? Especially a Sorayan wife, although the fact that she had human blood in her veins eased my fears somewhat. Soraya and Rohn have always had a difficult relationship. My father's death inside a Sorayan prison fifteen years ago only cemented the hatred between our two kingdoms.

But the signs mattered; for better or worse, my magic was telling me to take Sara as my wife. It wasn't until the day I met her that I understood. She strode into my ballroom, refusing to acknowledge the Fae courtiers who had gathered to meet their new Queen and walked right up to me. No curtsy, no respect, no fear. More than one of my bodyguards had drawn their weapons, fearing she intended to harm me, but all she did was stand there and look at me. She was tall, nearly as tall as me, her eyes as bright as the emeralds in my crown, that opalescent green that glows in the dark. Fae eyes. I nearly lost myself in them.

The hall had remained silent, waiting for me to put her in her place, and she knew it too because her mouth seemed to smile even though her lips did not move. I felt that smile inside me, and just like that, the bonding was real. I had doubted the strength of the bonding ceremony. She was human, after all. But as those thoughts slid through my mind, she tilted her head and examined me, her eyes dancing over my face, neck, chest, and lower. Everywhere her eyes touched— I felt it. Her gaze brushed against my skin, caressing me and... I blushed. Me, the King of Rohn and a Fae fully grown at thirty years of age— I blushed. But the heat rushing through my body was more than embarrassment. It was desire. My beast stirred; the fur on his back stood up, brushing against the underside of my skin. Sara's eyes had widened, and then she took a small step back as though she felt him too.

"Your Highness, My Lord." Snapping my attention back to the present, I see my soldiers waiting for me to dismiss them. I give the signal and turn back to the Fae standing beside my horse.

"What is it?"

"They've found another body, My Lord." I'm slow to understand his words, and instead of responding turn my eyes toward the sky again, searching for the hawk. She's still there. I watch as she circles above the castle, flying higher and out of sight toward the ocean. The ocean?

"Where was the body found?"

"On the banks of the Schoenberg fjord."

"Elf? Again?" The Fae's face twists with anxiety before he answers, but that look has already told me everything I need to know.

"Yes, My Lord."

Concealing my fear beneath a frown, I glance again toward the sky. The hawk is gone. "Here." I toss the reins in his direction and leap down from my horse. This situation is getting out of hand. Pure-blood Elves are nearly as rare as the white hawks, but this was the third Elf to turn up dead in the last four months. All of them drowned. Drowned— the hawk flew toward the ocean. What is the connection? Is there trouble in the Mer Kingdom? More than usual?

Frowning as I consider this, I push through the large wooden doors and enter the castle.

I ignore the warm cloak a servant holds out to me. What is it with the cloaks? The castle is warm enough. My magic has ensured that... but the court Fae will still insist on the old ways. My father always wore the royal cloak when he was inside, so I'm expected to do the same— even though I have been King for fifteen years and never once in those fifteen years have I ever needed a cloak for warmth. Brushing these thoughts aside with my usual impatience, I stride quickly toward the library, one of the only rooms in this castle where I can think straight. I need advice... from someone I can trust. For one minute only, I consider taking this matter to my council, but my magic warns me against it... that is not the help I need.

I have always associated the white hawk with news of Sara, but what if this has nothing to do with my wife? What if— and then I freeze in my tracks. Where is Sara? Is she safe? Dead Elves, white hawk, Sara. What is the connection between the three? And just like that, I know who I need to speak to.

SARA

Cork, Ireland

Do I love my husband? I consider my sister's question. This a curious question coming from Lilly, especially as she knows my marriage was an arranged one. How could I love him? I hardly know him... I mean, we're bonded, so I guess

I know him a tiny bit. His thoughts flit through my mind occasionally, but only when he forgets himself.

Lachlan is as remote and isolated as that home of his high up in the Rohn mountains. An icy fortress except for... I feel that familiar tingling and stirring in my body, a little reminder from my magic. He's not cold in my dreams. In my dreams, he burns through me, in me, his hands scalding me as they caress every inch of my body. After one of those dreams, I wake in a sweaty mess, aching, my hand between my thighs the only way to satisfy myself.

Wishful thinking or a premonition? Since discovering I'm a Seer, I have been learning to distinguish between the two, but I can never think clearly when it comes to my husband. It's hard to imagine the disciplined and stoic Lachlan has a passionate bone in his body – but that kiss. Our marriage was meant to stop a war, and once we'd achieved that, I would have left Rohn for good... but I couldn't bring myself to do it. And then my mom asked me to stay. *For Emuria's sake, the realm needs stability,* she had insisted. Was it guilt that made me stay? Was this my way of making up for not being around when my dad got sick?

Hardly a sound basis for a marriage. No wonder we failed. Frustration flays me, and I slam the front door with more force than it deserves. *You left him, Sara,* I berate myself. *Did you really think he would follow?* I shake my head at my foolishness. It's not like I was looking for love, but some warmth would have been nice, some indication that he noticed me around. When he finally kissed me, I thought, hallelujah, at last!! But no, like everything else with that infuriating Fae King, he was doing it for show, for a purpose.

I was so lost in his kiss that it took me a minute to realize the truth. I thought he felt the same overwhelming passion and heat until I noticed the Fae councilors gathered at the other side of the ballroom.

And then I felt like the biggest fool in that whole castle. Lachlan wasn't lost in passion; he was making a show of me. Putting me in my place and demonstrating to those awful Fae men how weak I am. When I pulled back from that kiss, he didn't even look repentant. He smirked at me like he'd just proven a point. And the most intelligent thing I could think of to do was run...just to prove to Lachlan and his awful advisors how foolish and silly I am. I'm sure they all had a good laugh at the young human Queen. The human part always said with a sneer.

"Sara, check the pot, will you? I think the water's boiling over." My brother, Cian, shouts from upstairs. Before I have a chance to respond, his girlfriend, Breanna, steps into the passage.

"I've got it," she shouts back up to him and brushes past me. As she does, she runs a soothing hand down my arm. "Hey, Sara."

Stopping in place, I squeeze my eyes shut to prevent my tears from spilling over. I can hide behind my anger with everyone else, but Breanna's different. It's impossible to lie to Breanna. Not only is she an Elf, but she is literally a mind-reader. After standing in the passage for a quiet minute, I follow her into the kitchen and flop down into the nearest chair.

"How was the gallery?" she asks over her shoulder "Busy today?"

"It was okay. As exciting as ever." I pull a face, and Breanna grins. My sister, Lilly, is away for a few months - touring Italy is what all of our human friends believe, but really she's in Emuria with her husband. And me— I'm working in her art gallery. But that's my fault for walking out of my marriage without a plan. Now I'm back in the family home and working for my big sister in a job that is as interesting as watching paint dry.

Cian strolls into the room and wraps his arms around Breanna, pulling her back against his chest. They look good together. Like us, Breanna is the product of a mixed marriage, and her brown skin is only a touch paler than Cian's. Her hazelnut-colored afro sits like a halo about her face and looks so cute it almost makes me miss my own afro. I fiddle with the long braids trailing over my shoulder.

Cian plants a quick kiss on Breanna's neck, and I avert my eyes. It's so weird seeing my twenty-two-year-old brother all loved up like this. He's too young to be so serious about a girl. *Who are you to talk, Sara? You're twenty-four and already married.* I accept that with a small sigh. Our time in Emuria has changed all of us. Our mom is now a Queen, Lilly is heir to the Sorayan throne and married to a Fae warrior... and besides, why shouldn't Cian love Breanna? Life is too short not to take love wherever you can find it.

"Where are the twins?" I ask, hoping to distract the other two from all their very public fondling. Cian looks over his shoulder at me and smirks as though he knows exactly why I'm asking. He releases Breanna, though, and turns toward me.

"Clodagh's working in the pub tonight. And Aoife is..." he pauses, and I know he's using his magic to get a sense of our sister, and then he grins. "One, two, three," he announces just as I hear a key turn in the lock and the front door open. I laugh at Cian. He's such a cocky shit that it's easy to forget what a powerful magician he is. He keeps his magic quiet— putting all his focus on the geeky, nerdy tech stuff he does. All that computer stuff that I have no interest in. I swear my brother is so good he could hack the government if he wanted to. Bloody nerd.

I'm surrounded by brilliance on all sides. My big sister, Lilly, is an accomplished artist. My geeky champion hacker brother is brilliant at everything he does, and now even the twins are outshining me. They both aced their final exams. I didn't even finish school. I left after my Junior Cert. My dyslexia made school a nightmare, and as all I ever wanted to do was climb, there didn't seem to be any point in staying in school. Now here I am at twenty-four with no other skills and too afraid to climb a hill, never mind a mountain. My career is in pieces, smashed against those same cliffs that killed Josh. Fuck! I am such a loser.

I look up as Aoife bounces into the room with a big smile. "I have a job for the summer," she announces brightly, and I sit up straighter, trying not to show my panic.

"I thought you were going to work in the gallery for the summer?"

"Oh, I will. Of course, I will, Sara. I wouldn't do that to you. I know you want out of it. I meant another job." She smiles sweetly at me and pumps soothing magic my way. The tension slips down my spine. Aoife is a powerful healer, and a dose of her gentle energy is better than any drug. She smiles at me again and then continues with her news. "There's this cute little bookstore on French Church Street looking for someone to work part-time."

"Oh yeah, I know the shop. They have a great sci-fi section," Cian interrupts.

Aoife smiles and nods excitedly. "Yes, that's the one. So, I can do both jobs. I'll do Thursday to Sunday in the bookstore and Monday to Wednesday in Lilly's gallery. And the best part is that it won't even feel like work. I love art and books equally, so it will be the perfect summer." Her smile grows wide, and she does a little happy dance around the kitchen.

I stare at my baby sister, trying to see her as the adult she is now. Although she's so petite, it would be easy to still mistake her for a child. Everything about the twins is small, dainty, and faery-like, which makes sense since they are faeries. They're identical twins but absolute opposites in personality.

Since they've finished school, they've been trying to find ways to look different too. They made a pact to change their hair so no one would ever mix them up again. They used to have long black hair, just like Lilly's, but now Aoife's hair is a sparkling silver color, and Clodagh's is red. Red— as in fire engine red, not like the orange hue that colors my hair. She also cut it short into a tiny bob that frames her delicate face perfectly.

Aoife's still talking about her summer plans, and Cian and Breanna are discussing their upcoming trip. All of them are excited and eager for the next few months. Clodagh's got her job in the pub, and Lilly and Aaronn are all loved up and exploring Emuria. Why does that make me want to cry? Everyone is racing ahead with their lives, falling in love, working, loving life... And me? All I can feel is grief— for Josh, my dad, my marriage even. My stupid arranged marriage. That really annoys me. I'm not supposed to like my husband. Marry him. Stop a war. Leave him. The end. That was the plan. But I'm still wearing the wedding bands around my neck. Lachlan put them there the day we shared our wedding vows and... I should take them off. But I push the thought aside. I know I'm not going to do it.

And now what? Everyone else knows what they want to do, but I can't seem to think about anything but my stupid husband, who probably hasn't given me a moment's thought since I left him.

Chapter 2

L*ACHLAN*
  Rohn Castle, Emuria

I stare into the fire, searching it for signs, even though I know that's not how my magic works. I can't force the Etain to show me signs. Sighing heavily, I shift in my seat, trying to get comfortable.

You haven't been comfortable in years.

I shake that thought off with the irritation my self-pity deserves. I'm brooding tonight. I know this, and I also know what a waste of time brooding is. It will not fix anything, yet I can't pull myself out of this morose mood. I felt Sara earlier, only a brief connection, and her mood was as bleak as mine. I took comfort in that— sadistic bastard that I am. She felt restless and edgy. I would have said sad if I believed my wife would take the time to feel anything other than annoyed.

And then those thoughts are immediately forgotten as I hear someone behind me. Booted feet on the stone floor, only steps away from my armchair. How did this Fae enter my chambers unannounced? Where are my guards? Rising quickly, I stand to confront the visitor but release a tired sigh when I see it's only my brother, Arlen. I summoned him two days ago, and I had begun to believe he would not come.

I remain standing as he approaches, and although it shames me to think it, I remember my father's mantra, *a King can never be too cautious.*

"Not like you to be caught unawares," Arlen says, voicing my thoughts. It reminds me that for most of our childhood, Arlen was always at my side, imbibing the same awful advice from our father.

Arlen's voice is sharp tonight, the usual humor missing, and even though I sent him away for his own good, I still feel guilty. *That wasn't the only reason you sent him away.*

But what was I supposed to do? Did Arlen really expect me to turn a blind eye while he made love to my wife? He didn't even have the decency to sneak around. The whole castle knew where he spent his nights. But he's looking at me as though I'm the one who did something wrong.

"Do you know where she is?"

I don't have the patience to tiptoe around the issue. I expect him to flinch, maybe flush, stutter an excuse but as usual, he shows no remorse. He's my brother, and I love him. Arlen is the only person I have ever loved, and his betrayal cut deeper than I would have liked. Not that I confronted him. I didn't even let on that I knew about the affair— to either of them. I sent my brother to the royal palace in Soraya, and I hoped that with him gone, Sara might see me at last. It seemed to be working because without my charming, funny brother around to distract her, she did seem to notice me. She let me kiss her... and then she ran away.

"I take it you've lost your wife again, Lachlan? A tad careless, don't you think?" He arches an eyebrow at me, and I bite back the angry retort I want to make. He's angry enough for both of us. "And? You want me to be your loyal sniffer dog and fetch her for you? You're the Master Tracker, Lachlan. You're the one bonded to Sara. You don't need me to find her. You can do that all on your own."

"Arlen, I'm worried about her." I ball my hand into a fist as my voice sticks in my throat, an image of those dead elves in my mind. "I need to know she's safe. I need." I stop again, unable to voice what I need. Arlen is looking at me closely now, his eyes narrowed and too perceptive. "There have been developments here." I'm prevaricating. I have to tell him. He won't help me otherwise. "Another Elf was found this week."

"How do you know Sara is in danger?" Arlen interrupts.

I scrub a hand over my face. "I don't *know* anything. Whenever a body is found, the white hawk circles above the castle and flies off toward the ocean."

"How many bodies so far?" he asks carefully, his eyes never leaving my face, as though he's searching it for clues.

"Two during the winter. Sara was still here. But since she left, another four Elves have been found, and every time since Sara's disappearance, that damn hawk arrives. I've come to dread the sight of it. Another body, another dead Elf but one of these days... I'm terrified it will be Sara's body we're fishing out of the fjord."

"How long has she been gone?"

"She left a week after I sent you to Soraya," I admit, a guilty flush heating my cheeks.

Arlen releases a small sigh, and his head drops forward, so I can no longer see his face. "Thank you, Etain," he mutters to himself, and I notice his shoulders slump in relief. "Clever girl. I'm glad she didn't wait." He's talking to himself, his eyes on the stone floor.

"What is that supposed to mean?" Is he suggesting that I'm a danger to my wife? That I would hurt her? Arlen doesn't flinch as I step toward him, my hand balled into a tight fist. My beast is restless and angry, ready to fight to protect what's mine.

His head pops up. "It means that if she hadn't left, you might have been fishing your wife's body out of the fjord, you bloody fool." His cold anger freezes me in place, but I still leave the armchair between us as a barrier— to stop myself from reaching for him and wrapping my hands around his throat.

I can protect my wife. Arlen's the one who put her in danger. As if he hears my thoughts, he adds, "I was the only protection she had in this awful castle, and you sent me away." I want to laugh at him, but I can tell he believes every word.

Pushing my anger down to a quiet simmer, I exhale loudly before I admit, "I don't know what that means."

Arlen shakes his head at me as though he can't believe he even has to explain it, and I feel my anger begin to boil again.

"Every Fae man and woman on your council wants her dead, Lachlan."

"That is not true," I refute quickly, refusing to give credence to such an accusation. "They are my council. They were father's council before that. Those Fae only want what's best for Rohn."

"Father was a brute, and so are the Fae who served him. They hate Sara and want her dead." The rage that surges through me then cannot be controlled, and I finally let out the roar that has been there for months.

"The council hates Sara because she was having an affair with you, you fool," I shout at him. "I don't know if you love my wife or you were just playing with her because you were bored, but everybody in this castle knew you were sleeping together. I *had* to send you away. The council was angry. I sent you away to *protect* both of you."

The sudden silence in the room has me sucking in a sharp breath. I never shout. I swore I would never be that sort of King. I would never be the King my father was, but all I can hear in my head now is my father's mocking laughter. I am his son, after all. Nothing but a brute and a monster. It is no wonder that Sara prefers my brother to me.

Arlen is staring at me in shock. His eyes narrow, a sure sign that he's analyzing everything that's just happened— understanding more than I want him to. Arlen has always known me better than anyone else.

Then he starts to laugh, not an amused chuckle, more of a doubled over, holding his stomach as he howls kind of laughter. When he looks at me again, tears are streaming down his face, and he wipes at them as he lets out a last rueful chuckle.

"Oh Lachlan, you bloody fool," he says with a shake of his head, another laugh making his mouth twitch, but he suppresses it and strides toward the fire, stretching out his hands to the warmth, shivering while he does. Arlen has always hated this castle and the cold, icy winters that seem to last forever. He reaches for the bottle of wine and tips some into a glass without asking.

I feel the frown on my face and try to wipe the expression away. I'm not sure what's just happened. Arlen drags the second armchair closer to the fire as though he would sit inside the hearth if he could. He folds himself elegantly into the chair and takes a sip of the wine.

"Lachlan, I'm only going to have this discussion once." He looks pointedly at the chair I was sitting in earlier, so I lower myself into it, and, following his example, I reach for my wine and take a sip. I have a feeling I'm going to need it. "You're my brother, and I love you," he continues. "I'd do anything for you, but sometimes you are the biggest fool in all of Rohn. Father was a brute, but he was never a fool— which was good because he needed his wits about him to keep that pack of Fae vultures in check."

I know he's referring to the council again. He's never kept it a secret that he dislikes my council. "Arlen," I start to defend them, but he interrupts me.

"Listen to me now, Lachlan. Hear me, because I swear I will never have this conversation again. I shouldn't even have to have it one time. You really are a blinkered fool." He pauses and shakes his head irritably. "Sara and I are not and never have had an affair. Everyone in this castle *knows* that. They know that Sara and I are nothing more than friends. They are using your jealousy to drive a wedge between us. Between all three of us."

"Arlen." I can feel my anger beginning to rise again. I never thought he would lie to my face like this.

"No." He stops me again and turns to face me. "Lachlan, I'm gay— and you are the only Fae in this whole bloody castle who doesn't know it. Why do you think they all hate me so much? Why do you think father hated me?"

And just like that— I see what's been in front of me all these years. Arlen has never once looked at a woman, not until Sara came here. "Does Sara know?"

"Of course, she knows." He rolls his eyes at me in exasperation. "Sara is a Seer, Lachlan. She knows everything. All of our dirty little secrets. That's why the council hates her."

"She's human," my voice trails off as I realize how empty my excuse sounds.

"Sara knows everything— about all of us." His voice is quiet, and his eyes are steady on me. I shift uncomfortably in my chair. I feel... stupid.

"But she's human. Sara can't be a Seer." Because I need to prove just how stupid I am.

"Oh, brother," Arlen says with a sigh, leaning back in the armchair. "Do you talk to your wife at all? Have you asked her about Josh or her father?"

"Who is Josh?"

"Her boyfriend." His simple answer roars through me, and that's all it takes for the beast in me to wake up, fur rising, growling, ready to tear things apart. "He's dead, Lachlan, settle down."

Heat scorches my cheeks. It's only ever Sara who brings out this reaction in me. I look away from my brother, and he gives me a minute to regain control of myself.

"What happened to the boyfriend?" I ask eventually.

"Climbing accident, they were taking a group out, something went wrong, and he died. That's the short version." Arlen pauses and then looks at me with that unwavering gaze of his as though he's trying to communicate more than his words suggest.

"She has nightmares, Lachlan. Those nights you thought I was making love to your wife. Yes, I was in her room with her, but not for the reasons you've been torturing yourself with. You could have just asked me." Arlen shakes his head sadly and stares into his glass for a minute. "Sara has horrible nightmares, and they've been getting worse since coming to Rohn. I was only ever a distraction on those nights, someone to talk to until she was tired enough to go back to sleep."

I can't understand any of this. Sara has nightmares. Rohn is making it worse. My brother is gay. My councilors are lying to me and—

"Sara climbs mountains?" is the muddled question that pops out of my mouth. "She hates mountains. She refused to go out with me whenever I suggested it."

"Sara is a professional climber or, at least, she was. She hasn't climbed since Josh's death."

And then I remember how she would pale anytime I suggested we go hiking. We were at dinner the first time I brought it up, her hand had jerked, catching my attention and I noticed it was shaking. She placed her wine glass on the table and tucked her hands in her lap while I pretended not to notice. All this time, I assumed it was the thought of being alone with me that frightened her.

"And her father? Where is he?"

Arlen sighs again, a long-suffering sigh this time. "He's dead, Lachlan." He lets that information hang between us for a long minute while I question everything I thought I knew about my wife. "He died one month after Josh, and then her mom disappeared. Shortly after, Aaronn kidnapped the whole family and brought them here to Emuria. Then her aunt promptly sold her to you in this sham of an arranged marriage."

"I didn't buy her," I growl, the only response I can think of. "She's not something to buy," I add for good measure, my mind still reeling from everything he's just told me.

"Glad to hear you say that. Sometimes it's hard to know how much of father there is in you."

I look away. That hurt. More than anything else he's said tonight.

"I'm sorry, Lachlan, that was a low blow," Arlen says quietly. I hear him sigh, and then he continues. "To put this simply, your wife has had a difficult time of it recently. And all that before she landed here in this den of vultures and treachery. I love Sara, Lachlan. As a sister," he adds pointedly. "All I ever wanted was to keep her safe." He lets me brood in silence then, and as I stare into the flames, I finally see what Sara's life in Rohn has been like for her... the isolation, the whispers that follow her around the castle, the barbed comments made by nearly every one of my councilors, the hatred. And if she really is a Seer...

"What do I do?" I turn toward my brother. "I'm worried about her. You know what that hawk means to me. That hawk is the reason I agreed to the marriage. The hawk and Sara are one. I'm afraid... for the first time in my life, I can't read the signs. I don't know what to do. I want to keep her safe, but if she's miserable here with me, if she's scared of me."

"Sara's not scared of you," Arlen interrupts impatiently. "She's scared of the mountains and her nightmares. More than that, she's scared of her visions. Her magic has been coming on strong since she arrived in Emuria. You must remember, Lachlan, Sara's had no training. There are days all she does is pace her room, crying because the impressions washing over her are so strong. She thinks she's losing her mind— and she's alone. I was her only friend here, and then you sent me away. You cannot blame her for leaving."

I drop into my heart, and immediately I feel her there. Sad. Lonely. Rubbing my chest, I try to soothe the ache but stop abruptly when I notice Arlen's gaze tracking the movement. Dropping my hand, I break the connection with Sara. I feel too vulnerable when I connect with her, too exposed.

"She's not scared of you, Lachlan," he reiterates. "It's her magic that she's most frightened of. She doesn't trust it."

Arlen's not like our father. He doesn't know what it feels like to have this beast inside him. He doesn't know that Sara has met my beast; she knows the horror inside me. He might be right about everything else, but he's wrong about this. Sara is terrified of me.

SARA

Cork, Ireland

Pushing my dinner plate away from me, I groan dramatically. "That was too delicious. I swear, Breanna, if you stay here any longer, soon I'll be the same size as the house."

"Hey," Cian objects. "I made that dinner."

"Sure you did. You keep telling yourself that." I wink at him, and while he pretends to frown, Breanna only laughs and kisses him on the cheek.

"I only put the finishing touches to it," she says, and I laugh at that.

"The finishing touches? As in the sauce? From my vantage point, all I saw Cian do was chop the onions."

"I turned the stove on," he mutters.

Breanna squeezes his shoulder. "That's okay. You have other skills," she teases, and seeing where this conversation is headed, I avert my eyes. I don't want to know any more about my brother's sex life than I do already. The walls in this house are thin.

I miss sex, I realize suddenly, and count off the months on my fingers...14 months without sex. That must be some sort of record. Aoife hops up and starts clearing the plates from the table, and Breanna slips out of my brother's arms to help her. Thank you, Aoife.

They load the plates into the dishwasher, working quickly together, and I marvel again at how seamlessly Breanna has slipped into our lives.

Cian starts describing some new tech coming to the market and how it will revolutionize how we do business, and I zone out. That's when I feel Lachlan tugging at my heart, searching, scanning, trying to get a sense of me.

I'm so shocked I don't think to pull my shields up. It's been six weeks since I left, and he hasn't reached out like this in all that time. I've had the odd sense of him, but it's felt more like he was just checking in, making sure I'm still alive, but this feels different. Personal.

Tentatively, I open myself and let him know where I am. It's only fair, I reason with myself. He is my husband, after all. He has a right to know where I am.

I'm making excuses. I want Lachlan to find me. As if he needs help, I chide myself not too gently. Not only are we magically bonded, but he's a Master Tracker. If he'd wanted to, he could have found me within an hour of me leaving his castle. The bitterness in that thought slaps the sentimentality out of me, and I shut down the connection.

It's been six weeks. *Wake up, Sara. If Lachlan is looking for you now, it's because he wants something, not because he misses you.*

"Who wants to go for a pint?" I stand abruptly.

Cian raises an eyebrow at my interruption. "You might at least pretend you were listening to me," his voice is heavy on the sarcasm.

"Come on, I can pretend to listen to you in the pub." I grin as I say it, though. Cian and I have an easy relationship. A no-bullshit relationship. He unfolds his long body from the chair and stands, reaching for Breanna's hand and tugging her closer.

"Pub?" he asks.

"Sure, but why don't you and Sara head across? Aoife and I will follow when we've finished cleaning the kitchen." Cian and I shrug at each other and head for the door.

"Don't feel like you have to stay and help," Aoife hollers after us, and we look at each other again and laugh this time. It's good to hear Aoife joining in the messing around. She was so quiet after our dad died— as though she wanted to disappear herself. But since our time in Emuria, she's different— still quiet, but she radiates with magic and confidence now.

Cian and I leave the house and walk across the street to the pub. O'Driscoll's is painted in big, black letters along the front of the building. The pub belongs to my dad's cousin and was a second home to us all through our childhood. We spent every Sunday afternoon in here, drinking orange cordial and eating Cheese and Onion Tayto crisps.

It was also the first place we all wanted to work in when we got older. It became an O'Driscoll tradition. Lilly was the first, of course; as soon as she turned eighteen, she took her first job here, and then a few years later, it was my turn, and so on and on. At the moment, Clodagh is working here, and she looks up from behind the counter as we open the door and push our way in. Her red bob haircut seems to shimmer in the dim lighting, and I wonder if she's using magic to get that effect. I glance around the empty pub; it's still early, another hour, and I'm sure the regulars will all arrive to keep my sister busy. She's pulling a pint as we approach, but she nods and reaches for a couple more glasses before we say a word.

"I made dinner. The first round is on you," Cian says as we reach the bar.

"I think we've already established that you did not make dinner," I snark back at him, but I'm already reaching for the wad of notes in the back pocket of my jeans. Pulling out a twenty, I place it on the counter. Clodagh nods her head toward the large table in the corner.

"Take a seat," she says, taking my money and turning away to ring up the sale.

"I want change," I throw over my shoulder, but she only gives me the middle finger in response. Cian laughs and leads the way to the corner booth. He slides along the leather bench, and I slip in next to him, glancing around as I do. This pub never changes. It's our one constant, and I love it because of that. The faded red carpet has been here for the last fifty years, and the dark blue leather stools and booth seats certainly haven't been changed in my lifetime. In fact, the only change I can recall in my twenty-four years is the time Eamonn painted the walls red. His regulars complained so long and hard that he shut the pub for a day and painted the walls back to their original green. He then grumbled for months after about ungrateful customers not wanting to move with the times. Although what made him think red walls was 'moving with the times,' I'll never know.

"Soooo," Cian draws the word out intentionally to get my attention, and I turn to look at him. "How's your husband?" I narrow my eyes at him in warning, but he only laughs. "I'm a Tracker, Sara. I felt Lachlan's magic in the kitchen only twenty minutes ago, so you can put that glare away." When I remain silent, he adds. "So, he knows you're here."

"He does now."

Cian nods. "Want to talk about it?"

"No." I swiftly change the subject. "What about you and Breanna? When are you heading back to Emuria?"

"Soon." He's frowning as he says it, though, his eyes narrowed, staring at the door, but then he shakes his head and blinks as he comes back to himself.

"What is it? Is your magic picking up trouble?"

Cian glances toward the entrance and frowns again. "Not sure."

But my magic has started tingling at the nape of my neck, shivering down my spine. Clodagh places the two pints on the table, and when I look her way, I notice her gaze on the entrance now too. The door opens—

Arlen. My gaze skims past him, searching. The tightening of his jaw and the concern in his eyes tells me he knows who I'm looking for, and he shakes his head. When his gaze leaves mine to scan the room, I want to crawl under the table in embarrassment.

Clodagh meets Arlen halfway across the room, barring his way. We might have always been Fae, but it took spending the winter in Emuria to activate our magic. Something that can never be undone and means we now have the senses to spot other Fae when they slip over into the human realm. Fae are powerful and, therefore, dangerous— always approached with caution. I watch as Clodagh speaks quietly with Arlen, and then she glances toward me. I nod at her silent question, and she lets Arlen pass.

I get up as he reaches the table. Arlen doesn't stand on ceremony or hold back the way his brother would. He folds his arms around me and holds me close. And, of course, I do the one thing I swore I wouldn't do again— I cry all over him. All because I miss my husband. My cold, hard, distant husband. There in the middle of the pub, Arlen holds me and softens all my pain with his soothing magic.

"You know why I'm here," he murmurs against my hair, my head still pressed firmly to his chest.

"Lachlan sent you," I whisper.

"It's time to come home, Sara. My brother needs you." He pushes me back and cups my face, using his thumbs to wipe the tears from my cheeks. I sniff and try to smile. I must look like such a mess. "Enough is enough, Sara. You've had time to grieve. Now Rohn needs its Queen." When I can't find the words to answer him, he adds, "You know I'm right." His voice is sterner than ever before, but yes, I know he's right.

The truth settles inside me, and my magic whispers in agreement.

Chapter 3

L *ACHLAN*
  Kingdom of Rohn, Emuria

Aaronn and Lilly's arrival in Rohn is a welcome distraction from the relentless brooding I've been doing since Arlen left for the human realm. I should have gone myself but...would Sara have listened to me? She is always so angry with me, so quick to fight. Sara would have refused to come back on principle.

Pushing myself out of the armchair, I stoke the fire—with a poker. Arlen would laugh if he caught me doing it, but there is something soothing about doing this with my hands rather than magic. I pace over to my bookshelf and retrieve the bottle of Irish whiskey I keep there and then rethink that. Lilly is with Aaronn, and I doubt she's a whiskey drinker. Replacing the bottle, I call the servant hovering in the doorway, request a bottle of wine and then sink back into the armchair by the fire while I wait for Aaronn and Lilly to be brought to me. Their visit is a surprise; I was under the impression my friend found the human realm more to his taste these days.

"What's with the long face? Is it possible you're missing your wife?" Aaronn's teasing questions and the laugh that follows them startle me. Once more, I'd lost myself in brooding. I stand to greet my friend, and Aaronn slaps a hand on my shoulder. His black face splits into a wide smile; married life clearly suits him. I don't remember him smiling like this before he met Lilly. "Sara's in Cork, Lachlan. There's no need to worry. She's safe."

"I know." I clasp his shoulder, but I struggle to smile. "Arlen is there," I add and glance at Lilly. She is shorter than Sara, and her brown skin is possibly a touch paler, or am I imagining that? "I hope you're staying for a few days. Sara will be here shortly." When I notice the frown in Lilly's eyes, I find myself making excuses. "She must, she needs ..." my voice trails off.

"Sara's not going to like being ordered back like that," Aaronn observes dryly, his knowing smile irritating me.

"It's not about what Sara wants," I snap. "Not now."

Sara's sister has gone quiet, and I shiver as I feel her magic scanning me. It's unnerving, her magic too powerful. The servant returns with the wine and glasses, and I wave him toward the fire. It's a bottle of red and will need a few minutes beside the warmth to remove the chill of the wine cellar.

"You're afraid," Lilly says suddenly, her eyes flitting around me. "For Sara?"

I open my mouth to deny this but turn away sharply and change the subject. "Your uncle will be happy to see you," I say to Aaronn. "Have you brought Breanna back with you? I know he misses her."

Aaronn ignores my diversionary tactics. "What's happened?" All traces of his good humor have vanished. I stare at him silently until I realize there's no point in not telling him the truth. His uncle will give him the news as soon as he reaches Torin. But I'm struggling to find the right words to explain it all.

"Has this got something to do with Sara?" Lilly asks, breaking the staring contest Aaronn and I are trapped in; I turn to her, and the concern on her face is enough to convince me.

"I don't know," I finally admit to her before turning back to Aaronn. "This morning, we fished a body out of the Schoenberg fjord." The silence lengthens until I'm forced to continue. "Elf."

Aaronn's eyes narrow, and his jaw tightens. "What was an Elf doing near the Schoenberg fjord?"

"It's not the first one."

"How many?"

"Seven dead this year."

"The gods, Lachlan. Have you notified the Mya?"

I don't bother to conceal my impatience with this question. "Of course. I've sent hawks to the Elvin council – and your uncle – with full reports of the incidents." I'm silent, my hands are balled into fists at my side, and I force myself to unclench them. "The seventh body was brought to me only this morning."

"Here. At the castle?" I nod. "Take me to them. I want to examine the bodies." He turns to Lilly, and she nods.

"Of course. If it will help," she says quickly.

"Aaronn, you can't ask that of Lilly." I'm shocked he's even thinking it.

"And why not?" Aaronn turns an incredulous look on me. "My wife is a powerful magician. She will be able to see the colors trapped in the energy field. That will tell us if they were afraid or shocked by their deaths. Clues, Lachlan. Information that we need if we're going to stop this."

"But—"

"Lachlan, this is personal. Have you forgotten that my aunt is Elvin? My cousins have Elvin blood in their veins."

"Of course, I have not forgotten. Why do you think I took this matter to your uncle first?" The look on Aaronn's face is intractable, and I relent with a sigh. If he feels that Lilly can manage this, then who am I to argue? Striding over to the door, I open it and instruct the servant I find there to find my advisor, Lars, and tell him that I need the ice room unlocked. When I return to the room, they both refuse the wine I offer them, and an awkward silence ensues.

"Is Sara well?" I ask and notice the flare of curiosity in Lilly's eyes. She's no doubt wondering why I need to ask her that.

"We left Cork five weeks ago, but she was," she hesitates and then adds with a wince, "fine."

I'm nodding, too tense to offer anything intelligent to that.

"Lachlan," Aaronn snaps my name impatiently and looks pointedly at the door.

"Yes, yes. Lars should have the ice room unlocked by now," I agree, but my feet don't move, and it takes Aaronn raising his eyebrows for me to huff out a frustrated breath and lead the way. I don't know why I'm reluctant to show Aaronn and Lilly the bodies. It's not like I've succeeded in solving these crimes, but the more people who know about this, the bigger the situation will become.

The ice room is in the furthest corner of the castle, two levels deep into the earth and built into the mountain itself. The passage to reach it takes us alongside the kitchen to a flight of spiral stairs, and as we descend, the temperature drops sharply. At the bottom of the stairs, I find Lars waiting for us, he holds the key card in his hand, but he's frowning his disapproval at the sight of my guests.

"My Lord, is this wise?"

"Yes."

I won't tolerate having my orders questioned. Not today. I notice the flare of irritation on his face, but that is a matter for another day. Taking the key from his hand, I tell him to leave and wait for the sound of his receding footsteps before I scan the lock and push open the heavy wooden door. Pocketing the key, I step into the room, Aaronn and Lilly behind me.

Ahead of us are the seven bodies laid out on seven narrow shelves, stacked one above the other. I hear Lilly's shocked gasp and, turning, see Aaronn place his hand on her lower back and pump soothing magic into her. She smiles gratefully at him but then nods and turns toward the bodies again. Her face is serious, a frown creasing her forehead as she studies them. She looks over her shoulder at Aaronn.

"Will I go first?" she asks, and when he nods, she walks slowly across the stone floor. This is literally an ice room, and all around us are large wooden crates filled with ice. Along the back wall are shelves where we keep the perishable food supplies. It's a long winter in Rohn, and high up here in these mountains, that means long, isolated months. During blizzards, it becomes nearly impossible for anyone to leave, and stores of food are a matter of survival. But it is Summer now, the stores are low, and the room is permanently locked.

I watch as Lilly examines the bodies. I trust Aaronn, but I have to wonder if his faith in his wife is misplaced. These are only bodies; the spirits who inhabited them are long gone.

I glance at the bodies myself, wondering what clues they will reveal. Each Elf wears the uniform of the Mya initiates— a green shirt and brown trousers. They are all male and all young. Their skin, usually a tawny brown, is almost translucent now.

Lilly has her back to us, and I cannot see the expression on her face, but when her shoulders start to shake, and I hear her sniff, her head bowing forward, I nearly call an end to this.

Instead, Aaronn steps up behind her and lays his hands on her shoulders. She leans into his touch but only for a moment before stepping away. He lets her, and I frown in confusion at that. How can he stand to see his wife suffer like that?

Lilly crouches beside the Elf on the lowest shelf and runs her hands above his body. She does this with each Elf. A quick scan that takes only minutes, so quick I'm not sure what information she could have gathered in that time.

When she turns back to us, her face is pale and drawn, and that frown on her forehead is back. She looks first at Aaronn and then glances at me. She opens her mouth to speak, but Aaronn shakes his head firmly and tugs her cloak tighter around her shoulders as she shivers.

"We'll talk upstairs. Give me two minutes," he tells her.

Aaronn steps away from the two of us and studies the elves, skimming his hands over them like Lilly did. When he turns back to us, he's wearing the same frown Lilly has on her face, and a communication passes between them as he looks at her. I see her eyes widen in disbelief, and then I remember Sara telling me that these two communicate telepathically. It's part of the magic of the bonding ceremony, and something Sara and I should be able to do, but neither of us have been brave enough to attempt it.

"Upstairs," I snap when they continue to communicate in silence.

When the ice room is safely locked up and we're back in the library, I pour us each a glass of the now warm wine and take a large sip, trying to thaw the ice from my veins. Lilly is hovering beside the fire, holding her hands out toward the heat, and with a wave of my hand, I flare the flames up higher and hotter. She smiles gratefully at me over her shoulder.

"Just like turning the thermostat up," she jokes, and I see Aaronn grin, although the joke is lost on me. I have never spent time in the human realm, so earthly references often go over my head.

"Well?" My eyes move from one to the other, looking for answers.

"They're not dead." The shock of that statement nearly knocks me over, but I'm saved that embarrassment when Lilly quickly interrupts.

"Aaronn, wait. I don't know if we can say that." I exhale loudly, relieved to hear something sensible. "Not for sure," she adds, frowning again. "But." She sits suddenly and takes a sip of her wine before looking back at me. "There was no sign of pain, shock, or fear. Nothing in the energy field to suggest an attack or accident. They are," she goes quiet for a minute and bites her lip. "Peaceful," she finally concludes.

"Sleeping," Aaronn interjects with quiet authority, and Lilly frowns at her husband again.

"Their hearts have stopped," I point out impatiently, frustrated with them for ignoring the facts, but Lilly shakes her head.

"Actually, no. There is still the faintest pulse of energy around their heart centers. A flicker, really. Impossible to detect physically. More energetic than anything." She turns back to Aaronn. "How? Explain it to me. What makes you so sure?"

"A Manifestor Magician can use energy to create physical objects."

Lilly huffs impatiently and waves her hand for him to go on. "Yes, and then the magician can pull that energy back—literally 'unmake' something. The way I did when we were fighting Cathmor."

A glimmer of a smile crosses Aaronn's lips. "When *you* were fighting Cathmor, my love. Not us."

Lilly blushes. "Fine. But I still don't get it. I pulled the energy out of the air and created the birds. Then I pulled the energy back to me, effectively killing the birds. But I could only do that because it was my creation. What you're suggesting." She stops and pales, staring at Aaronn.

"Yes," is all he says.

My eyes are ping-ponging between them. "Can one of you explain it to me?" I finally growl in frustration as the silence lengthens.

Lilly presses her lips together, her eyes on her husband. "Do you know anyone powerful enough to do that?"

"I don't know if that's the right question," Aaronn muses and paces away from us, sipping on his wine thoughtfully.

"Aaronn." My feelings are evident in the impatience in my voice, and my friend turns to me with a distracted frown, and then his expression clears.

"Do you understand what Lilly said about Manifestor magic?"

I nod sharply in response. Arlen has Manifestor magic. I've seen first-hand how he creates objects and then just as quickly takes them away again.

"I'm suggesting that somewhere in Emuria, a magician has been draining the energy from these Elves and is using it for some," he looks lost for a minute and finishes with a confused frown, "purpose."

"What is the question we need to ask— if not, who?" Lilly asks now, and Aaronn looks at her for a minute before answering.

"Why."

"Why?" I repeat dumbly, barely keeping up with these two.

"Why is someone draining their energy? Why does someone *want* their energy? What for?"

"Tell me again why you think someone isn't trying to kill them?"

"They're not dead," he says simply. "Besides, why kill Elves? Once they're dead, their energy is gone but put them to sleep and slowly extract their energy. Store it." Aaronn is pacing again.

"So, what do we do?" I ask. "We have to find out who's doing this."

"Yes," Aaronn says, nodding along, still thinking.

"But why are they doing this? Who would benefit from this energy, and can we retrieve it?"

"You think we can save them?" Lilly asks quietly from her seat beside the fire.

"I don't know." Lilly looks scared, but Aaronn has that stubborn tilt to his head that I remember from childhood. "I have no idea how to even begin." I notice he's looking at Lilly as he says this. Just when I feel like I've become irrelevant in my own castle, Lilly's gaze turns in my direction, and she smiles.

"Sara," she says softly. "We need my sister."

And just like that, the signs make sense. The white hawk wasn't warning me of Sara's death; it was telling me to fetch my wife home. We need Sara.

SARA

Cork, Ireland

Aaargh. My head hurts. I roll over in my bed, and my knee whacks off the wall, a sharp pain radiating up my thigh. What am I doing up against the wall? I always sleep on the other side of the bed, and then I remember— Arlen slept with me last night.

When Aaronn moved into our home, Lilly replaced the two single beds in this room with a large double bed, and there was nowhere else for Arlen to sleep. Not since Cian and Breanna have taken over what used to be my parent's bedroom, and the twins have finally got their own rooms.

I scrunch my eyes closed to block out the sunlight creeping through the blinds. Burrowing under the covers, I replay the previous night in my mind. Arlen's arrival and his news from Rohn. I quickly push that news to the back of my mind. I do not want my visions to come to me now. They will have to wait. My head hurts too much, and then I remember why. Breanna and Aoife joined us in the pub, and then we decided to go on to a nightclub after the pub. The one, two, three, I lose count of the vodka and tonics I drank as the rest of the night becomes a blur of dancing and drinking.

"Come on, sleeping beauty." Arlen is suddenly at my bedside, and I didn't even hear him coming into the room. "I like to test my brother's patience, of course, but this is a bit much even for me. He was expecting us back last night." He looks at the clock beside my bed. "It's almost lunchtime." I peek my head out from under the covers and glare at him. He is as handsome as ever, not a hair out of place.

"Do you wake up beautiful?" I mumble resentfully and burrow back under the covers. Arlen whips them off me, and I shiver and tuck myself into a ball. "My head hurts," I moan.

"Coffee will help."

The promise of coffee is enough to get me moving, and I stretch lazily and push myself up, edging over to the side of the bed. My head still hurts, and my mouth feels like sandpaper. I need water and coffee and... "Oh, I want a hot shower," I moan, then scrub my hands over my face and stand up. Arlen takes my place on the bed, stretching out his long legs.

"Don't be long," he tosses after me while I stumble blearily to the door. It's so long since I've had a night out. I can't remember the last time I partied like that, and then suddenly I do... New Zealand with Josh and some of the other tour guides. Before we flew out to the South Island, we had a night in Auckland. It was the one, and only time Josh and I slept together. We'd been flirting for months, but that night with enough drink in us to make us throw common sense out the window, we finally slept together. It was my number one rule— I never slept with any of the guys I worked with. Just that one time and three days later, Josh was dead.

When I return to the bedroom, Arlen is still in the same position, but he's flicking through one of Lilly's art books, a mesmerized look on his face as he studies the artwork. How this Fae survived growing up in Rohn is a mystery to me.

"Is this your first time in the human realm?" I ask, and he looks up with a grin, putting the book aside.

"I spent a summer in Dublin once, a few years back. Best summer of my life. I fell in love— more than once." When I roll my eyes, he grins.

"I honestly don't know how you've survived in Rohn all these years," I say, thinking of the cold, disapproving Fae I've met in my short time in that kingdom. There is no laughter in that castle, no fun or joy or... I frown, thinking of it now. Beautiful, yes, but so harsh, and those awful councilors that rule the castle. When I look back at Arlen, he's watching me closely. For once, there's no sign of his deflective humor.

"I was thirteen when my father died – it was easier after that."

"But you said he knew," I say in confusion. Thirteen seems young to be so sure of one's sexuality.

"When I was eleven, my father caught me flirting with one of the kitchen boys. I didn't know I was flirting, but he did. He knew. After that day, he wouldn't even look at me. Didn't say another word to me for two years... and then he died."

"But when did *you* know for sure?" I persist stubbornly.

"I was seventeen, and Lachlan finally gave in to my constant begging and let me come to the human realm. I fell in love. Fell hard." He gives a shake of his head and a small smile. "It all made sense after that. My father's behavior. His disgust with me. But it was good for me. That summer in Dublin put a lot of things into perspective. Answered a few lingering questions I had – like why a naked woman has never got me hard." He stares at me pointedly.

As I'm getting dressed as he talks, I burst out laughing. "Good to know."

He grins. "You're gorgeous, you know that— just not for me." He stretches lazily. "What about that coffee?"

"Absolutely. We're not going anywhere until I have coffee. The coffee in Rohn is like drinking caffeinated mud." I grimace dramatically, and Arlen laughs at me while I pause, knowing he won't like what I have to say next. "We have to tell the others."

"About the caffeinated mud in Rohn?" he asks, a confused frown on his face, and I roll my eyes but laugh despite myself.

"What you told me last night about the dead Elves. Breanna especially, she's half-Elf. It isn't fair to keep this from her." He sobers instantly, and after only the briefest pause, he nods. "I still don't understand what this has to do with me. Why does Lachlan want me," I almost say home but insert "back?" at the last minute.

"What I suggest is that you and your husband spend some time talking— get to know each other a bit," he says sarcastically, and the tone of his voice is so biting that I blink at him in confusion. "Try it," he says softening his words with a smile.

"Lachlan doesn't want to spend time with me," I say instead and pull a sweater over my head. It may be summer, but my experience of Rohn castle is that it is always cold there.

Arlen is laughing, shaking his head. "I can tell you for certain that's not true."

I glare at him, waiting for him to continue, but he doesn't say anything else. "I don't know what that means. He wouldn't spend time with me even when I was there— IN HIS CASTLE." When I turn around to look at Arlen, he's lost the grin. He looks uncomfortable. "What?"

"The thing is," he hesitates and looks down at his feet. "Those nights I spent with you in Rohn... when you couldn't sleep. It turns out I wasn't doing you any favors. Lachlan knew I was there," he adds quietly. I blush, remembering those nights. My hysteria, my tears, and then I realize what he's trying to tell me. Arlen nods. "Yes, Lachlan thought we were having an affair. That's why he sent me away."

I'm staring at him in disbelief— "But you're gay."

"It turns out Lachlan didn't know," Arlen says quietly and winces, embarrassed color slashing his cheeks.

"How is that even possible?"

He shrugs uncomfortably, "Lachlan can be stubborn, blind, preoccupied," his voice trails off, and it's then I notice the worry in his eyes. "He knows now," he concludes.

I watch him closely. "How did he take the news?" Arlen turns toward the window to avoid my eyes, and I hear him huff impatiently.

"He seemed more interested in how the news related to you," he says, turning around. I wait, and he gives me a tight smile. "I don't know. He heard me, at least."

"But how could he not know?"

"Rohn Fae are stubborn, stuck in the old ways, isolated from the rest of Emuria."

"And your brother? Is he stubborn and stuck in the old ways?"

"He's definitely stubborn." We both grin at that.

"I'm sorry he didn't acknowledge what you told him—finally, after all these years. Although I still can't believe he didn't know."

"He's lived his whole life in Rohn. Don't forget he was fifteen when my father died. He didn't have the opportunity to travel, and he's been shaped and guided by those vultures on his council."

"Is Lachlan like your father?" I'm scared of the answer, but I have to ask. "Is my husband a monster?"

Arlen goes still, eyes narrowing intently as he studies me. All trace of humor is gone.

"No, Sara. Lachlan is the best Fae I know. He will never hurt you." He's almost fierce when he says it, and my magic shivers down my spine, acknowledging the truth in his words.

Arlen places his hands on my shoulders and turns me around. "Now, it's coffee time, and while we do that, I can tell you all about Liam the Fire Fae, and once I've exhausted you with all my juicy stories about him, I'll take you back to your husband so he can exhaust you in other ways."

A laugh bursts out of me, followed quickly by a dozen fantasies playing out in my mind. Arlen takes one look at my face and starts to laugh.

"Seriously, when we get back to Rohn, I'm going to lock you and Lachlan in a room together. I have the magic to do it," he warns.

We're on our second cup of coffee when Cian and Breanna get home and flop down into chairs around the table.

Cian glowers at Arlen. "I blame you," he says. "I haven't had a night like that since..." he trails off.

"Since dad got sick?" I supply the answer, and he nods and falls silent. "Where are the twins?" I ask to change the subject.

"Aoife's gone to work, and Clodagh's still in bed."

"Can you wake her?" At his raised eyebrows, I grimace. "Sorry, but it's important. I need to talk to all of you before I leave." Cian takes one look at my face and rises silently, leaving the kitchen. I hear his footsteps on the stairs and glance at Arlen. I can sense his reluctance to discuss this subject, but I can't leave without telling Breanna.

Breanna's eyes move back and forth between Arlen and me, and then she asks. "You couldn't tell us last night?"

"Not the sort of discussion one has in a pub," Arlen says.

Upstairs I hear Cian talking and then a grumbling from Clodagh. I bite back a smile. She's going to be in a wicked mood. Clodagh's never been a morning person. I stand and pour two more mugs of coffee, handing one to Arlen. He takes it gratefully, and I sip on mine while we wait.

It only takes a few minutes, and Cian returns to his place at the table, taking Breanna's hand into his and squeezing it. Clodagh follows, stomping into the room, tugging a hoodie over her head. Pulling the hood up, she burrows into it and curls herself up into a ball on the nearest chair. She looks up at me, glares, and then holds out her hands for my mug. Grinning, I hand it to her without argument. She grumbles even as she's taking a sip, and I turn back to the coffee pot and pour out half a mug for myself before the pot is empty.

I'm the last to take a seat, and I glance at Arlen, wondering if he wants to take the lead. He shakes his head, so I turn my attention to the others.

"We're leaving after this and," I hesitate, but when I see the worry in Breanna's eyes, I know I'm doing the right thing. Her eyes narrow as she waits— she's a mind reader, after all. "There's a situation in Rohn." There's no delicate way to say this. "Elves are turning up dead along the banks of the Schoenberg fjord," I say as directly as I can, looking at Breanna the whole time.

"How many?" Breanna is pale, and Cian moves his hand to her waist, tugging her closer. She leans into him.

"When I left Rohn yesterday, six," Arlen says, and they all turn to look at him.

"Meaning that by now, there could be more?" Cian asks.

At the same time, Breanna whispers, "I don't understand."

"No. It doesn't make any sense," Arlen agrees with her.

"But what is being done?" Cian asks.

"Lachlan has been in touch with your parents, Breanna. They are aware of the situation and the Elvin council, of course.

"So, a whole lot of talking," Cian mutters irritably.

"I'm coming with you," Breanna says, looking at me. "Through the Portal." She glances at Arlen. "You're using the Rohn Portal, I take it?" He nods. "Good, then I'm coming with you, and then I'm going to Torin to see my parents, my family." Her voice cracks on the word family.

"Oh no, you're not. You're half-Elf. If some crazy Fae is killing Elves, you're staying here in Cork where it's safe," Cian says, turning her around to face him, two hands framing her face, but one look at Breanna and I know this is one argument my brother is going to lose.

And he knows it too. I watch his eyes slide closed, and he groans and presses his forehead to hers. "Okay," he says at last, and then he opens his eyes and looks first at me and then at Arlen. "We're coming with you."

"Clodagh?" I turn to my youngest sister. She's pushed the hood back from her red hair and is watching us all. I feel the power emanating from her, and I know she's tapping into her magic before she makes her decision. She shakes her head then.

"No. Aoife and I will stay here. Let us know when you need us."

Chapter 4

L*ACHLAN*
    Kingdom of Rohn, Emuria

Another day has passed, and there's still no sign of Arlen. We've gathered in the library again, me pacing before the fire, too restless to sit and wait, and Aaronn and Lilly on the sofa. I need Arlen to come home; I need Sara to come home. I need...and there's the truth of the matter. I need my wife. Is there a man alive who wants to utter those words out loud? If there is, I have yet to meet him. And in fact, I haven't uttered them out loud. It's enough to just admit them to myself. I'm ashamed of the hungry need I feel when I think of Sara.

Lilly is sitting tucked up against Aaronn with her head resting on his chest, his arm holding her close. She spent the last thirty minutes in the ice room trying to drag more information from the Elves - unsuccessfully. It was a ridiculous amount of time to spend down there in that cold, and all she could gather from the bodies was a sense of water. As the Elves were pulled from the fjord, this is hardly news.

Lilly's exhausted and resting in an attempt to regain her strength. Even from across the room, I can feel the hum of Aaronn's magic as he pumps soothing energy into her. I let eyes are closed, and she looks serene, her lips almost tipping up into a smile.

I'm trying not to watch them, but it's hard to look at anything else— they are so in love, so attuned to each other. Always touching, always catching each other's eye from across a room. Is this what a happy marriage looks like? I wouldn't know. I have no experience with happy marriages. I was eight when my mother died— my father beat her to death.

"Was there water in their lungs?" Aaronn asks suddenly.

"What?" I startle at the question, and Lilly raises her head to look at her husband, but he gently pushes her back down, cradling her against him, continuing to rub her back while he looks only at me. She huffs in frustration but doesn't argue with him. I almost smile at that; I can't imagine Sara being so docile.

"The Elves. When you found them. Was there water in their lungs?"

"No." I'm thinking, remembering. Three of the seven bodies were found on the shore, but the other four were pulled from the fjord— the rescue team pumped the bodies for water, needing samples to understand where precisely the elves drowned. But— "No," I repeat. "No water in the lungs." I stand and begin to pace. No water in the lungs. Not drowned. But they were found in the water. The hawk flew toward the ocean.

"Mer magic," Aaronn and I say simultaneously, just as we're interrupted by a loud knock on the door. It opens before I can call out, and I frown at the new arrival. My senior advisor, Lars, is standing there with his head bowed. A picture of respect... if I ignore the fact that he entered before I gave him leave to do so.

"A situation, my Lord." The sound of footsteps reaches us, and Lars frowns and glances over his shoulder. Turning back to us, he adds, "I must speak with you." He hesitates and looks over his shoulder again, his frown deepening. The footsteps are closer now. Outside the door, if I'm not mistaken, but still Lars stays woodenly in place, refusing to budge.

"Oh, do hurry up, Larry, no need to announce me. I do know my way around my own home, you know?" My brother's voice. The knot in my chest eases, and I force myself to stay put and not run for the door, snatch it open, and search the halls for my wife. Is Sara back?

At the sound of my brother's voice, Lars turned his head to look back into the passage. He is glaring at my brother. I see it even though he carefully wipes the frown from his face before he turns back to me.

"Your brother, my Lord, and the Sorayan Princess. And, on that subject, I have the annulment contract drawn up and ready for you to sign. Perhaps we may request a signature from the Princess since, by some miracle, she is here in Rohn." His voice is as dry as sandpaper and just as rough on my ears.

I'm staring at him blankly. Sorayan Princess? Annulment? What is he talking about? His long white hair is tied back today, but his beard is full, hiding his thin lips as they smirk. He thinks he's hiding this from me by bowing his head in respect. And then, finally, Lars steps to one side.

Sara walks into the room with Arlen at her back, and I forget all about my advisor. Sara looks shaken. Her brown skin is pale, and her hands balled into fists at her sides. Her eyes flick in my direction, but she looks quickly away and scans the library. She still wears her hair in braids, like she did when she lived here. They fall down her back, almost to her bum. And yes, she is as beautiful as I remember. Even like this, in an old pair of jeans and a sweater. Lars will have something to say about that.

When Sara lived here at the castle, he always had something to say about her clothes, her manners, her loud voice, and her even louder laugh.

Lars was never happy about my decision to marry Sara. It's the only time in my life that I've ignored his advice. Every criticism of Sara that followed our wedding felt like a criticism of me. And so I pushed harder and tried to mold Sara into the Queen that Lars wanted her to be.

It didn't matter how many gowns I ordered; Sara would inevitably be wearing jeans the next time I saw her, smirking at me if I dared to comment. It became easier to ignore the subject and the shape of her long legs in those figure-hugging jeans.

My brother has his hand on Sara's shoulder, squeezing hard. A week ago, I might have interpreted that in the way Lars intends me to see it. How many of my interactions with Sara have been orchestrated by Lars? How often was I made to see something in a particular light? Even now, Lars' glance flicks to mine, and I know he longs to make some barbed comment about Sara. I see the words forming in his mind, and if it were not for Aaronn and Lilly, he might have been brave enough to attempt it.

Arlen meets my gaze, unrelenting, steady. I notice his hand on Sara's shoulder tighten and watch as she gives him a tiny nod. They communicate effortlessly, my brother and my wife. The jealousy is swift and hot inside my chest. It burns like acid. I know he sees it in my gaze, but he continues to watch me steadily. His eyes calm me, *patience*, they seem to say. Sara, by contrast, won't meet my eyes at all. She walks swiftly across the room and hugs Lilly first and then Aaronn. When my friend folds his arms around her and holds her longer than I think is appropriate, I clear my throat. Aaronn glances at me, and at the fierce look on my face, he steps back from my wife, but he does it with an amused grin.

"My Lord." Lars' voice is impatient. He is standing with the door open, clearly waiting for me to join him in the passage.

"Later," I say firmly. Lars has been an advisor at this court for longer than I've been alive. He was my father's advisor before he was mine. Because of that, I've always given him leeway and allowed him access to me that I usually wouldn't give to anyone else. But after what I just witnessed, it is time for that to change. Relief surges through me, and my magic tingles along my spine, whispering *yes*. As though it's been waiting for me to see this.

Lars hovers in the doorway, disbelief etched onto his face. Is this the first time I've dismissed him? A lifetime of interactions with this Fae, and I can recall only one time that I did not take his advice. In every other exchange, I have allowed him to lead the discussion. To lead me. That realization is not a comfortable one.

"My Lord." Lars tries again to snag my attention.

"Come back in twenty minutes. I must see to my guests." Pausing, I glance at Sara on the other side of the room. She still won't look at me. "I have not seen my wife in six weeks, Lars. I'm sure state business can wait twenty minutes while a Fae greets his wife?" Raising an eyebrow, I dare him to contradict me. He doesn't. "Go. Come back in twenty minutes." I almost relent, and tack please on to the end of that command. I have always been polite with my staff; it has been a matter of honor for me. I will never be like my father, but...

Lars snaps the door closed, but not before I see the fury on his face. Turning, I meet Arlen's gaze, and we both smile, finding solidarity in Lars' anger. I want to tell him I'm sorry. I'm sorry that I ever took Lars' side over his. I'm sorry I believed the lies he fed me about Arlen's relationship with Sara. I'm sorry about so many things... things I can't undo.

"Lachlan." Sara finally addresses me, but she remains on the other side of the room, tucked between her sister and Aaronn. She is so unlike herself that I'm flustered and uncertain for a minute. I'm used to her challenging me and daring me to fight with her, but today she is subdued.

"Sara," I return her greeting. My voice sounds cold, and I regret it instantly. "Thank you for coming," I add, trying to make up for it. An awkward silence fills the room, and not knowing where to look, I glance down at the rug beneath my feet. As though I will find the answers to my problems woven into the red and gold fabric. But no, the carpet holds no answers, and I'm forced to look back at my wife. She is also staring at her feet.

"Right. Now that we've got that out of the way," Arlen says brightly, rubbing his hands together. "I have a monster hangover. Word of warning, Lachlan. Do not go drinking with your wife." He laughs, ignoring the silence that follows this pronouncement. "And sad as this may be, I fear the only solution is another drink." He strides across to the bookshelf where I hide my best bottle of Irish whiskey. "Anyone else?" he asks over his shoulder gaily.

I don't know if I want to kill him or celebrate him, but at least the color has returned to Sara's cheeks. She's smiling as she watches him pour a glass of whiskey.

"And I really don't want to share a bed with her again. She thrashes around like a drowning elf in the Schoenberg fjord." The sudden silence is deafening. "Too much?" he grins unrepentantly, enjoying our shock, and then the first part of his sentence comes back to me.

"You slept with my wife?" I ask quietly. Kill him. Definitely kill him, I decide now.

"Settle down, Lachlan. I shared a bed with your wife. I did NOT sleep with your wife."

"Shut up, Arlen," Sara snaps.

"Arlen," I growl at the same time. She smiles then, a small hesitant smile, but her eyes hold mine.

"He is," her voice trails off, and she looks at my brother uncertainly.

"Gay," Arlen announces brightly. "It's okay, Sara. I told you, Lachlan knows. He's just getting used to the idea."

"You didn't know?" Aaronn asks, shock evident in his voice.

"I am not discussing this," I growl instead of admitting to the not knowing.

I didn't know my brother was gay. It's not like not knowing what book he's reading or how he spent the night... he's gay, and he never told me. Arlen didn't trust me with something of fundamental importance in his life. Why? Why wouldn't he tell me?

"Lachlan?"

But why didn't I see it? When did I become so blind? Just like I didn't see how Lars was treating Arlen and Sara. My brother and my wife – not some random Fae in the castle but the two people who should be closest to me. Sara... I should have done more to protect her. I should have—

"Lachlan!" Sara's voice is sharp, and she's standing taller now, looking more like herself, and that softening in my chest continues. Soon I will be a puddle on the floor. "Are you listening?" she snaps.

Locking my gaze on hers, I see her sharp intake of breath as she feels it— the connection between us.

I wasn't having an affair with your brother, she says. Out loud? I'm not sure I saw her lips move, and then they do, curving up into a smile.

I am not in love with your brother, she says, her voice in my head. Telepathy comes with a Fae marriage, but we have never attempted it before. And then I feel something else, a shiver of fur as my beast stirs. Her smile slips away, and she frowns. Panic takes hold of my heart. No. I can't let my beast anywhere near Sara.

"I have business to attend to." Stumbling over my excuse, I flee the room, forcing myself away from her. Sara. My wife. That feeling of her inside me is opening an ache in my heart. I want more. I want everything, but so does my beast, and I'm terrified. What will he do to her if I set him free?

SARA

The library door slams shut and turning to Arlen, I raise my eyebrows, smirking to cover my hurt. "I thought you said he wanted me back." When all he does is pour himself another shot of whisky. "Annulment, Arlen? You heard Lars. Lachlan wants me back so he can divorce me."

Arlen replaces the bottle and shakes his head impatiently. "Lars wants the marriage annulled. That's not news. And not possible with a Fae bonding, as you well know."

"It's news to me that Lars wants the marriage annulled," I protest indignantly, ignoring the last bit he said. I don't want common sense to get in the way of my anger.

"Is it really?" he asks, his tone more mocking than interested. He returns the bottle of whiskey to the bookshelf and turns to face me, tugging at his shirt cuff with a distracted frown. Arlen is always impeccably dressed in tailored suits and is infuriatingly handsome. I have no idea how he's still single, and then he opens his mouth, and I remember... oh yeah, that's why. His wit is as sharp as his sculpted cheekbones. You could slice bread with either.

"I'm disappointed to hear that. Damn, I thought you were a Seer. I promised Lachlan I was bringing him back a Seer." He waves his hand in the air. "Alright, let's take you back to Cork. Lars wants the marriage annulled, so clearly, that's all there is to it. I mean, it's not like you and Lachlan want to stay married." He rolls his eyes. "Not like we can't carve ice sculptures out of the sexual tension in this room."

"Oh shut up," I growl and turn my back on them all, stomping over to the window. Arlen's not wrong, though. What was that? That moment of connection— so brief, so addictive. Lachlan read my mind. I've seen Lilly and Aaronn do that, and I always wondered what it felt like...

I stayed in this marriage because my mother asked it of me. Because it was the right thing to do. I wasn't there when my dad was sick. For once, I was going to be the daughter who did the right thing, and the result... I've felt like a fool and an imposter for six long months. No. I stop and correct myself. There were moments of connection before now. A look, a feeling, and those dreams.... that familiar heat flares inside me, leaving me aching.

"What was that you said about Mer Magic?" I hear Lilly asking Aaronn and turn around in time to see the excited nod he gives her.

"Yes. Mer Magic— it helps other Fae breathe underwater." He reaches for her hand and pulls her closer. They are always touching each other. It's sweet and— I'm jealous, I realize suddenly. I want Lachlan to touch me and look at me the way Aaronn looks at Lilly, as though she's his whole world. "Do you understand?" Aaronn is asking her now. When she shakes her head, he says, "I've only been to the Mer Palace once, but they had to use magic— a type of bubble, I suppose you could call it, so that I could travel underwater."

I notice Arlen is sitting up straight now and staring at Aaronn. His gaze is stern and focussed. "Mer Magic?" he asks. "The Elves weren't drowned?"

"No water in the lungs," Aaronn says. "And they're not dead."

"Wait. What?" At last, I've caught up with the conversation, and I stare at Aaronn, waiting for him to go on, but when he doesn't, I turn to my sister. She nods at me and then reaches for my hand.

"We've been waiting for you, Sara. We need your help with this." She smiles apologetically and then squeezes my hand. "Not that I want to ignore your marriage problems... but right now, Lachlan really does want you here. We need your magic to help us figure out what's happening to the Elves."

My magic is tingling at the base of my skull; it's a warning, and I scrunch my eyes closed. I already know this is going to hurt. The headaches that come with the most intense visions send me to bed for hours. Reluctantly, I open my eyes and nod, accepting my role in this. I am a Seer. This is my magic, and I can no more deny it than I can stop breathing. The other three are watching me closely.

"The bodies are here in the castle." I'm not asking. "Can you take me to them?"

"Lachlan has the key," Lilly says regretfully. "We must wait for him."

Arlen hops to his feet then and grins, his usual humor returning. "Now, now, what sort of troublemaker would I be if I didn't have a master key?" He pulls a chain out from under his shirt, and I see a key card dangling on the end of it. Lilly laughs.

"Are you this much trouble in Soraya?" she asks.

"Never," he says with a light grin. "Your mother is a goddess. I worship everything she touches."

"That's disturbing on so many levels," Lilly mock whispers to Aaronn, but she's smiling at Arlen while she says it.

"She touches me. Does that mean you worship me?" I have to ask.

Arlen blows me a kiss. "I've always worshipped you, sweet girl." He strides toward the door. "Now follow me, fearless ones, but let's be quick and quiet. At a guess, no one on the council wants us sticking our noses into this Elvin business."

I pull the library door closed behind me and follow Arlen as he leads us along the passage. Soon we're in an area of the castle I've never been to. Until now, the castle guards would only allow me to explore the eastern wing, but this side of the court feels different. Busier somehow, and then as the sounds and smells from the kitchen assault my senses, I realize why. This area of the castle is for the staff. I would never be welcome down here. My steps falter as I hear those Fae voices. The staff despise me, and they made that clear from my first day here. If I requested coffee with my breakfast, they would send me tea. Weak tea. The time I asked for extra blankets because my bedroom felt like an ice chamber, they sent two warm furs for my bed... infested with fleas. I had bites all over me for a week.

Arlen is leading us down a narrow passage that is dark and cold, even in the middle of the day. Wall sconces hold flaming torches that flicker as we pass them. I feel like I've stepped back in time, and the musty, damp smell that assaults my nostrils makes me want to tug my sweater up over my nose.

Arlen has reached a stairwell and is waiting for us. I can't help noticing how unusually somber he is. He offers me a tight smile and takes my hand to lead me down the stairs. Aaronn and Lilly are behind us as we descend deeper into the earth. The cold seeping into my skin makes me shiver. Arlen releases my hand and unlocks the wooden door at the bottom of the stairs.

Images wash over me before we even reach the ice room. As the door swings open, magic punches me in the chest, nearly knocking me down.

I feel Aaronn at my back, his hands on my shoulders steadying me, holding me upright. Seeing those bodies stacked up on shelves, one above the other, rips me up inside. Aaronn pumps his magic at me, and when I feel stronger, I nod for him to let me go and step toward the bodies. Arlen steps to the side, but he reaches for my hand and squeezes it quickly before letting me go.

I'm alone in front of the shelves. The others are standing behind me, waiting to offer me their support. I know this. I know I'm not alone in this. They will never let anything happen to me, but...

I don't want to look at the elves. They are all so young. Teenagers. No one told me they were children. I'd been led to believe they were part of an Elvin guard— protectors of

The Mya. Squeezing my eyes closed, I gather my strength before crouching down and forcing myself to look into the face of the Elf on the lowest shelf. I stay crouched like that for a few minutes letting my magic whisper its truth to me, and then I move to the next ledge.

Up and up. With each Elf, images wash over me. It feels more intense every time I do it, like waves crashing over my head, tossing me about in the surf. I remember that sensation from my surfing days— being dragged under, and every time I tried to come up for air, another wave would crash down on top of me.

That's how this feels. A wave of images bearing down on me, drowning me in sensation, and just as I'm coming up for air, another wave pushes me under. I'm sucking air into my lungs, trembling, shaking so hard I don't think my legs can hold me up. It's cold, and there's nothing but water... everywhere water.

"Enough." The voice is loud, cutting through the pain and the buffeting waves, and I turn toward it; fall into it. Although that makes no sense. I can't fall into a voice. But suddenly, that voice has arms and legs, and it's carrying me away. Away from the cold. Away from the water. There's a pounding in my head. It's so loud it hurts. My brain feels like it's being bounced around inside my skull. The vomiting will start next, and I hear a voice saying just that.

"She's going to throw up." It's Arlen. His voice is too loud; it hurts, and I'm scrunching up my eyes, needing the noise to stop.

"Ssshh," I hear then, soft now, soothing as I'm tucked against something hard and warm.

"Lachlan, Sara always throws up after using her magic."

And I do.

Now I know the warm, solid arms holding me belong to Lachlan, and— I'm throwing up on his chest. The smell of my own vomit is enough to make me gag and heave again. I feel Lachlan lower my legs to the floor and turn me around. He's holding me about the waist with another hand on my forehead as I bend double and throw up all over the stone passage and his shiny leather boots. *I'm throwing up on a King*, I think, and my world turns black.

Chapter 5

L ACHLAN

I'm so angry I want to throw someone across the room. My magic is tingling in my hands, and my eyes are turning from Aaronn to Lilly to Arlen. My gaze finally settles on Arlen, and I see him glance nervously at my hands and then look back up at me with a frown.

"Now, Lachlan, this was Sara's idea."

"But why did you agree?" I scrub a hand over my face trying to control my rage. "You know she's not trained for this."

"She asked to see the bodies."

"I don't care if she asked to see the moon. She doesn't have the training," I roar at him. "You saw what it did to her."

Lilly is pale, a worried frown on her face. "Lachlan, this isn't her first time using her magic," she says carefully.

"But not like this," I growl, and she nods and bites her lip as she considers what I'm saying.

"I don't think it's ever been this bad before," she agrees, but we all turn to look at Arlen for confirmation. He sighs and rubs his temples.

"I tried to tell you," he says, looking only at me. "Sara's magic overwhelms her. It can make her vomit, and she gets headaches." He frowns again. "But this is the first time she's passed out," and then adds, "as far as I know."

"Lachlan, Sara's visions started when she arrived in Emuria," Lilly says now, but Arlen interrupts her.

"Before that, actually. The white hawk came to Sara in a vision a few weeks after Josh's death."

"Whose death?" Lilly and Aaronn ask together.

I don't know whether to feel relieved that I'm not the only one she keeps things from or just frustrated that nobody seems to know anything about my wife. Arlen looks confused by the question and then guilty.

"I really need to learn to keep my mouth shut," he mutters more to himself than the rest of us.

"Arlen," Lilly's voice is tight as she stares at him, willing him to go on. I shake my head and huff out a breath, the anger draining from me.

"Josh was her boyfriend. He died in a climbing accident a few weeks before your father died." I try to keep my voice even for Lilly's benefit and look away when I see her eyes fill with tears. When Arlen glares at me. "You're not helping Sara by keeping her secrets." He hangs his head and doesn't argue.

I pace over to the window and stare out at the mountains. Mountains in every direction. Mountains that terrify my wife.

This section of the wall is floor-to-ceiling glass, and I've noticed Lilly never goes near it. She's scared of heights; I remember Sara mentioning it. I stare out at the mountains. They're a vibrant green and dotted with the small white daisy that grows everywhere at this time of year. The fjord is winking blue far below us. Beautiful, but still, it makes me shiver. Even though it's late afternoon, the sun is still high in the sky. It won't be dark for hours yet. I'm still staring at the view when I sense it... the white hawk. Dread skates down my spine. Another body? I turn back to Arlen. He's sitting now, his elbows on his knees, his head in his hands.

"The white hawk visited Sara in New Zealand?" I ask

"In a dream, but yes." He doesn't look up.

"That was months before the hawk came to me."

"Yes."

"You didn't think that information might be useful to me?"

"You didn't seem all that interested in your wife at the time," he throws back at me, irritation in his voice now. His head shoots up. "An annulment? You want an annulment—is that why you asked me to bring Sara back?"

I stare at him. What does it matter what he thinks? Maybe this is better. Perhaps if Sara believes I want a divorce, she will return to Cork when this is over. I ignore him and turn to Aaronn and Lilly.

"Do you know if Sara received any training in Soraya?"

Lilly shrugs. "Luneda separated us," she explains. "We weren't allowed to see each other."

"In other words, you have no idea what Sara can or cannot do with her magic." I head for the door, too tired to continue this conversation. "I need to get cleaned up," I add and leave without saying anything more. I discarded the sweater I was wearing when Sara threw up on me, but there are still dried patches of vomit on my jeans and boots.

Stepping into my chambers, I lock the door behind me. I strip as I cross the room, discarding clothes as I go. It's only when I'm standing under the hot spray in my large shower that I finally release the roar I've been holding inside. I punch the wall, letting the pain numb my rage.

"Stubborn, impossible woman," I growl. Why would she do that to herself? She must have known what it would do to her. I feel my fear shudder through me again.

When I found the library empty after meeting with Lars, it was easy to track them. Their combined magic had left a trail as bright as any blinking neon sign.

Stepping into the ice room behind them, the first thing I saw was Sara. She was trembling so hard her whole body shook. Her eyes had rolled up into the back of her head, only the whites visible, and the sight of her so far gone had frozen me in place.

I rest my forehead against the granite stone of my shower wall and pray for the first time in years. For what, I'm not even sure...but I'm scared. I should have protected Sara— if only from herself.

Sara. My magic stirs, and without questioning it, I flick the handle on the shower and step out, towel-drying and dressing quickly. Another pair of jeans, an old tee, and the warmest sweater I can find. The castle feels especially cold this evening.

Ignoring the voice of responsibility that tells me I should be checking on my guests, I let my magic take me to Sara. Outside her door, I hesitate, but when I hear movement within, I open the door and startle one of the castle servants. A young Fae woman stands beside Sara's bed with a glass clutched to her chest.

Looking at the bed, I can see Sara is still sleeping, so I pitch my voice low so as not to wake her. "Who gave you access to my wife's room?" My eyes are steady on the woman, and she avoids my gaze. That doesn't necessarily mean anything. Many of the staff are nervous addressing me.

"My Lord." She drops her gaze to the floor. "Master Lars sent me to attend to the Queen."

I glance at Sara again, her eyelids flutter as though she hears us, and I hear her breath hitch in her chest, but then it evens out again, and I return my attention to the serving woman.

"What's your name?" I ask her. "I don't recall seeing you before."

"No, my Lord. I usually work in the kitchen, but Master Lars sent me up here tonight," she repeats her earlier excuse and blushes prettily as she looks at the ground again.

"I see," I say slowly, letting my magic track the dark signature in the room. "Very well, you can leave now," I say abruptly. "I will stay with my wife."

"Oh!" She looks suddenly flustered. "I'm to give her this medicine. I was just about to wake her. I'll do that now," she says, quickly turning for the bed with the glass in her hand. "I'll get out of your way after that," she says with a smile a little too practiced for my liking.

Using my magic, I track quickly to her side, not giving her a chance to wake Sara, and she blinks and gasps suddenly as I'm by her side, plucking the glass from her hand before she has a chance to react.

She pales and backs away. It's only as she's hurrying out the door that I realize she never gave me her name. I look down at the glass in my hand. The dark magic I traced is coating this glass, and rage starts to burn low in my gut.

With the rational part of my brain, I realize I need to get this drink analyzed. I need proof, and slowly I release my stranglehold on the glass. Who can I trust with this? The Rohn court has always been riddled with treachery, but the darkness hanging over our castle recently seems especially strong... the Elves. Is there a connection between what is happening in my home and the fate of the Elves?

My attention is diverted by the sound of footsteps, and I wait for whoever is approaching. Sara's room is far away from my chambers and at the end of a long narrow passage. There is no reason for anyone else to be in this area of the castle.

Arlen appears in the doorway, a frown creasing his brow as he looks first at the open door and then through it. His eyes flick over me, then to the bed, and back to me, dropping at last to the glass I'm holding. He stands a little taller, and his eyes narrow as he takes in the scene. I feel my shoulders hunch forward defensively, readying for the accusation I see brewing in his gaze.

"The Fae woman I just passed in the passage?"

"Can you feel it?" I ask him now, looking down at the glass in my hand. Our magic works differently, so I'm never sure if we sense the same things, but he gives a sharp nod.

When we were kids, Arlen was my one ally in this castle, but I realize now that he likes me as little as the rest of my court. He might even hate me; I can't say I blame him. In my determination to maintain control of this court and follow the rules, I abandoned him. When my council moaned about his behavior, I allowed their opinions to matter. Arlen has every right to hate me.

"Who is she? I haven't seen her before."

"She said she works in the kitchen."

Arlen frowns suspiciously. "And what was she doing in the Queen's chambers? That's a long way from the kitchen." Before I can answer, his frown deepens, and he spits the answer at me. "Lars. He sent her here, didn't he? Is this enough proof for you, Lachlan?"

I've seen my brother eviscerate with humor, but this cold rage is new.

"When will you see what's going on right under your nose? Oh, gods! Lachlan, when will you wake up? When she's dead?" He points at Sara, and I suck in a breath as the pain rips through me. I can't look at her. The thought of what could have happened... if I'd been only a few minutes later...if I'd let my pride get in the way and not checked on her.

"Get this analyzed." I hold the glass out to my brother, and that's all it takes for the rage to drain out of him. I have to wonder at that; how different we are. His anger comes in a flash, and then he drops it and moves on, but mine sits deep inside me, brewing for years, raging inside me.

Arlen sighs now and pushes a hand through his hair, pushing it back off his face. He has our mother's more delicate features and has always been the better-looking one of the two of us. Is that why I was so quick to believe the lies about him and Sara? Arlen is better looking, younger, and, let's face it, more fun. He's just a better Fae. Sara deserves someone like Arlen. I follow his gaze to where it rests on the bed now.

"We should have left her in Cork, Lachlan. Rohn will kill her, just like it killed our mother."

I shove the glass toward him again. "I'm not father, and we're not going to let that happen," I promise him. He finally takes the glass from my hand and looks down at it with suspicion.

"Poison, do you think?"

"That's what we need to find out. Is Lars trying to kill my wife or just scare her off?"

"You have enough to charge him either way." Arlen's eyes narrow as he says this. Is he testing my loyalty to Lars? It hurts me that he feels the need to question me. Does he really think I would put Lars before him and Sara? I take a step closer and rest my hand on his shoulder, squeezing it hard. His eyes flick to my hand, and he frowns.

"Come morning, Lars will no longer be a member of my court. He will never have the power to hurt either of you again. I promise, Arlen." For the first time in years, my brother doesn't retort with something funny and sharp. He nods.

I drop my arm from his shoulder, and he turns for the door, but I can't let this go. "Arlen, I'm sorry. For all of it. Lars and... everything. Not knowing, not seeing. I'm sorry," I repeat, not knowing what else to say. He blinks in surprise, and I see the uncertainty on his face.

"About that." His voice falters, and suddenly he reminds me of the boy he used to be, and I want to smile. But smiling feels as unfamiliar to me as relaxing. Gods, I've turned into my father without realizing it.

"You are my brother, Arlen. Who you choose to love is your own business. It doesn't change anything between us. I'm only sorry you felt like you couldn't tell me."

He nods and, after a moment's hesitation, leaves me alone with Sara. I turn toward the bed and bite back a smile when I see her eyelids flicker. She's lying stiff as a corpse, and I know I shouldn't find humor in that...if I'd been any later, that might have been the outcome.

Sinking into the armchair beside the bed I wait, but she persists in the pretense. "I know you're awake," I whisper, certain that her head is still hurting. The way she squints at me through half-shut lids confirms it. Her eyes close again, but she rolls onto her side to face me.

"I didn't want to interrupt," she whispers. "Arlen needed to hear that from you. Your good opinion is everything to him." This woman has a way of pricking at the most tender parts of me, and I squeeze my eyes shut at the sudden vulnerability that washes over me. *A King must never allow himself to be vulnerable,* my father's hated voice in my head.

"So Lars is trying to kill me again, is he?" she asks softly, her eyes still closed. She doesn't see me wince, but she hears my sigh and cracks her eyes open again. "It's not your fault, Lachlan," she murmurs.

"Are you sure? The last time we argued, you told me all of it was my fault— although, if I'm being honest, I was never sure what 'all of it' encompassed. Our marriage? Winter? This wreck of a castle?" I'm rambling and shut my mouth abruptly. She chuckles but then winces and holds a hand to her head.

"Ssh, don't make me laugh. I need Aoife," she moans.

"One of your sisters?" I ask, and she nods, squeezing her eyes shut, tears on her cheeks.

"I'm sorry I can't bring her here to you." She nods again, and I gently brush my fingers over her forehead. She blinks up at me.

"Lachlan, I'm a little dizzy. I'm going to sleep some more. Try keeping me alive, will you? I still have to tell you what I learned from the Elves." Her eyes close, and she tucks her head down against her chest, curling into a ball like a child. I trace the line of her eyebrow with my index finger and then let my finger dip lower across her cheek, wiping the tears away. She moans, and I pull my hand back sharply.

I watch her in silence; she seems to settle, her features even out, and the tightness around her mouth softens as the pain lessens. I think she's asleep, but then she mumbles, "Lachlan, sorry about the boots." She stretches her hand out toward me, and I stare at it lying there on the white sheet. Slowly I place my hand over hers. When she doesn't jerk hers away, I close my fingers around her palm and hold it. My pulse is jumping, and my heart hammering in my chest – from nothing more than having her hand in mine.

SARA

When I wake again, it's dark, but the curtains have been left open, and the moon is shining through my window. It reveals my room— precisely as it was before I left for Cork. Nothing has been moved; nothing changed. It stood here waiting for me to return.

But there *is* something different. I can't put my finger on it, but I feel...something. It's unsettling, a dark magic, and then I remember the woman who was here earlier. She tried to wake me, held a glass to my lips. I remember now that I pushed her away. I thought she'd left, but then she was at my side again, but that time someone else was there— talking to her, stopping her. Lachlan.

I turn my head, searching the dark for him, find him asleep in the armchair beside my bed. His head rests against the wall, his arms crossed over his chest, and his long legs stretched out in front of him. I drink in the sight of him.

He's...mine, is the first word that pops into my head, and an embarrassed flush sweeps over me. He's not mine, not really. At least, only on paper and maybe not even that if he signed those annulment papers.

I look my fill, savoring every detail of him while I can. He keeps his dark beard neatly trimmed... I squirm as I imagine how it would feel brushing against my skin... and his shoulder-length hair, more dark brown than black like his brother's. And his eyes (when open) are a warm hazelnut chocolate, dark with flecks of amber light. His body is my favorite fantasy, powerful thighs, strong arms, and that broad chest. I want to rub myself against it...

"I know you're awake," he murmurs sleepily and I look away quickly, feeling my face heat up again.

"You didn't have to stay," I mutter into my pillow.

"I thought I might as well keep you alive. For a few more days, anyway," he says lightly, and I turn my head to look at him again. He's smiling at me, and all that heat rushes through me again. Lachlan never smiles at me.

"How are you feeling?" he asks now, the smile slipping from his face as he leans forward and studies me with concern.

I push myself up on my elbows and raise my head to look at him. His eyes find mine in the dark, his are glowing amber, and I shiver in response. There is something about the way his eyes change from chocolate to amber that gets me every time.

Lachlan notices my shiver and sits back in the chair, pulling his energy away from me. I feel the shift in the air around me, the sudden cold as though he'd been holding me while I slept, and now... he's not.

"I'm fine," I lie, not wanting him to feel like he has to stay with me.

"Hungry?"

"Starving," I admit and grin when he starts to laugh. I've never seen him laugh before, not like this. Not real laughter.

"What would you like?" He leans forward in the chair, rolls his shoulders back, and scrubs a hand over his face. My eyes are stuck on his raised arm, even through his sweater, I can see the curve of the muscle, the definition.

"I want..." I snap my eyes back to his face. "I want a grilled cheese sandwich." I say the first thing that comes to mind and one of the few things I can make myself. When he pulls his hand away from his face, he's frowning.

"I don't know what that is."

"How is that even possible?" I ask in disbelief and push myself up to perch on the side of the bed, only then realizing that I'm in my underwear.

Grabbing the blanket, I tug it over me, glancing quickly at Lachlan. He's already walking around the bed, keeping his eyes averted as he searches through my wardrobe until he finds my fluffy white dressing gown. The least sexy item of clothing I could possibly wear at this point. I blush as he hands it to me, but he doesn't notice as he's looking the other way, keeping his face angled away from me.

Slipping my arms through the sleeves I tie the belt quickly around my waist, feeling awkward and shy in front of him.

"You'll have to tell me what this mysterious grilled cheese sandwich is. Is it as gourmet as it sounds?" He smirks at me. "The kitchen might need instructions." He's grinning again and I'm drowning in the blast of sunshine that comes with that grin. "Come with me. We'll see if we can find someone to make it for you."

"You can't wake someone up. It's the middle of the night." I'm horrified at the thought.

"So?" He shrugs. "You're the Queen, and you haven't eaten."

"Don't be ridiculous, Lachlan. I can make a grilled cheese sandwich for myself." It's his turn to look horrified and I burst out laughing. "Do you at least know the way to the kitchen?"

He nods, still looking uncertain, and I want to cup his face and press my mouth to his frowning one. I want to feel his arms around me, and not because he's trying to make a point to his councilors. He stares at me, and his frown deepens.

"Sara?" His voice is a low growl, and I shiver and force myself to look away. Wanting my husband should be simple, but nothing with Lachlan is straightforward. Just look at this moment right now. Everything between us felt easy, but now he's scowling again. Why is he mad? Whenever I feel that connection between us, he pushes me away.

"I can wait for breakfast," I say to his back as he heads for the door. Lachlan doesn't respond. He only opens the door and waits there for me, not bothering to hide his scowl this time. "I'm serious, Lachlan." I cross my arms over my chest. "We don't have to do this. I'm sure you're tired. Why don't you put a spell on the door, lock me in, lock everyone else out? You know the one? I've seen Aaronn do it. Can you do that spell?" I'm rambling, but he remains quiet, waiting until I eventually snap, "What? Talk to me. You don't have to stay with me. Really, you can go."

"I want to stay with you." He doesn't say anything else, and I'm standing there, biting my lip uncertainly, when his mouth twitches into a small smile. "Really, Sara. I want to stay." Neither one of us moves until he nods toward the passage. "Besides, I'm intrigued by this grilled cheese sandwich thing that you can't live without."

He's teasing me. Lachlan the Grump is teasing me. "You have been missing out," I say. It's my version of an olive branch. Maybe we don't have to fight all the time.

Lachlan watches me as I step closer, and when I'm beside him, he reaches out gently and brushes his thumb across my cheek. That's it. Then he turns and walks out the door, leaving me in a puddle of desire on the stone floor.

Chapter 6

L ACHLAN

I might know how to find the kitchen, but I realize too late that it's been years since I was down here, and as I look around, heat flushes my cheeks red. Compared to Soraya or even the human realm, Rohn castle is primitive.

I've heard that from Arlen more often than I care to remember. Primitive, backward, stuck in the past... but I was a boy when I was named King. It took me years to realize there was another way to live. I'm embarrassed, not wanting to see Sara's face as she examines the kitchen.

When Arlen started traveling Emuria and reporting back to me, I fully understood how backward Rohn really is. I've made changes— slowly. I started with the heating, of course. As a Master Tracker with the gift of fire, upgrading the heating in the castle was the obvious place to start. Magic fire does not require the fuel that our old fires do, although....

I grimace as I notice the pile of logs stacked beside the wood-burning cooker. Getting my staff to avail of the magic is another thing altogether. They would rather labor with real fire than use magic. It is the Rohn way, my father always said. *We are not like those useless soft-handed Sorayans. We know how to use our hands. We are strong.*

79

And stubborn. With every change, I met more objections. When I replaced portions of the castle walls with sheets of glass to allow more natural light into the building... my staff nearly quit. A few of them did walk out, but they returned the next day, and although they grumbled, they resumed their duties.

After that, I kept my renovations to my personal chambers and the library. These are the rooms I spend the most time in, and at least there, I can relax without my father's ghost hovering over me.

The kitchen is dark, but I can see Sara standing in the middle of the room, turning around slowly. Her eyes are glowing green in the dark, cat-like, and I wish I could keep us like this... in the dark. I don't want her to see the full extent of the kitchen. How tired and old it is, but I sense her impatience. Reluctantly, I snap my fingers. The tapering candles dotted around the room flare to life. I'm watching her, so I catch her confused look as she blinks at me and then at the candles.

"No electricity?"

"No. Not down here." My voice comes out as an angry growl, and she raises her eyebrows, her eyes cooling as she regards me. "The staff won't use it," I mumble and turn my back on her. I don't want to see her disdain.

Sara dislikes Rohn; she's never hidden this from me. *A backward land with outdated ideas and practices* was one of the things she said to me at the start of our marriage.

As my eyes land again on the wood-burning stove and the iron pots above it, I cannot help but agree. Those pots have been there for a hundred years, maybe longer. I cast my eyes around with despair— everything in this kitchen has to be more than a hundred years old.

"Lachlan?" Sara waits for me to look at her, so I sigh and turn around. "Is Rohn," she hesitates, clearly trying to find a diplomatic way of asking her question.

"Lacking in financial resources?" I supply dryly and watch her mouth twitch as she tries to suppress a laugh. I shake my head. "No. Lacking in sense maybe, but not wealth."

She nods, still pressing her lips tight together, but the laugh bubbles up out of her anyway. It rolls over me. I love the sound of her laughter. The one thing I've missed the most while she's been away has been the sound of her laugh. Not that she ever laughed with me. No, she was with Arlen anytime I heard it, but it always made me pause in whatever I was doing.

"What's going on here?" Sara asks and waves her hand around the kitchen. I try to see it through her eyes: the old wooden shelves straining under the weight of the heavy iron pots. The flagstone floor that's cracked and worn to a shine in patches. Even the large sink is chipped along the top edge. I wince as I take it all in, my face heating again under her scrutiny. She's studying me, her head tilted to the side as she waits. Her green eyes flare suddenly, and I would love to know what thought caused that flare. I'm too scared to ask.

"I have an idea," she says, diplomatically moving on from her question. She opens the cupboards, searches for something, and then looks at me. "Lachlan, will you grab that frying pan?"

Walking toward the rack I reach for the nearest one.

"Yes, that one," she says. "Right, here's the bread." She pulls out a loaf of freshly baked bread, and the scent of the fresh loaf makes my mouth water. Sara is not the only one who missed lunch and dinner today. "What are the chances of us finding butter and cheese in this kitchen?" she asks as she places the bread on the wooden counter and starts searching again. "Is there a fridge?" She looks over her shoulder, a mischievous grin on her face. "Or is it a box lined with ice?"

She's teasing, but I still feel my face heat up in embarrassment. When I pull open the back door and step outside, her laughter follows me to the cold room. By the time I return with the butter and cheese, she's quiet. No sign of her mocking laugh.

She silently takes the butter from me and spreads it across the four slices. She follows this by slicing the cheese and preparing the sandwiches, and I feel that same old conflict twisting me up inside. It's such a simple thing she's doing, and yet, if anyone saw us, the council would be outraged. How dare the Queen of Rohn prepare food herself? *The rules are there for a reason.*

Sara hands the butter and cheese back to me and wipes the counter down. She doesn't look at me while she does this, and that easy laughter is gone again.

Rohn castle. It taints everything.

I return the butter and cheese to the cold room outside and find her waiting for me by the door.

"Now what?" I ask, glancing at the cold stove, but she only shakes her head firmly

"Nope. Now we got to the library," Sara says, heading for the passage before I can say anything else. I snap my fingers to extinguish the candles, plunging the kitchen into darkness. In the dark passage, her laughter floats back to me, and I hurry to catch up with her.

Sara walks fast, her long legs striding down the warren of dark passages. She's swaddled in that thick dressing gown, but the memory of her naked skin beneath it taunts me. The glimpse of her white lace bra and panties before she whipped the sheet over her body is burnt into my retinas. How sad is it that after six months of marriage, that is the closest I have come to seeing my wife naked?

Sara turns a corner and stops so quickly that I walk into her. My hands land on her shoulders and then I realize the reason for the abrupt change in her. One of the night guards is blocking the passage. He's glaring at Sara, his arm barring her way, but as his glance flicks over her shoulder, he notices me, and I watch him pale and step quickly to the side, bowing his head.

"My Lord," he mumbles, staring at the ground.

"I'm glad I didn't attempt this midnight feast on my own," Sara says lightly, but I hear the quaver in her voice and nudge her forward gently, my hands still on her shoulders. I want to tear that guard limb from limb. How dare he intimidate Sara? How dare he even look at her?

"Lachlan?" her voice is strained.

"Yes?"

Sara looks over her shoulder at me, and what she sees on my face makes her stop and turn around. My hands fall to the side. "Are you okay?" she asks quietly. I frown at the question. "You were holding me very tightly."

Comprehension dawns, and I glance down at her shoulders. "Did I hurt you?" I take a quick step back, out of arms reach.

"No," she says, her eyes steady on mine, and then she repeats it. "You didn't hurt me." I'm not sure I believe her, and she must see that. A mischievous grin slips across her face, briefly, and then it's gone. "Hold this." She hands the frying pan to me and loosens the belt around her waist. What is she doing?

Sara tugs her sleeve down, exposing one shoulder. "See? No bruises. No marks." She pulls the robe back into place and re-ties the belt while I'm still staring at where her naked shoulder was only a moment ago.

"Now come on, you promised me food. I'm going to be completely honest now and tell you that if I'd known the state of the kitchen, I never would have suggested grilled cheese sandwiches." She continues talking, her voice leading me through the castle as she fills the silence with a story about... I must be honest and say I don't catch all of it. I'm still thinking about her naked shoulder, and then I'm thinking about the night guard glaring at my wife. His Queen.

"The storm came out of nowhere, and we had to take shelter in a cave and wait it out, and all we had to eat was one protein bar and an apple— for three of us." She moves her hands in the air, punctuating the dramatic moments in the story, and as I watch her, I find myself relaxing, my anger slowly draining away.

Sara opens the door to the library, and once we're within, she closes it after us. "Is it crazy that I want to lock the door?" She laughs at her own question and strides across the room toward the fire. "Now, work your magic, Master Tracker. I want to see you make fire."

Placing the frying pan on the large stone hearth, I watch her in bemusement. I've never known her to talk this much. Is she finally getting comfortable with me, or is she nervous?

"A little of both, probably," she says. "My sister, Clodagh, can make fire shoot out of her fingers." She laughs and then frowns at me. "What? Why are you looking at me like that?"

"What's a little of both?" I ask slowly, and when she frowns in confusion, I add, "You said a little of both, probably."

She shrugs. "The answer to your question— probably both. I'm still nervous but also more comfortable with you." She bites her lip then, and I notice the uncertainty in her gaze.

"Sara, I didn't ask you a question." I rub my hand down my jaw, feeling the scrape of my beard against my palm. "Out loud," I add, to be clear. She frowns, and then her face clears, and she smiles brightly.

"We did it again? Cool." She accepts it so readily, as though our telepathy is something to celebrate. I don't feel that way; I can't. Every time she gets inside my head, I'm terrified. My beast is there waiting to meet her. I can't have her inside me. Ever.

SARA

I see the change come over him, and I want to scream in frustration. *No, don't retreat. Don't shut me out.* But of course, I don't say that. I pretend not to notice the scowl on his face as he stares at me, and I expect at any minute to be sent back to my room with no dinner— as punishment for contaminating the air he's breathing.

I don't understand this man. This Fae man, I remind myself and realize that, of course, how could I? His life has been so different. I have no point of reference with which to understand him. I can't possibly know what worries him or what fears keep him up at night, sleepless, prowling these castle hallways.

The tingling starts, dancing down my spine, and in my mind's eye, I see Lachlan walking the passages. It's late, even the lights in the halls have been extinguished, but he doesn't need the light. He knows every stone in every hallway. He's walking toward my room, getting closer, and then he stops outside my door. And nothing. He stands there. I don't know what he's thinking, but that familiar scowl crosses his face, before he turns and leaves.

I turn away and crouch by the hearth to shield my face from him. What keeps this Fae King up at night?

"Can you light the fire?" I ask, keeping my voice light and unconcerned. I fiddle with the sandwiches, turning the slices over so the buttered side is on the outside. I refuse to look at him. I also refuse to believe he will send me away hungry. A few months ago, I might have thought him capable of that. But after hearing his apology to his brother, I don't believe the angry, brooding vibe he's giving off. It's a shield for something else. It has to be. *Wishful thinking, Sara. Maybe he really is that angry.*

I don't have to look up to know Lachlan has got the fire going. I can feel the heat warming the top of my bowed head, and the orange flames cast a warm light beside the hearth. I look over my shoulder and catch him staring into the fire, that brooding scowl still firmly in place. I feel a nervous flutter in my belly at the sadness I sense radiating from him.

Oh, Lachlan. My heart softens, and instantly his eyes snap to mine. They seer into me, the amber in his eyes flares brighter as he leans forward and takes the frying pan from my hand. His arm brushes against my shoulder, and a little frisson of energy skitters down my arm, tingling through my fingertips. I push my lips tight together to silence the automatic moan his touch induces.

No. I can't solve my marriage problems with sex. If Lachlan and I are going to find a way to get along, sex will have to wait.

Or maybe sex will fix everything, my magic is taunting me now.

Lachlan holds the pan over the flames and stretches out his other hand to me. I grasp it, and he pulls me to my feet. Again, that sizzling energy brushes my skin, and I swear my magic is cackling at me like some wizened old hag.

Stop it!

"Stop what?" Lachlan asks with a frown, a concerned look in his eyes.

"Oh, sorry. Not you. I was talking to... my magic," I finish awkwardly, embarrassed heat creeping up my cheeks. He doesn't laugh.

"You talk to your magic?"

I distract him by leaning closer to the flames and reaching for the sandwiches in the pan. He nudges me back firmly.

"Don't burn yourself."

"I just want to turn them over," I mutter, relieved that my ploy worked. "Hold the pan closer, please." I turn each sandwich, so both sides fry evenly, then I rub my hands in anticipation. "I am so hungry." And then I have an idea. "Do you have wine?"

"I do," he says it cautiously, though, suspicion in his gaze.

"What?" I ask, trying to look innocent.

"You never drink wine with me."

"I also never eat grilled cheese sandwiches with you, yet here we are." I make a ta-da gesture with my hands.

"What are you up to?" he asks, not falling for it.

"Ssh, don't ruin it, Lachlan. We're actually getting along." To punctuate that statement, he scowls at me, but this time his scowl only makes me grin. "You see, I don't believe that anymore," I say, pointing at his face.

"My face?" he asks with what appears to be genuine confusion.

"Yes, that angry scowling look— I think it's a lie."

"You think I'm lying to you?" he asks slowly, and if the look on his face is anything to go by, he thinks I'm a raving lunatic. I might be. I could be at home in Cork right now. I could be going on a date with a nice, ordinary man who doesn't scowl at me, whose servants don't try to murder me in my bed. In fact, he probably wouldn't even have servants because he'd be human and not a King. No brooding. No scowling. I risk another look at Lachlan, and yes, that scowl is still firmly in place.

"Do you want to go back to Cork?" he asks quietly, but nothing about his tone suggests the question is innocent.

"Do *you* want me to go back to Cork?" I don't address the fact that he read my mind. He seems to stress every time we do that, and then just like that, the way he rushed out of here earlier makes sense. He wasn't trying to get away from me...well, he was, but not for the reasons I thought.

Lachlan's scared of connecting with me. His councilors are scared of me too. I've realized that Seer magic isn't appreciated in the same way as Manifestor magic. There's not much fun in having someone tell you things about yourself you'd rather no one else know. I grimace at the thought and then force myself back to my earlier mission, scanning the room for the wine I know he must keep here.

"What are you looking for?" he asks without turning around, and for a moment, I stare at his broad back, his shoulders hunched defensively.

"Wine and glasses," I answer eventually, and he nods toward the bookshelf.

"There should be a bottle over there. I don't think we finished it last night."

I find the bottle where he indicated and hold it up, grinning when I see it's half-full. I'm hoping a glass of wine will help Lachlan relax. I don't know why this is so important to me tonight. Why tonight after six months of marriage?

I tug out the cork and pour the wine into two glasses. What does it matter if we clear the air tonight or tomorrow or... Frowning at the two glasses of wine, I stop my wandering thoughts. Lachlan has been reading my mind. Has he read all of this? Heat rushes to my cheeks at the idea. God, this bonding stuff is complicated. I reach out tentatively, trying to feel him but—

"I'm right here, Sara. Ask me what you want to know." I feel the rebuff as a physical sensation, an energetic pushback as he places me firmly outside his energy field.

Taking a deep breath, I exhale it slowly. So, Lachlan can control this connection between us; he can choose not to let me in. Right. So that is what I need to learn. I can't have my husband reading all my thoughts.

"The sandwiches are done," I announce, glancing at the pan. He pulls it away from the heat and frowns at the toasted bread.

"I'm not convinced they're worth all the effort it took to make them."

I force a laugh and take a sip of my wine before placing the two glasses on the side table beside the hearth. Lachlan hands me one sandwich, and I curl myself up in the nearest armchair and tentatively take my first bite, burning my mouth on the melted cheese and huffing irritably, holding a finger to my burnt lip. When I look up, Lachlan's watching me.

"What? It's delicious, just hot. Go on, eat," I tell him, and he lowers himself into the armchair beside mine and sensibly waits a minute for it to cool down before taking a large bite. I'm nibbling around the edges of my sandwich as I wait for his verdict. He takes another large bite and nods at me. I smile and sink back into my seat. We eat in silence.

Swallowing my last bite, I reach for my wine glass and take a sip. I'm feeling more like myself already and let myself snuggle back into the armchair, tucking my legs underneath me. Lachlan leans back in his chair and stretches his long legs out in front of him, his eyes close as he sips on his wine.

"I meant it," he says suddenly. "You can ask me anything."

"I know." My answer surprises him, and he turns to look at me.

"You're not scared of me?" I shake my head slowly, looking for signs of his scowl returning.

"Are *you* scared of *me*?" I ask him, teasing him.

"Terrified," he says with such sincerity my heart skips a beat. I want to reach out and comfort him, but instead, I wrap one arm around my waist and hold on tight. God, I wish that didn't hurt so much. "Sara, do you want to go back to Cork?"

I open my mouth to snap back a retort but then stop. I could lash out at him; I could fight back. It's what we do, and then even that statement feels like a lie. That's what I do— not Lachlan. I fight. I get angry, and I pick a fight. I've been fighting with Lachlan since the first day I met him.

Why? Because I walked into that throne room and I saw him. Him. Confrontational would be a polite way of describing my behavior that first day. I was terrified— and then he looked at me, really looked at me, and I felt the connection between us. The magic that binds us together, and for the briefest moment, I felt held...safe. His eyes had flared from chocolate to amber, and I felt...imagined that he wanted to reach for me, pull me closer, but then his beautiful eyes turned hard and flat.

The look on his face nearly broke me. Not this man—not from him. I'd been dreaming about him for years. *Dreams aren't real life, Sara.* Yet there he was, this man, standing in front of me, looking at me with cold disdain. My heart broke, and everything I knew about myself splintered into a million pieces.

Chapter 7

*L*ACHLAN
Emotions flit across Sara's face and she pales... I can't read her, but my question prompted this flood of pain washing over her. I've hurt her again and without even knowing how. Sara would be happier in Cork without me.

I admit I don't know how to talk to her. I have a knack for saying the wrong thing. I miss the social cues that most Fae, and even humans, seem to understand. Kings can have sex, but we're not allowed to date. The stupidity in that decree has left me wholly ill-equipped to have a relationship with my wife.

You could take her to bed, my beast whispers, *that's one way to make her forget her pain.*

One way to cause her more pain, I snap back.

Talking to my magic. Sara says she does the same thing. I turn my gaze back to her. She's staring into her glass, her eyes shining with tears. I don't know what to say to her. As I watch, she gives her head a little shake, and then when she notices me watching her, she smiles widely.

"I'm sorry, what were we talking about?" she asks.

"You would be happier in Cork."

The smile slips, and she tilts her head to the side as she looks at me. "That isn't a question." For a second, I'm distracted by the elegant line of her neck. All I can think about is brushing my lips along it, tasting her skin, and inhaling her scent.

I drag my eyes back to her face. She looks annoyed, and I can't tell you how relieved that makes me feel. I hate it when she's sad. "I am your husband. Surely a man knows what his wife wants."

Color slashes her cheeks, and every muscle in her body tenses as she prepares to leap from her seat. I have to bite the inside of my mouth to stop myself from laughing at her, but then her eyes narrow, and she huffs indignantly.

"Remind me why I married you again?"

"To stop a war."

"Oh yes, that," she says dryly. And then, because I'm a masochist, I bring up the subject again.

"Sara, would you like to go back to Cork?" I don't even know what I want her to answer.

"Lachlan, can we not talk about Cork tonight? Do you mind?"

I nod even as I feel heat flood my face. I've done it again, missed those little social cues that others would have picked up on. My brother certainly would have. "Of course." I stand stiffly, avoiding her eyes. "I apologize for being thoughtless. You are exhausted. Let me walk you back to your room."

Sara sighs but uncurls her legs and places her feet on the floor. I hold out my hand to help her, but she ignores my hand and frowns at me.

"Lachlan, are you tired?"

"No. I don't really sleep much." Sara nods as though she expected that answer. She still hasn't taken my hand, and I let it fall to my side.

"I really don't feel like going back to my room." She shudders. "Not yet, anyway."

I wait for her to continue, but when the silence stretches into an awkward tension between us, I turn and take my seat again. I'm still waiting, trying to take my cue from her. What does Sara want? She's still looking at me, her gaze unnervingly steady.

"Will you tell me why I terrify you?" Her tone is deceptively casual, but the look in her eyes suggests the question is important to her.

Turning, she places her wine glass on the floor beside her chair. The light from the fire illuminates her face and brings out the red tint in her hair. When she turns back to me, she's dropped all pretense of casual, and she's biting on her lower lip, a concerned look on her face.

"Is it because I'm a Seer? I get that a lot," she says as though she feels a need to reassure me. I don't know how to answer that. Sara's sincerity is unnerving when I'm used to her fighting with me.

"I didn't mean it," I say at last.

"I don't terrify you?"

"Not exactly." How do I explain this without terrifying *her*? How do I do it and not give myself away? I stare into the flames until I hear her sigh.

"I don't understand you," she finally says, and the honesty in that simple admission undoes me.

"How could you?" I smile to soften my words. "We're from different worlds."

"But what about you?" she asks. "Have you spent time in the human realm?"

"None." She nods as though my answer doesn't surprise her.

"What a match we are." She sighs and stares into the flames. "Why did you marry me?" she asks suddenly, catching me off guard again.

"The signs told me to."

"Do you always follow the signs?" she asks.

"I try to."

"And now..." her voice trails off. "Now, you're stuck with me unless...you want the marriage annulled?"

"Do *you* want the marriage annulled?"

"Lachlan, for the love of all that is sacred in this realm, can you not answer my question with another question." She glares at me. "Please give me a straight answer."

"We're bonded by magic, Sara." I frown at her. My own frustration rising. I swear she's the only one who ever talks to me like this. No one else would dare. Sara raises her eyebrows impatiently, waiting for me to continue. "An annulment is impossible. I've never discussed it with my council, and we have no annulment contract to sign. There. Is that what you wanted to hear?" I snap. "There's no way out. You're stuck with me forever."

Sara's silent for a long time after that, first watching me and then turning her eyes toward the fire. "Okay," she says, and I stare at her incredulously. She nods resolutely and says it again. "Okay. So, this is it— we're married." She swivels her gaze back to me, tucks her knees up to her chest, and wraps her arms around them. "So, tell me everything," she says. "If we're going to spend forever together, I should know something about you."

I stare at her, but all she does is look right back at me expectantly. "Am I scowling again?" I ask eventually because I'm nearly sure I am.

"Yep, but don't worry. I can ignore it," Sara says with her trademark grin. "Tell me about the signs that told you to marry me."

So that's what I do, and when I've told her everything, she's silent, a thoughtful expression on her face, but she still doesn't tell me what she's thinking.

"Arlen told me the White Hawk visited you too." I leave that hanging between us, hoping she will expand on it, but all she does is nod slowly and then change the subject.

"Have you been married before?" Whatever she sees on my face makes her laugh. "I'll take that as a no. What about girlfriends?" she asks.

I shake my head again. "Not allowed," I explain, and as I watch, her eyes widen, and I smirk and shake my head in amusement. "I'm not a virgin. Sex *is* allowed."

"Of course it is," she mutters, but her eyes skitter away from mine.

"And you?" I ask, torturing myself with the question. I'm already jealous of every man who's ever touched her. She shrugs non-committedly.

"Not really. Nothing serious. I was always working, and I had a strict no-dating policy with my colleagues." She notices my frown and rolls her eyes. "Arlen told you about Josh." She lifts her head off her knees and turns to stare into the flames.

"He told me about the nightmares." She nods as though that makes sense but keeps her face averted.

"Josh and I weren't dating. Not really. We flirted, and then we slept together one time. The occasional kiss." She turns back to me. "It wasn't serious."

"The nightmares?"

She shrugs. "Josh died in front of me." Irritation flashes across her face. "It wasn't that, not just that. I dreamt about the accident before it happened. I knew."

"You blame yourself."

"Of course I do." The irritation is directed at me this time. "I *didn't* follow the signs," she adds pointedly.

"Sara, you were a human living in the human realm. How were you to know the difference between a dream and a sign?"

She looks suddenly heartbroken and curls in on herself, wrapping her arms around her knees in a tight stranglehold. She tucks her head against her knees. "You would have followed the signs," I hear her mumble.

"I'm Fae. And a Tracker. I've been studying signs since I was a boy." Her head pops up at that.

"Yes. You're a Master Tracker. Arlen is a Manifestor..."

"I don't hear a question."

"You both have magic, but this castle is...." She hesitates. "So, what's going on here? You have magic, but this castle runs on candle power," she jokes. I sigh and scrub a hand down my face. I'm so tired of defending my home. I'm just tired, is the simple truth. I've been fighting the council on this subject for fifteen years.

"Rohn Fae hate change," I say eventually, and I'm preparing myself for the disparaging look in Sara's eyes, but she only shrugs.

"Of course they do. Everybody hates change, Lachlan. That's understandable. But surely they want to be comfortable and warm? I don't understand the poverty I see in this castle." She looks around then. "Well, not this room. I love this library, and I really love the glass wall. I think it's genius. Was it always there?" She turns to look over her shoulder at the wall. It's a black surface now reflecting the orange glow of the flames, but during the day, it draws the landscape into the room, so when I'm working here, I feel like I'm in the mountains.

And then her words hit me. Poverty? There's no poverty in my castle. There's a difference between poverty and a lack of modern comfort, and I'm about to growl this thought, but something happens. Sara distracts me with a smile and an understanding look, and instead of hearing criticism, I hear her enthusiasm for this room, and my bristling pride settles down.

I tell her about the changes I've made to my home... the more comfortable furniture, the glass walls, and larger windows to allow more natural daylight into the castle, the use of magic fire to heat the rooms. There are still so many changes I want to make, and as Sara gets excited, I find myself telling her about them. Her eyes flare green, and then she offers her own ideas and asks questions about life in the mountains during the long winters. We talk for so long that the darkness outside is fading to dawn when she yawns and stretches her arms over her head.

"I don't like my room, and I really don't want to go back there," she says suddenly and shudders. "But I need to sleep." She sits up straight, her eyes wide. "I'm so sorry. I should have told you what I learned from the Elves. We've talked about everything except what really matters." Her eyes are heavy, though, and she smothers another yawn.

"Tomorrow. Lilly and Aaronn will want to hear your report." Sara yawns again, and I frown as I consider my next words. "Sara, you said you don't like your room."

"Sorry. Was that rude?" She grimaces, which makes me smile.

"You did say you like this room, though. And if you like this room, you will probably love my chambers. They're even nicer than this." I joke to lighten the atmosphere, but Sara freezes in the act of standing up. She looks at me and then away again but doesn't say a word. I would almost say she's holding her breath.

"I want you to move into my rooms." Her head pops up again, her eyes widening. I add quickly, "I have more than one bedroom." When she doesn't say anything, I explain my strange request. "Sara, I'm worried about you being alone on the other side of the castle. I'd feel better if you were closer."

My beast is practically purring in anticipation, and I'm doing my damndest to push him back.

"I won't... I mean, you'll be safe from me. I only want you to be safe." My cheeks feel hot, and I know I'm blushing. I feel like a teenager talking to his first love.

Still, Sara says nothing, and I'm forced to look at her. She's watching me, and my beast is climbing to his feet, his fur brushing against my insides as he sniffs the air, catching her scent. Sara senses him. I see the knowledge flare in her eyes, but she doesn't look away. She leans in closer.

"Is that your magic?" she whispers. My breath feels trapped in my chest, and I can't find the words to answer her. I'm terrified that if I open my mouth, it will be a growl I emit. Even now, I feel it building in my chest, and I leap from my seat and prowl to the glass wall. Squeezing my eyes closed, I take a deep breath and release it slowly.

"Lachlan? Tell me what's going on."

"I can't," I grit out and huff out another long breath as I push my beast back. "You're safe," I tell her, worried that I've frightened her. "I will never hurt you," I add.

"I'm not afraid of you, Lachlan."

Hope is such an ephemeral feeling, so quickly extinguished, but tonight it flickers to life inside me.

SARA

Lachlan won't turn around and look at me, but I can see his reflection in the glass wall, and he looks tortured. His eyes are squeezed shut, his head bowed. Power emanates from him. He has the strength of a dozen Fae— no wonder the Fae in this castle are afraid of him. He could toss any of them across the room without blinking. Even now, his hands are bunched into fists at his side, and I watch as he forces them open and slowly exhales, his shoulders drop down, and then he opens his eyes and catches me watching him in the glass.

His eyes flicker with that amber vein, watching me, tracking me. Shivering, I wrap my arms around my waist. I'm not cold. It's anticipation.

"I won't hurt you," Lachlan says again, still not turning around. As though he doesn't trust himself even as he makes that promise. I nod at his reflection, unable to look away. Lachlan's eyes hold me captive, but he squeezes them shut, breaking the spell, and turns. Just like that, his magic is sheathed, tamed. I can't tell if I'm relieved or disappointed.

"Will you move into my rooms?" Lachlan asks me now, and I see the uncertainty that flicks through his gaze again. He is two different men. This one is shy and uncertain, and the other... I shiver again.

"I would feel safer if—" He drops his head, and I hear the sharp breath he sucks in as though he's in pain. "Lachlan?" I step closer. "Are you hurt?" His head shoots up, and he offers me a tight smile.

"It's okay, Sara. Come, I'll take you back to your room."

"Lachlan, I was going to say I'd feel safer in your rooms. You don't have to talk me into it. I always feel safe when you're with me."

He frowns again, and, wow, this man is hard to read! What have I done now?

"Good." He snaps this response and scowls at me. When I don't move, he snaps again, "Come then, I'll show you where you'll be staying from now on."

"Okaaaay," I draw the word out and raise my eyebrows— a silent demand that he explain himself. Lachlan ignores that and strides for the door. I have no choice but to follow him. In the dark passage, he stops abruptly and turns to me.

"You said you don't believe my scowls anymore," he says gruffly. He pulls me close and presses his lips to my temple in a quick kiss. "Thank you," he whispers against my skin and then releases me and walks off.

I'm left reeling, a slow warmth washing down my body. Hurrying to catch up with him, I feel a new lightness in my steps. Maybe Lachlan doesn't hate me; maybe he even likes me a little bit.

His chambers are nearby, and unknowingly I've walked past the door many times. If I'd known where he spent the nights... no, I would never have invited myself into his rooms. Not with the way he always avoided me. Lachlan opens the door and waits for me to enter before stepping in after me.

"Sara." Lachlan waits for me to turn around. "I'm locking the door, but the code is 325. I won't ever lock you in here. Is that okay?" His voice softens as he asks this.

A vision slips through my mind. A young Lachlan locked in a room— nothing as comfortable as this. Bare, dark, damp. He can't be more than five years old. In the room with him is an animal, a large cat creature, chained to the wall, snarling and angry. Lachlan is curled up in the corner of the room— the chain stretches, stopping only inches from him. I see scratches on his arms and legs. The door on the other side of the room is locked, claw marks scratched into the surface of the wood. Lachlan can't escape. He's trapped in that room with that wild animal.

The vision vanishes as quickly as it came, but tears fill my eyes. I blink them away and avert my face.

"Sara? What is it? Have you changed your mind? Will I take you back to your old room?"

"No." I don't mean to sound so fierce, but I'm angry, so angry. I want to protect him. I want to hold him close and make everything better, sweeter. *I'll love you forever*, I want to whisper. But he's giving me that frown again and stepping back, making sure to keep a distance between us. And that makes me see red. Stepping closer, I jab my finger into his chest— angry enough not to care.

"I am not scared of you," I say. "Have you got that, Lachlan? I'm not scared of you. I know you won't hurt me." I jab my index finger into his chest one more time.

"But—" he starts.

"No," I snap, needing him to listen. I need him to hear me this time. Grasping his face in my two hands, I hold his head still. His eyes flare with shock, but he doesn't move; he doesn't push me away. "I am not scared of you. I will never be scared of you." A flash of vulnerability in his eyes replaces the scowl, but then his face goes carefully blank and cold, and oh, I hate that expression even more than I hate his scowl. "And don't you dare look at me like that, King Lachlan of Rohn. I forbid it." I sound ridiculous, I know, but it works. His mouth twitches, and then he laughs and steps back. I let him this time. "No more talk of hurting me, okay?" My voice is steadier now. His laughter vanishes, but he nods.

"Let me show you where you'll be sleeping," he says, and I follow him through what looks like a cozy sitting room. Along one wall is a long window that showcases the Duana Mountains. On the other side is an open hearth, and in the middle of the room is a two-seater brown leather couch and two matching armchairs, all positioned around a rustic hand-carved coffee table. It's masculine but comfortable.

Lachlan is waiting for me on the other side of the room, beside two closed doors. He opens the one on the left.

"You can use this room," he says, holding the door open so I can walk through. "We'll fetch your clothes tomorrow." He nods to the other side of the bedroom. "There's a bathroom through that door. I have my own. We won't have to share." Lachlan stops suddenly, and color slashes his cheeks. It makes me want to kiss him and demand that he tell me what thought caused that sudden blush. But he turns away quickly and steps out of the room. I want to call him back and ask him to stay with me, but I don't dare do that.

Lachlan turns around, and I think maybe he's read my mind, but no— "The main door is locked. No one can get in here."

"Except for Arlen. He has the master key," I say unthinkingly and then wince. His brother is still a sensitive subject between us, but Lachlan rolls his eyes instead of scowling at me.

"Of course he does. I should have known." He looks like he might take a step closer but only taps his hand on the bedroom door. "There is a key for this door, too, if you want to lock it."

I shake my head. Lachlan stares at me for a long moment but then turns abruptly, closing the door as he does. I'm left staring at that door wishing for something more but just a little relieved that I'm alone. This day has been a whirlwind of emotion after six weeks of living in a void. Now I'm back in Rohn, I feel like I've been dumped in a storming ocean, visions pounding me from all sides.

Needing to sleep, I drag myself to the bed and tuck myself beneath the warm quilt. Woolen blankets are piled at the bottom of the bed, and I drag them up and around me. It's not cold in here, but I feel alone suddenly. Isolated from the people who love me. I roll over onto my side and tuck my arm beneath my head as I look through the window. It's smaller than the one in the sitting room, and from this angle, all I can see is the sky, growing light as dawn approaches. I yawn again, my eyes heavy. I like this room, I think to myself and sink into sleep.

Chapter 8

L*ACHLAN*
    I glance impatiently at the seating area in my library and then move the armchairs around, facing them toward the sofa. I instruct the servant hovering outside the door to fetch another chair and place it with the others to form a circle of sorts, with all the seats facing each other.

I've already instructed my staff that we're not to be disturbed, but once the others arrive, I lock the door to ensure it. Arlen ignores my carefully arranged seating and moves over to the glass wall, his back to the rest of us. Aaronn and Lilly take the sofa, and Sara chooses the armchair she sat in last night. As my gaze lingers on her, she turns to look at me, so I walk to her side and take the seat beside her.

"Arlen." I point at the remaining empty seat, but he shakes his head. "Please?" He frowns but gives in to my request and walks across the room to take the remaining seat.

"Is there a reason for this drama and intrigue, brother?" he asks with his usual sarcasm, but I see the worry in his gaze as his eyes flick between Sara and myself.

"Firstly, Arlen. I don't want you to worry about Sara. She has moved out of the western wing of the castle." I pause then as I consider my next words, but I feel I should explain myself, as awkward as it is to do that in front of the others. Glancing at Sara, I add, "I was thinking of you when I installed you in that wing of the castle. I wanted you to feel safe; I didn't want you to feel like I was on top of you all the time, breathing down your neck." Sara's eyes flare a deep green, and Arlen starts to laugh.

"Well put, Lachlan."

I glare at him in confusion but then notice that Lilly is suppressing a smile and that even the ordinarily stern Aaronn has his face averted. I seem to be the only one missing the joke. Blushing, I'm aware of being one step out of sync with everyone else. I am tongue-tied and uncertain again, a boy pretending to be a King.

I feel a light touch on my arm, and looking down, I see Sara's hand resting there. She waits for me to look at her, and then... there she is, inside me again.

They're laughing because they think I want you on top of me, breathing down my neck. It's me they're laughing at.

As I stare at her, she blushes and averts her gaze. For a moment, all I do is stare at her, and then her words hit me and my own blush deepens. I turn my scowl on Arlen and send him a stern warning.

"After what happened last night," I continue coolly, ignoring the fiendish grin on my brother's face. "Sara has agreed to move to the room next to mine."

Lilly sits up straighter, instantly serious. "What happened last night?"

"Last night." I glance at Sara with a frown and then plunge in with the truth. "Lars tried to kill Sara."

Nobody says a word until Arlen takes over the telling of it. "Poison," he informs Aaronn and Lilly. "Lars sent a young Fae woman to Sara's room. Lachlan interrupted her trying to give it to Sara while she slept."

Lilly pales, and Aaronn immediately places his hand on her back, but it's me he's looking at, and if the danger in his eyes is any indication, Lars better hope he doesn't run into Aaronn any time soon. "Where is he?"

"Gone, and the Fae woman is dead. Her body was found this morning." Sara jerks in her chair, and her eyes go wide. "She was trying to kill you, Sara. She doesn't deserve your sympathy," I mutter impatiently.

"But maybe she didn't know."

I reach over and clasp her hand. The gesture doesn't go unnoticed by the others, but for now, I ignore them and squeeze it gently – just enough to get her attention. "Lars wants you dead, Sara. Why?" She looks past me; her eyes are distant.

"He's involved," she says at last. When we all look at her in confusion. "With the dead Elves," she adds. "The Elves met with Lars in a, a," she trails off and hums in frustration before jumping to her feet suddenly. She moves to the window and paces back and forth in front of it.

"Sara?"

Her hand shoots up to halt my question. "I'm trying to work out the location. It wasn't a cave or a house or a..." Sara trails off again and tugs at her braids in frustration. "I don't know, but it was cold and wet." She stops and stares out the window. "Water," she says suddenly. "They were in water. That's the feeling. Water all over my skin but not dark. It was bright, and a turquoise light shone from the ceiling. They weren't scared. They were all there together in this... space. It was enclosed and underwater." She sighs and looks back at us. "I'm sorry. I know that doesn't make much sense."

Frustration is evident on her face. Nobody says a word. Aaronn and Lilly seem shocked that the source of the trouble has come from within Rohn castle. I am not. It's no coincidence that the Elves were turning up in the Schoenberg Fjord. I look down on those waters every day. Are they being left for me to find – like a trail luring us into something...a trap?

"Lachlan." The urgency in Sara's voice grabs my attention, and I'm across the room before she can say anything more. It's not until I'm behind her that I see what's caught her attention. The white hawk is back. Sara looks mesmerized as she watches it, a smile in her eyes, but she shivers then, and her eyes roll back.

"Trouble coming," she whispers, and then she moans and shakes her head, tears running down her cheeks. "No." She breathes the word and stumbles. I catch her, my hands wrapping around her shoulders and holding her upright. The tremors start in her arms and pass through her body. She turns in to me, and I know it's an automatic response. I'm the nearest one to her. She would have done the same with Arlen or Aaronn, but for once, I'm glad I'm the one she reaches for.

Holding her close, I rub my hand up and down her spine, soothing her. "Tell me what you saw." She shakes her head, and I tighten my arms around her. "Remember what we talked about last night?" Her trembling stops, she's listening. "To follow the signs, you must first believe in them."

"I'm scared," she murmurs, so quietly I'm the only one who can hear her. This woman, she's breaking my heart. Pressing my lips to her temple, I kiss her before easing back and looking her in the eyes. She stares back helplessly and then nods. "Cian," she whispers. "My brother – one of the bodies," her voice trails off into silence.

"But he's in Cork." I hear Lilly's instant rebuttal, and Sara stiffens in my arms and then looks at Arlen. I release her and stand back. Sara rejoins the others. Arlen looks embarrassed now, his gaze swinging between Lilly and Aaronn.

"I'm sorry," he says at last. "After everything that happened yesterday, I forgot to mention it."

Sara reaches for Lilly's hand. "Cian and Breanna came through the Portal with us." She glances at Aaronn. "They left immediately for Torin; Breanna wanted to see her family, and Cian wouldn't let her go alone.

Lilly pales, and I notice Sara is still shaking. She clasps her hands together and then sinks into the armchair, leaning forward and cradling her head in her hands.

Arlen meets my eyes from across the room, a determined light shining in them now that makes me nervous. It's the same look he always got when we were kids, and he was about to do something reckless. He turns toward Sara. "Sara, sweetheart, look at me, please." The easy endearment brings a sour taste to my mouth, but I swallow it back.

Sara raises her head and smiles at Arlen. I shouldn't feel this jealousy. I have no right to feel it. Arlen can make her smile, if he can reassure her... surely, I want that for her. So what if I'm not the man to do it?

Arlen walks over to Sara and kneels in front of her. He takes her hands in his. "Sara, can you tell us everything you learned yesterday? It might not make sense to you but between us... maybe it will help." She nods slowly, and Arlen looks over his shoulder at Aaronn. "Will you help? Your Influencer magic can stabilize her while she accesses her visions."

I remain at the window, watching as Aaronn stands behind Sara's chair and places his hands on her shoulders. She sits up straighter, her eyes meet mine over Lilly's head, only for a few seconds, and then she closes her eyes.

SARA

The cold washes over me once more. Yesterday I believed the ice room was the source of the cold, but today I know that my location has nothing to do with it. This cold is what the Elves felt before...

"I'm cold and surrounded by water. It's all around me. My hands are so cold they're almost blue. But I can breathe. There's no water on my face or on my chest. No... my face and chest are warm, protected from the water. My limbs are freezing, though."

I talk them through all the physical sensations I'm experiencing. The cold, the exhaustion, my eyes closing. I want to sleep. I want to rest, just for a few minutes.

"Sara."

"Let me sleep," I murmur.

"Sara. Wake-up. Now."

Someone shakes me, and a stinging slap to my cheek forces my eyes open. "Ow." I glare at Arlen as he looms over me. "Was that really necessary?"

"Yes," he says grimly.

I hold a hand up to my face, I can still feel the sting of his slap on my cheek, but I also feel disorientated, not quite in my body. Shaking my head, I puff out a loud breath, hoping that's enough to steady me.

Arlen and Aaronn are debating the best method for visioning, and Lilly is interrupting them with her questions before the conversation turns to the information I just related... which is hardly anything when I hear it back in their words. The Elves were cold and tired! Well done, me, a great bit of detective work that was.

I shake my head again, roll my shoulders back, and I'm ready. "Okay, let's do it again," I say to the others.

"Sara." Lachlan's voice is firm and cuts through the chatter from the other three. "You don't have to do this." He's frowning as he says it, a fierce expression in his eyes as he looks only at me, ignoring the others. I want to kiss him right now. Shock replaces that frown, and his eyes widen as he stares at me.

Oh shit! Did he just read my mind?

Somebody steps in front of me, blocking Lachlan. I look up and see Arlen studying me with a concerned look on his face. Taking a deep breath, I nod at him and try to focus again on my magic.

"Sara, we'll try that again, but we're going to use Lilly as a guide. Her voice will direct you through your visions. Think of it as a lifeline to the present."

"Arlen –" Lachlan cuts in, he sounds angry.

"Lachlan," Arlen snaps his brother's name and turns to face him. "Yes, she does have to do this. You want to protect

Sara, but this is *her* magic. She has to use it, or it will turn on her. You know this." Arlen sounds so grave and unlike himself that I see Lachlan pause and study his brother. His gaze flits to mine, and I nod.

"It's okay. This is important," I tell him.

Lachlan turns away and paces over to the window. His back is rigid, and his hands are bunched at his sides. I wish I could hold him right now, soothe him. I watch as his hands relax, and he hangs his head and releases a sigh.

Focus, Sara, his voice whispers in my head.

"Sara." Arlen's voice drags me back to my place in the middle of the library, and I look up at him. "Did you understand what I told you earlier? Lilly's voice is your anchor, your lifeline. You need to follow it. Don't let the visions take over. Do not—"

"Arlen," I interrupt him, then reach for his hand and squeeze it. "I understand." My eyes stray past him, but Lachlan still has his back to us, his face turned toward the window. Aaronn returns to his position behind me, and I feel his hands settle on my shoulders. Lilly kneels in front of me and takes my two hands in hers, and I force my gaze away from Lachlan and look at my sister. I see the worry on her face, but she keeps her eyes steady on mine.

"You can do this," she whispers.

Closing my eyes, I take a deep breath to steady my nerves and release it slowly. Lilly guides me through the vision. "You're in an underwater room with Lars and the Elves." I let myself drop back into the vision but always with her voice leading, asking questions, guiding me— directing what I see and hear.

"They are excited, talking about a new energy source. A clean, renewable energy source. If they can perfect it, the forests won't need to be cut back for fuel. There's a lot of talk about protecting the forests and protecting the Mya. I don't understand; something about hydropower being amplified by this new energy source."

Lilly keeps asking me questions. I hear Arlen and Aaronn whispering to her, adding their own questions. The only voice I don't hear is Lachlan's. I want him here with me. It's his hands I want on my shoulders, not Aaronn's.

My magic pulls me deeper into this ocean world, water clouding my vision. A brush of fabric against my shoulder. A halt in Lilly's questions. I'm far away from the room but within it at the same time. It's the strangest sensation. A floating and then a sudden grounding as Lachlan's hands settle firmly on my shoulders. His thumb brushes up the back of my neck to let me know he's with me. As if I wouldn't know the difference between Aaronn's impersonal touch and Lachlan's possessive hold.

Lilly and Arlen are debating again— a whispered conference, but Lachlan remains quiet, soothing me with that gentle caress of his thumb up and down my neck – and then Lilly's voice tugs on me again, and I'm leaving the room, following the trail of her words.

"Sara, I want you to go back further. To the day the Elves decided to leave the Mya Initiate School. What made them leave the woods? Why were they near the ocean? Who lured them under the water?"

"They weren't lured. They went willingly and with the Mya's blessing. There was a celebration to bless their journey.

There's a lot of excitement amongst the initiates. The ten strongest are chosen to join this," I'm struggling to find the right word, "project. No, experiment. Yes, it's an experiment. They don't know if it will work, but if it does, it will mean huge advances for the realm."

Lilly has gone quiet, her questions trailing off into silence, but I need her voice to bring me back. Without it, I'm falling, my vision blurring, going black. A hard squeeze to my shoulders and Lachlan growling my sister's name stops me free falling into darkness.

"Sara, I want you to follow my voice back to the present. That's it. Keep following my voice until you're back and ready to open your eyes. I'm right here. Can you hear me?"

I nod, sucking a deep breath into my lungs as I blink my eyes open. Lachlan keeps his hands on my shoulders the whole time, his fingers biting into my skin as though he's afraid to let go. I reach across my chest and place my hand over his. It's only then his hands relax, and I hear him exhale. He doesn't move his hands away, though, and I keep my hand over his, anchoring him there at my side.

"How are you feeling?" Lilly asks, still crouching in front of me, concern creasing her forehead. I see her eyes flitting all around me, and I know she's using her magic to scan my energy field. Her eyes linger where my hand rests on Lachlan's, and she smiles. Glancing up at Lachlan, she nods before pushing herself up and turning to the others.

"Well, what do you think?" She directs the question to the group, but she looks at Aaronn, who is frowning and staring into space.

"Before we discuss this." Lachlan interrupts them, and the others turn to us. "Sara needs to go outside. She needs to feel the mountains under her feet." The other three stare at him in confusion. Arlen even starts to object, but he doesn't get a chance. "No arguments," Lachlan snaps. He pulls me to my feet and puts an arm around my waist.

"He's right," I say to Arlen and then grin when he rolls his eyes.

"He's always right." I hear him mutter.

Lachlan's arm tightens around my waist, and I lean into him. Being in nature is the quickest way to ground back into my body. That's why I always craved the mountains after being stuck inside for long periods. We're only five steps outside the massive front door, and I feel the change in me. My head stops spinning, the cold air brushes against my flushed skin, and my heart rate slows. I no longer feel like I'm trying to catch my breath.

"How did you know?" I ask Lachlan, resting my head on his shoulder.

"It was the same for me when I learned to use my magic. Afterward, I had to be outside." A few Fae are in the courtyard, but they are studiously ignoring us, their eyes averted.

"Where are you taking me?" I ask as he continues to walk us toward the gates. I know that just outside those gates is a path that leads down the mountain, along the back of the city. There is a hole in the wall there. It's how I've escaped Rohn before – but I doubt that's where Lachlan is taking us.

"Correct," he mutters, but there's a rumble of laughter in his chest.

"We're not escaping?"

"Unfortunately not," he says and then laughs again. "But along that path is a boulder where we can sit a while." He leads me through the gate and down the path.

"You can let go of me now," I say, but he only shrugs and keeps me pressed close to his side.

I know the boulder he means as soon as I see it; it's large and almost flat on top and sits a few feet to the left of the path. Lachlan climbs up in one large step and then holds out his hand to pull me up. His hand tingles against mine, sending electricity up my arm, and I shiver with the contact. He drops my hand and turns to view the Duana mountains and the Schoenberg Fjord below us. It's a picture of blues and greens.

"Sit," he says gruffly, pointing at the boulder. He's avoiding my gaze, but I can't bring myself to tease him right now. When I'm sitting, I look up at him expectantly. "Now lie on your back and place your hands palms down on the boulder." He's turned his back on me again. Almost as if—

"Sara." He's using his commanding don't-mess-with-me voice. "Lie down."

I ease back onto the rock, close my eyes, and turn my hands, so my palms rest against the boulder. A surge of power flows into my hands, up my arms, and floods my body. I gasp at the sensation, and my eyes fly open in shock. Lachlan still has his back to me, and my eyes slide closed as the energy surges through my body. My back arches off the rock and then collapses down. I'm breathing heavily. It's the most incredible feeling. I'm tingling all over my body. It's better than any orgasm I've ever had. My eyes pop open with that thought, and I notice Lachlan waiting, his body still turned stiffly away from me. Did he know I would feel this way?

A little embarrassed, I blink the question away and push myself up, crossing my legs. I look down at the view, enjoying the silence. I haven't enjoyed the mountains since Josh's death, but today feels different. I feel as if I've made peace with... something.

"Your magic," Lachlan supplies the answer, turning around at last. He sits beside me but still won't look at me.

"Can you read my mind all the time now?" I ask and feel instantly embarrassed by the X-rated thoughts I've been having about him.

"X-rated, huh?" he teases, finally turning to look at me. I blush and swat his arm in embarrassment.

"Ssh, how long have you been reading my mind?"

"I can't do it all the time," he admits and looks away again. "Right now, our magic is merged— after what happened inside. I put a trace on you to make sure we could pull you back to us if you passed out." I shiver at the thought, and that familiar scowl appears on his face. "Your magic can be dangerous, Sara. You're so cavalier with it." He breaks off and looks away, and the silence between us feels heavy until he shakes it off abruptly.

"But no, I can't read your mind all the time. I'm new to this bonding magic as well. We should get some help with it. Some guidance. Your sister might be a good person to ask. Lilly and Aaronn seem to have mastered it."

"You mean, learn how to read each other properly?"

"I was thinking more that we need to learn how to manage our boundaries better. A lesson in how to stop our thoughts bouncing back and forth between us."

"Oh." He's right. I know he's right.

"Sara?"

"Hmmm," I mumble before glancing back at him. He's looking at me with uncertainty, an embarrassed flush on his cheeks. "What?"

"Never mind." He turns his head away. "We should get back," he says, but before he can stand, I grab his arm.

"Wait. What were you going to say?"

"It doesn't matter." But he won't look at me.

"Lachlan, please tell me." His eyes narrow in irritation as he glances at my hand on his arm, restraining him. I drop my hand, but then he huffs impatiently.

"In the library, you said," he grimaces and corrects himself, "you thought about kissing me. Did you mean it? Or was that just..." He shrugs and throws me a helpless look. "You know, like does it mean something else," his voice trails off, and he looks away with a frustrated frown.

"What else could it mean?" I ask with a laugh, but when his jaw tightens and he stands abruptly, I quickly stop my laughter. "Lachlan."

"Just leave it. It was a pointless question. I was curious, that's all. I don't always understand the colloquialisms that humans use. Was it as straightforward as it sounded, or does that phrase mean something else?"

I stand up cautiously, nearly afraid to spook him away. "I wanted to kiss you. It was as straightforward as it sounded," I say steadily, forcing myself to look him in the eyes.

"But why?" He looks genuinely confused, and the heat drains from my body at his cold, analytical expression. "I'm trying to understand, Sara. Why in that precise moment did you want to kiss me?"

What can I possibly say to that? *The truth*, my magic whispers.

"I always want to kiss you." I watch as his face shuts down, and that hard, flat look returns to his eyes. Why does it always hurt so much?

Lachlan turns and jumps off the boulder, waiting for me to follow. He doesn't hold out his hand to help me down and the shock of his rejection feels the same as being dropped into a glacial lake. I can't breathe for a minute. My legs are shaking, but I manage to make it down the boulder without falling on my face.

I concentrate on brushing my jeans down just to avoid looking at Lachlan, but I still feel the stern look he gives me. I don't look up until I hear him turn away and begin to climb the hill.

"Except for now," I mutter to his retreating back. "I definitely don't want to kiss you right now. I could happily throw stones at your hard, stubborn head. That would be infinitely more enjoyable than kissing you right now."

He doesn't respond to my quiet muttering, but he hears it, and, childish as I am, that makes me feel better.

Chapter 9

L*ACHLAN*

 I stare at the list in front of me, growl, and hurl my pen across the room. It bounces off the wall of my small study, spattering blue ink onto the cream rug. I can't work, I can't sleep, I can't think straight... all because my wife has wedged herself into my head. Her thoughts, her face, her lips. *I always want to kiss you.*

After returning Sara to the library, I left her there with her family and proceeded to my study. Arlen had already disappeared, and that should worry me. Trouble follows my brother around like a love-struck fool. Sighing, I scrub a hand down my face and stare out the small window beside my desk. It's only mid-afternoon, and I know I should return to my guests, but for now... for now, I need to be away from Sara and her *I always want to kiss you.*

Damn that woman for always finding a way to get inside my head. What was I supposed to say to that? Nothing. And that clearly wasn't the correct response if her anger was anything to go by, and those quiet mutterings... although they were mostly entertaining.

But no, I have to clear my head. I need to concentrate on this matter with the Elves. Hence, the reason I'm sitting in my study working. I stare down at the list I've compiled and curse loudly. Even locked away in my study, I can't escape her.

1. Find out why the Elvin council withheld this information from us.
2. If ten initiates were chosen, why have we only found seven bodies?
3. Sara wants to kiss me all the time. Why?
4. Source a reliable tracker to find the missing elves.
5. Sara's lips on mine. Will they be as soft and warm as I remember?
6. Send a rescue team to search the fjord again.
7. Peel that green sweater from her body and run my lips down her throat.
8. Appoint a guard to protect Sara while I'm away from the castle.
9. Kiss her breasts, suck her dusky nipples into my mouth.
10. Send out a water patrol to track for Elves below the surface.
11. Undo the button on her jeans, and tug them down over her hips.
12. Run my tongue up the length of one long thigh.
13. I always want to kiss you.
14. Sara's mouth on my chest.
15. Sara's lips around my cock.

Aaaargh! This is intolerable. Scrunching up the list, I toss the crumpled paper across the room. I can't think about anything but her. "Fuck." This isn't working. Nothing is working.

Striding across my study in three steps, I yank open the door. Another three steps, and I'm across my bedroom and stepping into the shower. Flicking the dial to ice-cold, I strip out of my clothes, dumping them where I stand. The cold water hits me, sharp pinpricks that sear into my skin. I force myself to stay where I am. Discipline. Control. I am in control of my body. Control is all that matters...but I have no control around my wife.

Why don't you just take her? Then you'd be able to concentrate again, my magic taunts me.

You'd like that, wouldn't you? I growl back.

I would, actually, my magic chuckles.

Things are bad when my beast is the one making sense.

Besides, you don't need a tracker to find those Elves. You have me. Release me. Let me find them, he growls low, the sound vibrating deep inside me. *Let me find Lars; I know his scent. I can track him. I can kill him for daring to touch something that belongs to us. Sara is ours. No one else gets to touch her, no one gets to even look at her without our permission. No one—*

"Enough," I shout loudly enough to cut through his rant. It's not the first time he's whispered threats like this. Any man who's come close to Sara ends up on his kill list. "Enough," I say again, and although he growls in frustration, he lets me push him back. I turn the water pressure up and blast myself with the frigid water.

Enough is right, though I see again the hurt in Sara's eyes, and that tangled-up place inside me squeezes tight.

Returning to the library an hour later, I find only Aaronn and Arlen seated by the fire. I raise my eyebrows as I look around the room.

"Sara wanted to talk to Lilly before we leave for Torin," Aaronn says, correctly interpreting my look.

"When will that be?" I thought he would stay to see this case resolved. I was counting on his help.

"We've been talking," Arlen interjects while I glower at the two of them. "This matter involves the whole realm, not just Rohn. It's clear both the Mya and the Mer are involved."

I frown at his neat conclusion. "We do not know that the Mer court is involved."

"Of course not, brother, but there is a Mer presence in those visions. These are the questions we need to have answered. The only thing that is clear is that it's no longer about one power-hungry Fae. This is too organized.

Sinking into the nearest armchair, I sigh heavily. My brother is right. "I have sent out a tracker unit to scour the fjord again. There might still be three more Elves in the water."

The only sound in the room is the crackling of the flames in the fireplace. Standing again, I reach for the whiskey and three glasses. After pouring a measure into each, I hand them out and return to my seat.

"Does any of this make sense?" I ask at last. "Did anything Sara say explain why the Elves are turning up in the fjord?" I hate not having the answers, especially if it's something about my kingdom. And I'm furious that Lars is involved, and I never saw it; I never realized that he was up to something... something. What?

"A clean energy source... tapping energy directly from the Elves. Since they discussed it being a renewable source, I'm assuming they didn't intend to kill the source— but did they go too far? Was it an accident?" Aaronn muses as he stares into the flames.

"And who's behind it?" Arlen interrupts. "Lars wouldn't do this on his own," he mutters with a frown. "He has to have someone backing him. But who? And why would they involve Lars— of all the Fae..." his voice trails off, and then his gaze snaps to me. "Unless it's because of his position in the Rohn court, he was close to you." Arlen's stare sharpens, seeming to see right through me. "Lars had access to you— more access than any other Fae. The Elves were found in the fjord below Rohn castle... brother, I'm willing to bet all my magic you're involved in this."

I raise my eyebrows coolly and cross my arms, pushing my beast down, although he's already clambering back up and growling low in my ears.

"Oh, settle down." Arlen rolls his eyes impatiently. "Tell him to stand down, Lachlan. I'm not accusing you, either of you," he says pointedly, ignoring my glare. "I said you're involved somehow. Someone is doing this to you, I mean. Targeting you."

My beast is soothed by Arlen's explanation and settles back down, but I'm horrified— first by the fact that he knows about my beast and second that he's just outed me in front of Aaronn. I can't bring myself to look at my friend. I'm too busy glaring at my brother.

"Lachlan, every Tracker has a predator within them. You're not unique in this." Aaronn's voice is steady and reasonable as it cuts through the fraught silence and breaks the staring contest Arlen and I are involved in.

My eyes snap shut as Aaronn's words penetrate. "I know, but this is different. My beast is stronger than most," I admit quietly, turning to look at Aaronn. "He's... dangerous, wild."

Arlen sits up straight, his eyes going wide. "That's why you keep pushing Sara away. I could never understand it." He shakes his head in amazement. "Sara excites the predator in you. No, don't deny it. There's a power in you every time Sara is near. Your magic is stronger. It's amplified." His eyes glow with excitement as he leans forward. "Lachlan, this is a good thing. Why are you trying to push her away?"

"You're afraid of your beast," Aaronn supplies the answer quietly, in the same steady voice he always uses. "You're afraid you won't be able to control it, and he'll hurt Sara."

I nod sharply and look away, too ashamed to say more.

No one says anything for the longest time until Arlen asks, "But why would your beast hurt Sara?" He looks completely baffled by the conversation; all I want to do is change it.

Arlen will never understand what it's like having a beast inside. He will never understand the fear I live with every day.

"When has it ever hurt someone you love?" Arlen continues unrelentingly. "The gods know I've given you enough reason over the years. Even those months you thought I was sleeping with Sara— your beast still didn't hurt me."

"I control him— with everyone else, I can control him, but with Sara... I have no control." My voice breaks as I admit this, and I can't bring myself to look at them. "I have no control," I repeat. "None. She gets inside and... I'm scared." It hurts to say it out loud, and I watch the other two look at each other in silence. I squeeze my eyes shut. I don't want to see the look on their faces after that admission.

Aaronn and Lilly should take Sara with them. At least they can keep her safe. They can all go to Torin... or Arlen... my brother can take Sara to Soraya. She can stay at the palace with her mother.

"Have you considered the possibility that your beast, your magic, has been waiting for Sara all these years? The signs brought her to you for a reason, Lachlan." Aaronn's voice is steady and measured, with no sympathy or fake encouragement. "You can't control him around her because you don't have to." He pauses. "What if Sara can control him herself?"

"And what if he hurts her?" I growl back, barely concealing my impatience with him.

"What if he doesn't?" Aaronn counters. "What if he protects her? What if he loves her?"

I release a rough laugh at that. "My beast knows nothing about love, Aaronn. He wants to fuck Sara, own her, dominate her." My words are ugly. I mean to shock them into silence, but the silence that follows is not heavy. Arlen is grinning, his laughter just below the surface of that grin, and his eyes are on the door behind me. Aaronn looks amused, and when I turn and find Lilly and Sara in the doorway, even Lilly looks like she's holding back a laugh.

The only person who isn't laughing is Sara. Her eyes sweep me from head to toe, with confusion and something that looks like hurt in her eyes. Then she turns and walks out of the room as fast as possible.

"Fuck," I mutter under my breath and then turn and glare at Arlen and Aaronn. "This is your fault." I head for the door. "Don't leave before I get back," I say over my shoulder, running after my wife.

SARA

I'm running to get away from that room, and those words... the passages are a blur, and when I finally stop, I have no idea where I am. Looking around, I realize I don't recognize this area of the castle. A long, narrow window lies in front of me, and a passage runs to the left and right. Along this passage are more doors. Where the hell am I?

I can't go back to the library. Not yet. Placing a hand on my cheek, I can feel how hot my face is. I'm so embarrassed. I press my forehead up against the cold window. I will not cry over this... they're angry tears, but still... just no. I can't believe Lachlan would say something like that about me. I'm his wife. He can't talk about fucking me...

He didn't. Lachlan wasn't saying *he* wanted to fuck me. He said his beast wants me.

Oh no, that explains so much. The way he blows hot and cold all the time. His magic desires me. That spark between us... it's not Lachlan. It's the predator within him... who wants to fuck me. Not love me, fuck me. That word is very specific.

I feel like I'm going to throw up— there's a churning in my stomach and a pain in my chest. I press my cheek against the cool of the window, trying to concentrate on the sensation of cold glass against my skin. Why do I keep letting him hurt me like this? I can't, I can't—

Two hands land on my shoulders, shocking me out of my pain, and I lash out, kicking back with all my strength, twisting and turning.

"Sara, it's me." Lachlan's voice is rough and low in my ear as he tugs me tight against his chest. His one arm clamps around my arms to stop my flailing, and the other wraps around my waist.

I stop struggling as soon as I hear his voice, but I'm shaking now. It's adrenalin; that's all it is. I want to cry but bite down on my lip to stop my tears. Lachlan hears the whimper I try to muffle, and his arms tighten, squeezing me to his chest.

I've never felt safe in this castle, and I can't help that the first thought that went through my mind a minute ago was that this time Lars would succeed. This time his minions would kill me, and it would all be my fault because I'd got myself lost. I'd run away again. Run away without protection.

Lachlan's holding me firmly, his arms nearly too tight, but I don't want him to let go. At least with him here, I know I'm safe. He presses his face into my hair, and his breath is warm on my neck. The coarse scrape of his beard against my cheek soothes me. Even the unsteady heave of his breath is a comfort, and now I'm not sure if he's shaking or if it's me.

It's me, of course. Lachlan has no reason to shake, and that thought rains a cold dose of sense down on top of me.

"Sara." Lachlan turns me around and wraps his arms around me, pulling me close. He cradles my head against his shoulder. I don't know why I let him. "I'm sorry." His voice is low and rough against my ear. "I'm sorry I scared you, and I'm so sorry you heard...that. What I said in the library. I'm sorry."

I feel his lips against my temple, and I remember all the other times he's done that...held me like this, like he cares. I give him an angry shove, but I might as well be trying to push a mountain out of the way.

"Lachlan, let me go." He drops his arms immediately and steps back. I glare at him.

"I'm sorry," he says again, but I'm tired of his apologies.

"Explain. Right now. Last night you said that you would never hurt me. Guess what, Lachlan? You're hurting me. I'm hurting." Tears are running down my cheeks and I scrub angrily at my face. "Why is it okay for you to sit there with the men talking about how you want to fuck me, but I—"

"I don't want to fuck you," he interrupts, a note of desperation in his voice, but all I hear is *I don't want you*, and tears start to fall again.

"Fine. I misunderstood. You don't want to be my husband, you don't want to kiss me, you don't want to fuck me. Got it— what do you want?"

He looks shell-shocked for a minute, then he steps closer and gently tugs me into his arms. He moves slowly, giving me time to push him away, but I'm blinking at him through my tears, too upset to know what to do with him. He leans down and presses his mouth to mine in a soft kiss, gently at first and then harder.

"Lachlan." I'm still not ready to give up this fight. His hand comes up to cup my face, and he tears his mouth away and rests his forehead against mine, his lips only inches away.

"I don't want to fuck you," he whispers. "I want to make love to you every minute of every day. All I think about is you." He presses a soft kiss to my lips. "Your mouth," he murmurs then. "I've lost hours of my life thinking about your lips." His lips are firm on mine, controlling as he nips my bottom lip gently and brushes the spot with the tip of his tongue.

"Oh," is all the coherence I can muster as he tugs me closer and deepens the kiss slowly, masterfully. He's in control, and I'm lost in the sensation of his lips on mine.

A discreet cough reaches through the fog, and I blink my eyes open in a confused daze. I didn't dream it. Lachlan is standing in front of me with his arm still wrapped around my waist. I stare at the pulse jumping in his neck and then look up, but he's not looking at me; he's frowning at someone over my shoulder.

"Excuse the interruption, My Lord."

Spinning around quickly, I find a castle servant standing two feet away, his eyes concentrating fiercely on the stone floor.

"My Lady," he adds and gives a little nod of his head in my direction without looking at either of us.

"Yes?" Lachlan's impatience would terrify an army. I cast a wry look his way. His mouth almost twitches into a smile, but then those lips flatten into a hard, disapproving line. "What is it?"

"My Lord, the Commander is leaving and requests an audience before he departs."

I'm trying to work out who he's talking about, but Lachlan nods impatiently and waves the servant away. He still has me pressed to his side, his hand splayed possessively against my hip.

Turning slowly, I look up at him. He brushes his thumb across my left cheek and then my right, wiping my tears away. It's a simple gesture but so tender my heart squeezes tight in my chest. I'm too scared to believe any of this is real. He will be staring at me with that horrible, cold stare any minute now.

"But you won't kiss me if I look at you like that," he says quietly, his hand cupping my cheek. "*Your* words. You'd rather throw rocks at my head than kiss me when I look at you like that." He leans down and presses his lips to mine—too quickly, and then he steps back, his hands dropping to his side.

I feel bereft without his touch. Lachlan starts moving away, but when he realizes I'm not following, he turns back, and uncertainty flickers in his gaze.

"Lachlan, you haven't explained anything." Frustration is edging out the softer feelings. "You can't just kiss me and walk away." He raises his eyebrows in confusion. "I'm not something on your 'to do' list: appease wife. Tick." Something bright flares in his dark gaze, but he tamps it down. "Lachlan, I'm serious. Kissing me doesn't fix this. I need an explanation. I need—"

He hauls me into his arms, and his breath is warm on my neck as his teeth clamp down on my earlobe. He sucks it into his mouth, and I shiver. I'm instantly weak in his arms and equally frustrated with myself for feeling that way.

"Lachlan," I moan— in objection, I'd like to think, but really, it's closer to surrender as I angle my neck, offering myself up to his mouth.

"Sara, I know what you need," he promises as his mouth trails down my neck. And then, just like that, he steps back, and I'm left cold and dazed without his arms around me.

I growl in frustration. "Stop doing that. I swear, Lachlan, if there were rocks in this passage, I'd be throwing them at your head right now." He laughs, and the smile he offers me is so wide and easy that I see a glimpse of the boy he used to be and nearly trip over my feet. He reaches for my hand and presses a quick kiss to my palm.

"Let's hear what Aaronn wants to say. Okay?" His eyes catch mine, checking in with me, and that brush of his magic against mine soothes me... enough for me to nod.

But he looks anything but soothed— the amber in his eyes flares brighter, and his hand around mine squeezes tight, pulling me close to his side.

Chapter 10

L*ACHLAN*

The wooden door is intricately carved. I rest my palm on it for the longest minute of my life, too scared to go inside. The carvings of the red-tailed hawk and wild amber lily are as familiar to me as my own fingers lying across them. It's a beautiful door, and I've seen it thousands of times.

I've spent my entire life sleeping behind this door. In these chambers. Even after my father died and the council wanted me to move to the King's chambers in the west wing— I refused. I wouldn't spend a single night in those rooms— where my father slept, where my mother died.

Oh, the gods, this is a mistake. I glance up and down the passage, relieved to see I'm still alone; there's no one around to see me hovering outside my door like a blushing virgin. By now, everyone in the castle knows Sara has moved into my rooms; the court also knows I was kissing my wife in the passage like a horny teenager.

I don't want to imagine the gossip that will spread if anyone sees me standing here, too scared to go inside. Too afraid to sleep with my wife.

But how can I go to Sara with these ghosts in my head? How can I go to her at all? With the others here, it had seemed almost an easy thing... my beast would never hurt Sara.

But that's not how the Rohn beast works. Love means nothing to the beast. My father beat my mother to death... his beast took control of him instead of the other way around. Ironic since my father spent so much of his life preaching to me about the importance of control.

His way of teaching me how to control my beast was to beat me. He would beat me until my beast was a snarling, raging force within me, and then he would step back and tell me, "Now, control it. You are in charge of the beast. Even now when he's at his most vicious. Control it." My father would spit insults at me, waiting for me to attack him, and if I did, he would beat me unconscious. His beast asserting its dominance over mine.

Oh, the gods, I can't do this tonight. Sara deserves so much more than me. Curling my hand into a fist, I turn away from the door just as it flies open.

"Don't you dare walk away. You've been avoiding me all afternoon." Sara. Fuming. In a rage but even more beautiful for it. My queen. Mine. My beast purrs in anticipation, and I squeeze my eyes shut to push him back. Not now.

"Lachlan?" Sara's voice is softer now, hesitancy creeping into it. "You said we would talk after the others left," her voice trails off uncertainly. "They left hours ago," she says it as if I don't know this fact. As if I wasn't there at her side to see them off. As if I didn't immediately find a reason for us to be apart.

"I have a kingdom to manage. I can't be at your side every minute of the day, Sara," I snap and squeeze past her, avoiding her eyes as I do.

She steps to the side, and even without looking at her, I sense her frown, her simmering frustration. But I can't be with her now. Not with my beast so close to the surface. If I look at her, I will want to touch her and... I don't know how to do that without letting the beast out. He's always close when she's with me.

"Lachlan."

Freezing halfway across the room, I wait, but I keep my back to her. I don't know what it is about Sara that makes it impossible for me to ignore her... even if it's for her own good. She says my name, and I come running, but tonight, something in her voice scares me.

It sounds like determination. And then I feel her hands on my back, lightly sliding up, settling on my shoulders before brushing down my arms.

I'm holding my breath, praying she'll let me go. Her touch keeps me there as effectively as iron shackles. I can't move as she presses her body to mine. Her breasts brush up against my back as her arms wrap around my chest, and she holds me tight. That's all she does, but already it's too much.

I don't even recognize my voice or the groan that slips from my lips. I'm breaking apart. The cracks forming are wide enough for my beast to slip through, fur rising in anticipation.

"No." Squeezing my eyes shut, I push myself out of her arms. "No, Sara." I shove her away, and she stumbles back a step, but I can't even apologize. My beast is ready to rip those clothes from her body. He will... I have to get away.

Stumbling into my bedroom, I slam the door closed behind me. The click of the automatic locking system is loud in the sudden silence.

Sara didn't say a word after I pushed her away. Nothing. And I couldn't bring myself to look at her, to check if she was okay. Did I hurt her?

Looking down at my clenched fists, I don't see hands. I see claws. It's my imagination. I know this. My beast is not a physical thing, but I see him anyway. Claws where my hands should be. Claws that will rip Sara's soft skin.

Sinking to the floor, I bow my head over my knees— this fear is tearing me apart. I'm broken and twisted up inside. The beast is growling in frustration, and I'm that same small boy locked in a room with an angry leopard.

Its iron chain rubs against its neck, scraping it raw, and there's a blood stain against its white fur, a wound that festers and irritates. The leopard growls low as it stares at me, then pounces. The chain yanks it back, but those claws rip at my trousers, and a thin bloody streak appears on my leg. I see it through the tear in the fabric.

Face the beast, boy. Kill it. Destroy it.

I never did kill it. It was the one command I could never obey. No matter how many times my father put me in that dungeon. No matter how many times that leopard lunged at me in the dark, stuffy room. My father killed it in the end— in a rage so bloody I still have nightmares about it. But in my nightmares, I'm the one in the rage, tearing that leopard apart with my bare hands. Blood pooling on the stone floor, splattering across the walls, blood on my hands and face.

And I'm that boy again, cowering in a corner, covered in blood, terrified and alone with the mutilated leopard. My nightmares are all around me, eating me alive. It's not the leopard, spine shattered, limbs torn asunder... it's Sara on the ground at my feet. It's my mother as I saw her last, neck snapped, eyes lifeless.

"Ssshh, I'm going to make this better, okay?"

Sara is kneeling behind me; she wraps her arms around me, and I shudder, fear seizing me. Her actions are slow and cautious, though... as if she can sense the wild animal in me. I'm frozen stiff in her arms. I don't have it in me to push her away a second time, but the fear inside me crawls up my throat, wanting to howl.

"Sara, please, you have to go away." I manage to squeeze the words out and curl tighter in on myself, tucking my hands against my chest— as if that will stop them from reaching for her.

If she answers me, I don't hear her. But she does sit back on her heels, giving me some space. She doesn't leave, and I feel her hand on my back, rubbing up and down my spine with a light soothing touch.

I don't know how long we stay like that. The nightmares are playing out behind my closed lids, but throughout those long minutes, I feel Sara's hand on my back, soothing. Nothing else. A gentle touch up and down my back. Sometimes I hear her murmur meaningless words, reassuring nonsense that I know better than anyone will do nothing if my beast escapes.

When the nightmares recede, it's the shame that follows and the self-hatred. Here I am— a King. On his knees, howling like a child. Heat rushes to my face, and I'm no longer hiding my beast from Sara's eyes.

Now I'm trying to conceal the red stain flooding my cheeks. But she must sense the change in me because her hand disappears from my back, and her voice is on the other side of the room when it comes again.

"Your room is nicer than mine," she announces, and I can just imagine that curious glint in her eyes as she looks around. So nosy and interfering and— "So, explain," she says abruptly, and the sudden tension that statement elicits has my chest clenching in fear.

I don't want to look at her. I don't want to explain what she's just witnessed, but I push myself onto my feet, forcing my legs to hold me upright.

"Why do you get the nicer room?" she asks, and I hear her stride across to the large window.

Relief shudders through me, and I look up. She has her back to me, and I release my breath. She's dressed for bed. I didn't notice this earlier, but I do now.

My feet take a step back, and my fingers curl in on themselves. I can't think past the vision of my wife here in my bedroom in a red silk nightgown. It caresses her body and brushes against the floor when she moves. I can see every soft curve through the light fabric.

"The view from here is..." her voice trails off, and she spins around suddenly and jumps onto my bed, falling like a starfish across the wide mattress. The gown falls open, revealing one naked thigh.

"Sara." It's an agonized whisper. She ignores me.

"Yep, just what I thought," she announces, her eyes fixed on the window. She won't look at me. "You can lie in bed and still see the mountains. Can you see the sunrise from here?" she asks, finally turning to face me.

She rolls over onto her side, tucking the gown around her legs, and I release the breath I was holding. I don't believe the innocent look in her eyes or the casual way she pushes herself off the bed and returns to the window.

"Sara."

Nothing. She ignores me again. Trailing her fingers along the window she surveys my room, looking everywhere but at me. Next, she pops her head into my bathroom. I blink, and she's disappeared inside it.

"And your shower is twice the size of mine." I hear her say, probably from within my shower.

"I'm twice your size," I mutter to the empty room.

"Mmmm, yes, you are." She's standing in the doorway, her eyes running appreciatively up and down my body. If my legs could blush, I swear they would be bright red now with the look she's giving me.

"Sara."

She sighs loudly. "Fine," she says.

"Fine?"

"I'll let you share this room with me. How about that?"

"Sara." I'm trying to do the right thing here. Why can't she sense the danger she's in?

SARA

My pulse is hammering in my neck, and the blood rushing through my veins is so loud I can hardly hear my voice. I have no idea what I'm talking about. All I know is that if I stop talking, Lachlan will ask me to leave. He will push me away, and I can't... not again. I won't leave him, not when he's hurting.

"How did you get into my room?" His voice has that hard quality to it that usually pushes me away, but as I hesitate, his frown straightens into a thin angry line.

I've seen him use this exact look on his soldiers. It's not a pretty look, and I feel myself trembling slightly. Not because I'm scared of him. I know Lachlan will never hurt me, but he will hurt himself trying to protect me.

"Before Arlen left, I convinced him to give me the master key."

Lachlan stares at me, his eyes hard and flat— the expression I hate the most, but then he sighs and looks away.

"I'm surprised he gave it to you." And then he laughs; the sound is hoarse and rough. "No, I'm not. You always get what you want, don't you, Sara?" His eyes are back on me, piercing and a little angry. "And now?" he asks roughly. "Since you won't leave me alone, what do you want now?"

I stare at him, and the silence stretches on between us. I'm trying to do what Lilly told me to do. *Don't react. Get out of your head. Drop into your heart. You'll be able to feel Lachlan. No matter what he says to you – you'll know the truth by feeling him, reading him.*

I can't do it, though. I swear there's nothing to this Fae's heart but a hard stone wall... a wooden door, a snarling leopard, and pain, so much pain and fear...

"Sara." Suddenly Lachlan's at my side, his hands on my shoulders shaking me. "Sara." His voice is frantic. "To all the gods, woman, would you stop doing that?" He glares at me. "I don't want to lose you, Sara." He sounds fierce, the growl in his voice more audible than usual.

I blink up at him and then try to move my shoulders to dislodge his iron grip. When he realizes what I'm doing, he pales and drops his hands, taking a quick step back.

"I was trying to feel you," I explain softly.

His scowl deepens. "What?" But before I can answer, he snaps, "You have no business being inside me or feeling me."

He strides over to the other side of the room, putting as much distance between us as possible. He keeps his back to me. Shielding his expression from me, I realize. He doesn't want me to feel him... or know him.

Lilly's words are still in my head. *Don't react. Everything in Emuria is about feelings. Your thoughts will only confuse you.* I keep my voice steady when I speak next.

"I asked Lilly for advice," I say to his back. "She said I must drop into my heart to know what you're feeling. That's what I was trying to do."

"I told you to find a way to STOP us getting inside each other's heads."

"Hearts," I interrupt him.

"What?" he growls the question as he turns.

"Hearts, not heads. We have to feel each other's hearts, and then we'll be able to communicate without words." His face pales as he stares at me. "Lachlan?"

"And what did my heart feel like, Sara?" His voice is so cold I shiver, and he smiles bitterly, observing it. "Well," he continues harshly. "What did my heart feel like? What caused that fear I saw in your eyes?" I'm silent for so long that he scoffs. "You don't want to feel my heart, Sara. You don't want to be anywhere near it. I wish you would believe me." There is so much pain and loneliness in his voice that it hurts me.

"I felt a stone wall, a rough old wooden door bolted on the outside. On the inside are large claw marks scraped into that wood. I smelt fear and rage... but mostly fear. It's everywhere. I felt it on my skin and tasted it on my tongue. It tasted like blood, fresh blood."

Lachlan stands as silent as those cliffs outside his window, his expression as stark and lonely, and then he starts to laugh, but the sound is ugly. I squeeze my eyes shut and put my hands over my ears to block out the laughter. It's only my stupid pride keeping me in that room. My feet want to run. I don't want to see that look on his face. The ugly sneer, the bitterness.

I don't know how long the laugh lasts, but when he's silent, I open my eyes and find him on the floor, leaning against the wall. His head is resting on his bent knees, and he's silent but for the ragged breaths that shudder through him.

Stepping forward, I lower myself to the floor beside him. My shoulder brushes his, and he flinches, but I don't move back, and eventually, he sighs, and his shoulders relax next to mine. After a few minutes, I rest my head on his shoulder and slip my hand onto his lap. He stiffens and holds his breath. But in the next instant his breath rushes out of his chest and his hand finds mine. We lace our fingers together so tight it almost hurts.

Chapter 11

L*ACHLAN*

I wake with Sara in my arms, my right thigh is wedged between hers, and my arm is draped across her waist. I freeze as I realize I'm cupping her breast. Carefully I lift my hand and let it lie on the sheet beside her, pretending an innocence I don't feel.

At some point during the night, we moved from the floor to the bed, and, for once, my beast was quiet and let me sleep. Sara's presence soothed him. It was enough to hold her, my nose pressed up against her neck.

I don't know what Sara thinks of me now. I can't... my mind shies away from the conversation I know she will insist on having.

Last night, her revelations about my heart took my feet out from under me. Literally. The shock of her knowing about my past...about that room. No one else knows about those early years, not even Arlen.

Now Sara knows all my dirty secrets: my beast, my cowardice... how could I fight with her after that? Not when I know she's right— even after all these years, I am still that five-year-old Fae boy locked in a dark room with an angry beast.

That is at the heart of who I am. Sara deserves a King for a husband; instead, she has a terrified boy. I hate my weakness, I hate my—

"Lachlan," Sara murmurs my name as she turns around. Her eyes are still closed, but she slips her arm across my chest and squeezes. "I can hear you frowning," she mutters irritably, scrunching her nose and burrowing her face into my neck. "Not before breakfast, please. And coffee, I need coffee." She pries her eyes open and looks at me. "Coffee," she mumbles again and rolls out of my arms. "And that's saying something," she adds, stretching her arms over her head and rolling her neck. "The coffee in this castle is disgusting— to be blunt."

Climbing off the bed, she strolls over to the window. I find I can't take my eyes off her. Her braids fall down her back to just above her bum, but she gathers them up in one hand and pulls them over her shoulder. The tilt of her head shows off her long neck, the simple gesture so elegant I want to hold onto this image forever... Sara is silhouetted by the morning light, blue sky, and green mountains behind her. This is the Rohn I want.

"And I'm still prepared to drink it," Sara says suddenly, continuing where she left off. It makes me want to laugh out loud. "I need caffeine so bad that I am prepared to drink that dirty mud the kitchen tells me is coffee." She turns away from the window but avoids my gaze. "Why is that? Why is the coffee so bad here in Rohn?" She's fiddling with one of her braids and looking around the room as if searching for something.

"Sara."

"You have to know that there is no good excuse for bad coffee. It's a little thing to fix. In fact—"

"Sara." She stops at last and flicks her gaze in my direction. The uncertainty I see there makes my heart clench. "You don't have to do that."

"What? Talk?"

Pushing the covers back, I follow her over to the window. She watches my every step, her eyes widening slightly as I stop in front of her.

"Are you telling me not to talk? You know that's just rude. You really shouldn't tell your wife not to talk." Her voice falls to a whisper as I reach up and cup her face. I brush my thumb across her lower lip and press it firmly to her mouth when she looks like she's about to start talking again. Her eyes narrow in warning, and if I had to guess, I would say she's considering biting my thumb just to prove a point.

"We both know you're talking because you're nervous."

Her eyes narrow into long thin slits, but then she rolls her eyes and looks away from me, so I drop my hand to my side, although all I want to do is wrap it around her waist and tug her closer.

"What else am I supposed to do when you go all broody and silent?" she asks.

She waits for me to say something, but I don't know how to answer that question. I know I'm a miserable bastard. It's not like I haven't told her that myself. It's not like I haven't wondered a hundred times why she would choose me. But she's still waiting for an answer I don't have, so I give her the only response I can.

"I have no idea." And then I remember my surprise for her and turn for the door.

"Lachlan!" I can hear the frustration in her voice, but I know she will love what I have for her.

"Hold that thought," I tell her pulling open the bedroom door. "I have a surprise for you." As I intended, she follows me into the sitting room. I only get two steps across the room when I hear her gasp.

"You didn't!" She squeals in excitement and pushes past me. "A Nespresso coffee machine," she gushes, running her hand along the top of the machine, caressing it, and sighing again.

Sara spins around and jumps on me, wrapping her arms around my neck and her legs around my waist. She drops kisses all over my face and leaps down as quickly as she leaped up.

I'm left standing there like a love-sick fool, just blinking at her with a stupid look on my face as Sara spins back to the coffee machine.

"This will be the best cup of coffee you've ever had in your life," she's saying, but she could be speaking in Mer for all that I can make sense of her words. She keeps talking, though, not requiring any input from me, and miraculously all those hard edges in me soften.

She's studying the selection of coffees with rapt attention, her finger gliding across the boxes of coffee. Tugging her gently back against my chest, I press my mouth to her neck. She submits with a soft sigh, angling her head to the side, so I bury my face in her neck and nip gently at her ear lobe.

"The coffee is for you, Sara. I have enough trouble sleeping. Caffeine would only make it worse." I press a lingering kiss to her neck, then step back, putting some space between us. "I'm going to have a shower. The machine is connected to a globe and will run for the next century off that power source. You will never run out of coffee again."

"Globe?"

"A renewable power source the Mer developed." Unable to resist, I press another kiss to her neck.

"How did you do this?" She's looking back at the coffee machine with love in her eyes which makes me smile.

"Being King has its perks, Sara." I laugh and tug her closer, wrapping her up in my arms for a minute. "I sent someone to the human realm to fetch the coffee. I'm very good at giving orders," I whisper in her ear, and she shivers. "Enjoy your coffee." I brush my knuckles down her neck, enjoying the little gasping sound she makes.

"Lachlan?" her voice is hesitant, and she's still got her back to me. "Can we talk," her voice trails off, and my heart squeezes tight.

"I need to work for an hour, but after that... will you spend the day with me?" I ask gruffly, hating how needy I sound. Sara still won't turn around, but she nods and fumbles with the coffee, grabbing a box from the shelf and popping one of the pods into the machine.

The hour in my study drags by, and I spend most of my time looking at the closed door rather than the pages on my desk. On the other side of that door is my bedroom. On the other side of that is Sara's bedroom, her bathroom, her shower. I want to carry her into that shower... I want to...

"Concentrate," I growl. I have one more missive to send, and then I'm free to spend the day with Sara. Surely, I can concentrate for five more minutes.

Glancing back at my desk, I read over the letter I was writing to King Muir. I've summarised as concisely as possible the events of the last two months, detailing the number of Elves found and my concern that there might be a Mer connection to these events.

That was the most challenging part of the letter to write... King Muir is volatile at the best of times, and the last thing I want is for him to take offense to my letter. I am not accusing him of anything... but somebody in his court is involved. I'm hoping Muir will work with me to uncover the truth.

I'm hesitating, though. I know Arlen is right and that all of Emuria must be informed of these events, but a part of me is still reluctant to involve the Mer court.

Aaronn has already left for Torin, where he will call for a meeting between the tribes and the Elvin council. Arlen has taken the news to Soraya and, with the Queen's help, will relay a message to the other two kingdoms.

That leaves only the Mer Kingdom; I can't ask anyone else to do this. I have always had a good relationship with the Mer royal family, but they are a tempestuous race, prone to violent mood swings.

I can handle them but Sara... I don't want to leave her behind in Rohn, but I also don't want to take her to a place where she could be in even more danger than she is here.

This familiar tug and pull on my heart is maddening. It's been this way since I married her— my need to keep her safe is constantly at war with her need to follow her magic.

Enough.

I sign the letter with my magic, an unhackable, impossible-to-forge signature, and open the small hatch window beside my desk. As I wait for one of the specially trained red-tailed hawks, I roll up the letter and slip it into a copper cylinder. When the hawk swoops low outside my window, I lean back and wait, enjoying the spectacle. It's the same every time I call one of these beautiful birds to me. It's hard to imagine there are Fae who hunt these majestic birds for sport.

With wings stretched wide, the hawk circles, slowly beginning its descent. It lands on the metal perch, tucking in its wings and surveying me with arrogant disdain. I feel laughter rumble in my chest as I remember an earlier argument with Sara at the start of our marriage. She accused me of having the same arrogance and conceit as the court hawks.

Wiping all humor away, I reach forward slowly and gently so as not to startle the bird and attach the copper cylinder to its leg.

"Aescheles," I say the name clearly but only once. These hawks are well-trained and have never let me down before. Withdrawing my hands, I watch it fly away before closing the hatch. My gaze swivels automatically to the closed door. Sara.

My beast purrs in anticipation, but I don't know what I'm feeling. I've been hard all morning, since waking with

Sara in my bed. But even that physical evidence of my desire is not enough to wipe out the fear I feel.

What if the beast protects her? What if the beast loves her? Aaronn's words to me in the library.

What if I can make love to my wife without hurting her? My pulse beats faster at the thought, but a knock on the door slows it right back down.

What now?

All I want is one afternoon without interruptions.

"Lachlan?" The door opens, and Sara stands on the threshold, an uncertain smile on her lips as she tries to gauge my mood. "Are you hungry?" she asks. "You didn't have any breakfast." She's still hovering in the doorway.

"Come in. I've just finished." I wave her into the room before adding, "Close the door." The door clicks shut, and I'm holding my breath as I wait for her to turn around.

Sara scans my face uncertainly, her eyes widen, and her teeth clamp down on her bottom lip. I don't say a word as she walks toward me. I can't. My nerves have tied my tongue up into a tangled knot.

My study is a small room. Four steps, and Sara's beside my desk. Her breath is a little shallow, the pulse in her neck jumping.

"Nervous?" I ask cautiously.

She shakes her head. "You?"

"Yes," I admit. Sara swallows and then nods as though my answer makes sense. I wish it didn't. I wish she knew nothing about my beast.

Sara edges around my chair. The soft fabric of her dress brushes my legs as she perches on my desk, her legs swinging.

I close my eyes to lessen the intensity of the moment. When all she does is wait quietly, I have to smile. If she was nervous, she'd be talking.

"What?" she asks. I open my eyes and find hers, the green in them is flaring brightly, and I lean forward and rest my hands on her thighs, nudging her dress up as I do.

"We're going to take this slow," I say, tearing my eyes away from her legs to look up at her. She nods. "Let me lead, okay? I need to be in charge."

"This time," she consents, a mischievous sparkle in her eyes. My fingers graze her thighs, nudging her dress higher, and her breath catches, her eyes opening wide.

"Lift up," I murmur. Placing her hands on the desk behind her, she pushes down and lifts her hips up for me. I slip my hands under her dress and tug her panties free, dragging them down her legs so slowly she squirms on the desk and moans her objection.

I smile at her impatience, and she blushes and looks away.

"Sara." I wait for her to look back, and when she does, I tuck a finger in the collar of her white dress and pull her closer, pressing my lips to hers. "I've been waiting a long time to do this, don't rush me."

"But—"

"No, I'm in charge."

"This time," she insists stubbornly, still kissing me.

"Lie down." Her mouth frames a question. "Lie down," I repeat. She glances over her shoulder and then lowers herself to the desk. "Open your legs." She freezes, her thigh muscles tensing. I wait, and slowly she relaxes and spreads her thighs a little wider. "More."

Again, I wait, and she parts her thighs a little wider for me. She's naked from the waist down and spread before me, and... my beast is quiet. He's not trying to claw his way out of my skin. He's not whispering obscenities in my ear.

SARA

"Lachlan?" Raising my head to look at him, I'm forced to admit that this is not the most dignified position I could hope to find myself in.

Lachlan's staring at me with a frown, and that's definitely not the expression a woman wants to see on a man's face when he's looking at her lady bits.

His eyes are glued to the juncture between my thighs, and the frowning silence has gone on so long that I'm developing a complex.

Are Fae women different down there? I mean, I like a bit of grooming as much as the next woman; I might not be bare, but I keep things neat, a thin strip of trimmed hair up the middle, but... maybe Fae women go entirely bare, or perhaps they don't wax at all or maybe their vaginas are a different shape.

"Lachlan." I push myself up, and his eyes finally find mine, but he doesn't look repulsed or confused or anything other than sure. He growls low in his throat, a rumbling sound that moves through me like a heat source. "Lie down."

"No."

"Sara. I thought I was in charge?"

"Not until you tell me why you're looking at my lady bits like they're going to bite you."

"What?" He looks down at my waist and back up again. "What?" he repeats.

"Are Fae women different?"

"Different?"

"Down there," I snap. God, why is he making this so difficult? I squeeze my legs shut and try to wriggle off his desk, but his hands are like vice clamps on my thighs. "Look, it's fine, Lachlan. We come from different worlds. There are bound to be...differences. If my vagina is... that is, if you don't want to, you know, it's fine." I finish lamely, flustered and embarrassed.

His hands don't move, and I'm forced to look at him. His mouth is curved slightly in the left corner, and there's laughter in his eyes. And my cheeks are so hot now I want to hide my face away. Hide me away. This is so embarrassing.

"Sara, lie down." When I don't move, he adds, "Lie down, and I'll show you how much I don't like your... lady bits." His mouth kicks up again at the side as he tries not to laugh. "Please lie down. I want to taste you." He sounds so patient, so calm, and I'm falling into a molten fire with every coolly delivered phrase that falls from his mouth.

Lying back down, I'm holding my breath and waiting, but again nothing happens, and I can't take this agony any longer.

"Lachlan," I snap and then feel the brush of his lips above one knee. His beard scrapes against my leg, just below the warmth of his mouth, and oh, I never knew beards could be so sensual.

Pushing my thighs apart, he runs his tongue up my leg, all the way to my hip. I'm panting from the anticipation alone. But then he pulls back and starts again on my other leg, tracing the same journey with his mouth up and up, getting closer all the time. I want to scream. I want more.

"What could possibly be interesting about my thighs?"

"Everything," he mutters roughly before lifting my legs up and hooking them over his shoulders. And just like that, his mouth is where I want it to be, where I've dreamt of it being for so long.

There's magic in his tongue and in his large fingers as they part me and slip inside. His two fingers are thrusting in and out of me as his tongue swirls around the most sensitive part of me, and I'm coming apart in seconds, too tightly coiled to drag this out.

"Lachlan, yes," I scream as my orgasm surges through me, wiping out everything that came before this. "More," I whisper as I lie on his desk, dazed, spots dancing before my eyes. "I want more," I whisper and hear him chuckle softly as he lowers my legs to the desk and helps me sit up. He pulls me onto his lap and tucks my head into the crook of his shoulder.

Sighing contentedly, I snuggle closer. "And you were scared of that," I murmur and press my mouth to the juncture between his neck and shoulder. When I wriggle in his lap, he groans and clamps a hand to my hip.

"If you want that more you were talking about, you're going to have to stop wriggling about on my lap," he says through gritted teeth and lifts me, so I'm straddling him.

"Are you frowning again?" I tease and drape my arms around his neck, tilting my hips against his, just to hear the groan that slips from his mouth. He's so hard and big... so big it gives me a moment's pause.

Glancing down between us, I reach down and cup him. His hand lands on top of mine. I don't know if he means to keep my hand there or drag it away. I'm not sure Lachlan even knows.

"I've been hard all morning, Sara." He rolls his eyes then and cups my face dragging my mouth to his. "I've been hard for months. Since that first day, you walked into my throne room and refused to kneel before me."

He deepens the kiss. Moaning, I rub myself against him, needing to be closer. "Sara." His hands clamp around my waist, and he nudges me back. I moan my objection and continue pressing kisses to his neck. "Sara, baby. I need to talk to you."

"Now?" I groan.

"Yes." I hear the laughter in his voice. "Sara, I don't know what's going to happen." His voice falls away, and I shift back. He looks so unsure of himself. "Usually, I can control him."

"Your beast?"

He nods. "But with you— I can't. Your magic amplifies my magic, my beast. He's stronger when you're with me and—"

"You're scared he's going to hurt me?" I finish for him. He nods and looks away. "Lachlan, baby," I croon with a teasing smile, and when he finally looks back at me with a question in his eyes, I add, "You know, I've never really liked it when men call me baby. There's something weird about it, you know? Because I'm not a baby, I'm a woman."

He frowns. "Okay, noted. I won't call you baby again."

"But when you say it." I ignore his irritation, sliding my fingers into his hair and tugging hard to ensure I've got his attention. His eyes narrow, and that amber flicker passes through the chocolate brown. "I think I might like it." His eyes flare fully amber, and I lean in close and whisper in his ear. "Why don't you let *me* worry about your beast?"

And then I hear what I've just said and burst out laughing. I laugh so hard tears stream down my cheeks, and I drop my head onto his shoulder. "There's a phrase I never thought I would say. It sounds like something from a bad porn movie." I'm still laughing.

"Porn movie?" he asks, which sets me off again.

Howling with laughter, I press kisses to his face. "Oh, Lachlan, I love you so much. The next time you have a free week, we're going back to Cork, and I'll introduce you to everything. Bad porn, good porn, frappucinos, my favorite bands, the best movies of all time...."

Lachlan has gone rigid beneath me, and it's not until my laughter drains away that I realize what I said. Looking at him nervously, I see his eyes are squeezed shut, his jaw locked.

"Lachlan?"

He shakes his head once, heaves in a breath, and lets it out slowly as though he's in pain. Clambering off his lap, I smooth my dress back down over my hips. He lets me. He still won't look at me, and after minutes pass in this tense silence, I walk out of his study. Quickly— before he can feel what he's done to my heart.

Chapter 12

L ACHLAN
    I fucked up.

There's no other way to say it. But to all the gods— those words. *I love you so much.* The pain in my chest is a vice, squeezing, squeezing. I can't breathe. *I love you so much.* I can't. I just... can't.

No one has ever loved me before... Arlen. My brother loves that phrase, loves the word love. He throws it around casually at all the most inappropriate moments. Arlen loves coffee, he loves me, he loves his new stallion, he loves cake. He once told Lars he loved him... a blatant lie. It means nothing. It's only a word.

But Sara? What does it mean when she uses it... *I love you so much.*

Impossible. Sara's spent most of our marriage angry with me, hating me, now she desires me... now she loves— No. She can't. I'm unlovable. I'm a brooding, angry Fae with a beast where a heart should be.

Unlovable.

To all the gods! I tug on my hair in frustration. I'm not even likable most of the time. Sara can't love me. I exhale loudly, relief filling my chest as I breathe back in. Forcing myself to unclench my fists, I let my head drop back and stare at the ceiling. Cold, grey stone is all I see, but it cools the heat in my blood, and the panic eases.

She can't love me. She doesn't. Not in the way I understand it. It's only a phrase, something to sum up her enthusiasm, her enjoyment. She was on a high after her orgasm. It's only a word. It doesn't mean anything. But... she left. I hurt her.

Regret slams into me, chasing my panic into the background. No matter how often I promise her I won't hurt her— I keep doing it. The regret tastes bitter on my tongue, and, to all the gods, I can't sit here while she's somewhere in the castle, hurting and alone.

Using my Tracker magic, I'm out of my study and tracing her through the castle. I've never appreciated my speed more than I do right now. I find Sara in the library, curled up in one of the armchairs in front of the fire.

As I appear in front of her, she looks up, a startled expression on her face. I watch her cautiously, noting the sad tilt to her lips and the bright sheen in her eyes. I've made her cry— again. The leather armchair folds around her like the arms of a lover, and now I'm jealous of a chair!

Not giving her a chance to argue with me, I bend low and scoop her up into my arms. With my Tracker magic, we're back in my bedroom a minute later. By the time I'm standing at the foot of my bed, Sara is dizzy, holding a hand to her head... and then I regret my haste. That was thoughtless of me. I should have at least warned her before I did that.

Sara shakes her head slowly from side to side and blinks her eyes a few times.

"So that's what it feels like," she mumbles. Her dazed expression clears, and she slaps a hand against my chest. "Put me down, Lachlan." She narrows her eyes when I don't release her. "There was no need for dramatics. We could have talked in the library as easily as in here."

"I don't want to talk."

"Don't," she hisses at me, so angry I have no choice but to let her go. Lowering her to the ground, I take a step back. She's still glaring at me. "Don't," she repeats again but then her bottom lip trembles, and she clamps her teeth down on it.

"Sara."

Her hand flies up to stop me, and she turns her back and paces over to the window. "Don't," she mumbles again when I step nearer, but I ignore her warning and wrap my arms around her.

I need to hold her. Sara's hurting, and that's tearing me up inside. She feels stiff in my arms, still angry. "Not angry," she murmurs in response to my attempt to read her. "Embarrassed, hurt, rejected, alone," she intones in an empty voice.

It's the alone bit that hurts the most. I know what alone feels like; I would never want that for her. Not Sara, who is like sunshine, bright and vibrant and so full of life she's impossible to contain or tame.

Squeezing her gently, I press my lips to her temple and murmur, "You're not alone." She doesn't respond, so I turn her slowly to face me. Her eyes are glittering with tears, but she won't look at me. "Sara, baby— in a strictly I-respect-you-as-a-woman-and-there-is-nothing-infantile-about-you sense," I add, trying to get a smile out of her. It doesn't work.

"You can't keep pushing me away," she says instead. "Lachlan, how long do we have to play this tug-and-pull game? We're here. We're married. We lo—"

"Don't say it," I interrupt quickly. Sara pauses and frowns at me.

"Why not?"

"Because you don't mean it."

"What?" Her eyes flare with temper so suddenly I'm forced to take a step back.

Weighing my words carefully before I speak, I look out the window at the mountains around us. Right now, I wish I was out there instead of in here facing Sara's anger.

"Sara, it's not that you don't mean it. I'm sure you think you mean it." I'm floundering here, and Sara has gone as still as one of the boulders on the mountain outside my castle. "It's just that my understanding of love differs from your understanding of love. It means different things to us."

Her eyes narrow into tiny slits, and I realize I'm not helping my case. I try again, though, my words tumbling over each other as I try to make it up to her.

"You love everything, Sara. Your enthusiasm for life is a gift." I reach for her, placing my hands on her shoulders, needing to touch her. "You have that in common with my brother— you're so alike. Charming, funny, vibrant, you love everything that brings you a moment's joy."

"A moment's joy? So, you think I'm fickle." Her voice sounds so unlike her – flat and lifeless. "I fall in love every day. Is that it?" Sara shrugs my hands off her shoulders and steps back. "At least I know what you think of me— before I made the mistake of sleeping with you."

How could this conversation have gotten so out of my control?

"Sara, I didn't say you're fickle. Your love of coffee has endured for years," I say, attempting a joke, but again it falls flat. I feel desperate now as I feel her shoring up her defenses, slipping away from me. She's silent, waiting. "Sara, please."

"Please, what? Please fuck me? Your beast wants to fuck me, is that it, Lachlan? Your dreaded beast that's so terrifying you can't let me get close... but you can let him fuck me. That's okay, is it?"

I've never seen her so angry.

"You are your beast, Lachlan. Your beast is you. When are you going to get that? There is nothing to control, nothing to lock away. Your father lied to you. Your father was the beast – not his magic. His beast didn't kill your mother. Magic didn't kill your mother. He did. Your father killed your mother."

Her words land on me like boulders tumbling in a landslide burying me alive. I can't breathe.

"There's no wild beast. There's just you and your magic, Lachlan." Sara's waiting for me to argue with her, but I can't find enough air to suck into my lungs. "And if I tell you I love you, Lachlan, it's because I love you. Don't you dare—"

"You can't love me." The air rushes back into my lungs, but I feel half-crazed by the lack of oxygen. Her face is a blur as fear clouds my vision.

"Why can't I love you?" she shouts back.

"You just can't. You don't." My voice is desperate. My beast clawing to get out of my skin, making a lie out of her earlier words. My beast and I are not one— he's wild and needs to be controlled. She's still arguing with me, though, as if she can't feel the danger all around us. As if she can't sense my beast getting ready to pounce.

"What does it matter if I tell you I love you? I'm not asking you to love me back."

"That's not the point," I roar at her.

"Why?"

"Because when you change your mind, I will break. When you take your love away, I will never recover."

Silence follows my outburst. Her hands drop from her hips to hang at her side, and slowly my beast settles back down inside me.

Sara sinks slowly down onto the edge of the bed. She sits there, staring at me, and a storm of emotion passes through her eyes before she stands again.

Sara will leave me now. I've been preparing myself for this all along.

But she doesn't leave. She takes hold of the hem of her dress and tugs it over her head. She's naked beneath that dress, and I'm instantly hard, my beast waking up. Sara doesn't wait for my reaction. She walks to the top of the bed, tugs the covers down.

"Come to bed, Lachlan."

SARA

Lachlan hesitates, and I hold my breath, waiting to see what he will do. The moment drags out; it could be one minute, it could be ten. I don't know. Time has lost all meaning. All I can see is Lachlan standing in front of me, so beautiful and strong but vulnerable, almost broken by his admission.

He tugs the shirt from his jeans, his eyes never leave mine, and I'm the first one to break eye contact, my eyes dropping as he pulls the shirt over his head. This is my first time seeing Lachlan without a shirt on— after all the arguments, the kisses, the brush of hands, and six months of marriage. Now he's standing here in front of me, and he's so magnificent that I feel suddenly shy and inadequate.

I mean, I'm okay to look at. Let's put it this way, no man has ever kicked me out of bed, but... if I'm honest, I'm a little out of shape since I stopped climbing. A little soft around the edges. I certainly don't look anything like this Fae with his broad chiseled chest, all sharp planes, delineated muscles, tight belly, and...

His jeans drop to the floor, he kicks them to one side, and my own stomach clenches. He's not looking at me, and as I stare at him, color steals across his cheeks, and his eyes creep to mine— almost shy.

"Lachlan," I whisper his name and pull the covers back to let him in. His eyes slide down my body, lingering on my legs and passing back up my chest. His eyes stop on the gold wedding bands around my neck and a flash of amber passes through the brown. Heat curls over my skin.

When he slides in next to me, we lie on our sides, looking at each other. I see the vulnerability in his eyes, and I want to kiss it away, tell him again how much I love him. I want to tell him that I've been dreaming about him for two years; I've loved him for two years. But his confession is still hanging in the air. It might as well be trapped in a giant speech bubble above our heads. *When you take your love away, I will never recover.*

The room is warm, but I want *his* warmth. I want his skin against mine. I scoot closer until our bodies brush together. He lifts his hand and rests it on my hip, a little hesitant, hovering there lightly and then more firmly until his fingers are digging into my soft flesh. His cock is hard between us, nudging at my belly and... I want. That hasn't changed. I want more. I want everything. Amusement flares in his eyes, and I know he's reading me.

Lachlan tugs me closer, his hips nudging mine. "Sara, I want to kiss you." His voice is rough and low, and I feel it everywhere, brushing against my skin. Nodding, I tip my face up a little. My mouth is so close his breath tickles my lips. I want... and then his mouth is on mine, and it's better than any kiss we've shared before. This kiss is infused with all the truths we've shared today. It's full of love, although he hates that word so much.

Lachlan is kissing me with gentle precision, his one hand on my jaw, holding my face still. By the time his mouth is on my neck, and his hand is brushing over my breast, I'm lost. I'm writhing on the sheets, arching into his touch, begging him for more. His mouth closes around my nipple, and I feel a sharp pain as his teeth nip at my tender flesh. Is it possible to come from this alone?

Lachlan's magic feels like it's sliding under my skin, dancing with my magic... and then I hear a purr and feel the brush of fur inside my veins. His heart. Blinking my eyes open, I stare up at Lachlan.

He lifts his head from my breast and meets my gaze. His eyes are fully amber, with no sign of the soothing brown in their depths. His eyes trace a line down my body, over my breasts to the apex of my thighs, and the amber flares bright. His beast growls low in appreciation, and I feel it shiver inside me, but when his eyes meet mine again, chocolate is bleeding into the amber. Uncertainty crosses Lachlan's face as he watches me.

Oh, my love, I want to murmur those words, but I don't. I can't let him fear this; I can't let him fear his beast. Nudging Lachlan onto his back, I switch positions and lean over him. I see the anxiety that moves across his face and brush a kiss to his tight jaw. His eyes are squeezed shut, and I know he's pushing his beast back, controlling the urges charging through him.

"Lachlan." I kiss him lightly on the mouth, feeling the soft warmth of his lips under mine. His hand comes up to cup my head and hold me there. "Open your eyes," I whisper. When his eyes blink up at me, I see a marbled chocolate and amber pattern in their depths as he battles to push his beast back. "I'm in charge this time," I whisper.

He stares at me in silence and then nods.

"First rule." I clamber over him and straddle him. "Relax." He does the opposite. His jaw tightens, his eyes close, and his fists are now bunching around the sheets on either side of his hips. I press a kiss to his neck and then lower, trailing my mouth toward his stomach. "You're not listening," I murmur. "Relax."

"I can't." He sucks in a sharp breath as I brush my tongue over the head of his penis. When I take him in my mouth, his hips arch up, and he groans loudly, his hand landing forcefully on my head, holding me there.

I smile around his cock and suck him deeper. "Sara." It's half plea, half reproach. "You can't. You mustn't. I'm losing control, Sara. I'm losing...." He groans roughly, and his hips start moving in a thrusting motion as he pushes himself deeper into my mouth. "Sara, Sara." He yanks me away from him, and I'm on my back suddenly with Lachlan between my thighs.

He's looking down at me, his eyes glowing with a magical amber light. No trace of uncertainty. No hesitancy. He waits, and I reach up, cup his face, and pull it down to mine. As his lips meet mine, he thrusts into me. Hard. So deep, I bite down on his lower lip and then suck it into my mouth as he moans. A rumbling moan comes from his throat, and deep within, I hear an echoing growl.

"Yes, Lachlan, yes."

He doesn't speak. Not one word, so I wrap my arms around his neck and hold on tight. He's fucking me. There's no polite way to say it. Possessing me. Owning me.

My beast wants to fuck Sara, he wants to own her, dominate her.

"Yes," I scream as my orgasm hits. "Yes, yes, yes," I mumble again and again as Lachlan's orgasm echoes through me. His one hand is on my hip, holding me in place. His other hand is closed in a fist in my hair. He won't let me move, but I don't want to. I want this. I love this man so much that I will break if he doesn't feel the same way.

Chapter 13

L*ACHLAN*
     My magic hums gently inside me. Sara trails her fingers down my back, a light scratch of her nails and then a gentle brush back up with her knuckles, and my beast is purring in contentment.

"I'm squashing you," I say eventually and roll over onto my back, tugging her to my side. I keep my eyes closed, though. I'm still too nervous to look at her.

Let me be clear, I could feast my eyes on Sara all day: her long legs and perfect up-tilted breasts. Her elegant neck with the gold wedding bands wrapping around her brown skin. It's been months since I've seen the gold bands. I wasn't even sure she still wore them... I hoped.

There isn't a part of my wife's body that I don't want to worship. But I'm not ready for her eyes. Her knowing gaze. Or the censure, the condemnation, scorn. Fear would be the worst.

Sara wasn't afraid, though, not once. I was there. I was pushed to the back as my magic took control, but I was still there— a voyeur, watching as my beast fucked my wife. Just as I said he would. There was nothing gentle about it. He dominated her, took, demanded.

Satisfied her, hums my magic with a hint of swagger. All I can do is sigh. Yes, Sara was satisfied.

When I finally work up the courage to open my eyes, hers are closed, and my heart pinches anxiously.

"Sara?" I tighten my arm around her. "Sara? Look at me. Please." She opens her eyes slowly, and I fall into those green pools. The connection hums as it binds us deeper together. "Tell me," I whisper before pulling her head up to mine and gently kissing her.

She whimpers and presses closer, almost frantic with her need to be near me, inside me. "Baby, easy." I soothe her with kisses and gently rub a hand up and down her arm. Cupping her face, I hold her still. "Tell me," I say firmly, calmly, despite the fear clawing its way up my spine. Did the beast hurt her after all?

Sara freezes and stares at me with a flare of panic in her eyes, and then, just as suddenly, she drops her head onto my shoulder.

"I'm sorry. I'm fine. Lachlan, I'm fine. I don't know what's wrong with me. It was just intense," she mumbles this excuse into my chest, no longer looking at me, so I roll her onto her back until she's under me again.

"Intense good or intense scary?"

She blinks up at me, and a small sigh slips out. "Intense great." Then she adds quietly. "I like your beast."

It's ridiculous to feel jealous of myself. My beast, my magic— mine. It's me she likes, and yet, not me. She guesses my thoughts; I see the knowledge in her eyes and then in the mischievous smile that slips across her face.

"Lachlan, you are the only one here who doesn't like your beast." While I'm processing that, her legs wrap around my waist, and she tips her hips up, rubbing against me, and that's all it takes for my cock to grow hard again, throbbing and needy. "Yes," she says with a smile and a little nod, encouraging me.

I take my time sliding into her heat, enjoying her moan of impatience and the arching of her back, and then the impatient tilt of her hips as she pushes up to meet me. I grip her hip and pin her to the bed. She glares at me. It makes me smile, and I press my mouth to hers.

"Slowly, this time. Okay?" She nods.

I slide my hand up her side and she tilts her hips up to meet my thrusts. Again and again, but slowly this time. It's my turn. My turn to love Sara. And there's that word again—such a complicated word, so hard to understand.

Her breasts are so beautiful, I draw one nipple into my mouth, suck on it gently, and she writhes beneath me. The gasping, breathy sounds falling from her mouth only make me harder. Push me to my limits.

Slipping my hand between us, I trail my fingers down her belly to where our bodies meet and place my thumb over her clit, pressing down gently as I angle myself to give her as much pleasure as possible. I can feel her tension building, her inner muscles squeezing around my cock. Her eyes go wide, and she gasps out my name.

Her head falls back on a silent scream, and I bury my head in her neck and my cock deep inside her as I find my release.

We lie like that in silence, still wrapped up in each other, neither of us willing to let go.

"Lachlan," her voice is hesitant and muffled against my neck. "It's a bit late to be having this conversation, but I couldn't help noticing that we didn't use condoms. Are you not worried about pregnancy? Or disease? I mean, I'm clean. I'm not saying I'm not, but shouldn't we have used condoms?"

I pull back and roll over onto my side, lying next to her. She rolls to her side, too, and trails her fingers along my chest.

"Sorry." She winces as her eyes flick nervously up to mine. "I know this is not the most romantic conversation to have after...that. And that was amazing, by the way," she adds nervously.

Pressing a finger to her lips, I lean forward and replace my finger with my mouth, kissing her deeply. She responds instantly, her hand circling my neck to hold me close until I break the kiss.

"It's okay. We can talk about this." I tug her against my chest, wrapping my arms around her. "I'm not worried about disease. Fae don't get sick, Sara. There are no diseases here in Emuria."

"Oh. Lucky you," she murmurs.

"Lucky us." I laugh and press my mouth to her forehead. "You're Fae too, you know. And pregnancy happens differently here too. It takes magic to conceive a child."

"What?" She pops up and looks down at me. "But what about the Fae who don't have magic?"

"They visit a magician when they're ready to start a family and...yeah. It works like that."

"What about us? Will we need to visit a magician?"

"No." I pull her back into my arms and press her head to my chest again. "For us...when we decide to have kids, our magic will do the rest. If we intend a child, then we'll conceive one."

"So, Fae can go around having as much sex as they want without worrying about disease or unplanned pregnancies?"

I laugh and squeeze her tight. "As much sex as we want, yes, that is the plan."

"I like that plan," she says with a mischievous grin as she slips her thigh over mine.

Stepping out of my bedroom I grind to a halt as I see Sara waiting for me. She's dressed in jeans, a tight-fitting green sweater, and a brown leather jacket. She's dressed for travel.

"Sara?"

"You didn't think you were going alone, did you?"

"I'm a King. I'm never alone," I say dryly but maintain my stern expression. Sara shouldn't want to come with me, but she hums in frustration and throws her hands up.

"Fine. Then I don't want to be alone." I open my mouth, but she glares. "And don't you dare say I'm a Queen and never alone. I'm coming with you, and nothing you say will change my mind."

"Do you even know where I'm going?"

"Aescheles." She shrugs and looks at me like I'm the fool here.

"Right. Do you know anything about the Mer Kingdom? About King Muir and his family?" Sara shakes her head, and a frown turns her lips down as she considers my words. "They are...unpredictable." I will not insult them, so I choose my words carefully. "Wild. They can be savage. They think nothing of tossing their visitors into the shark-infested waters around Aescheles."

Her eyes grow wide. "Lovely," she mutters, but she still hasn't lost that determined look in her eyes.

"It helps to keep Aescheles free from invasion," I add, trying to soften the picture I'm painting of them. "Sara, they're dangerous." I suck in a breath and continue. "They hate humans," I avert my eyes then as I add, "and King Muir hoped for an alliance between our families. He always intended to give his daughter to me in marriage."

Her eyes widen but other than that— nothing. Her face is carefully blank.

"Nothing was formalized. I never agreed to it. Kira and I have never said more than five words to each other." My excuses are stacking up one on top of the other. My tongue will tie itself up into knots if I keep going. I clamp my mouth shut and wait.

"Even more reason for me to come with you," she says finally, and I groan in frustration.

"Sara, they hate you. King Muir will try to kill you."

"He can try." She grins then and throws me a wink that is so typically her. All sass and recklessness, and I love her so much that the thought of being apart from her is hurting me. There's an ache in my chest where my heart should be. But if the Mer hurt her and they will try...

"Sara, I'm serious. If not for *your* safety, then do it for me. If you get hurt, if you—" I can't even say it. "Please." She raises her chin and stares me down – a match for any Queen – and I know I've lost. "Tell me why. Why do you want to come with me?"

"My magic told me to." Her response was as straightforward as she always is, but the foolish part of me wanted her to say she couldn't spend a day without me. I close my eyes and inhale deeply, trying to quell this feeling of losing control. I hear Sara step closer and feel her arms wrap around my waist. She rests her head on my shoulder. "Trust my magic, Lachlan. The same way I trust yours."

Clamping my arms around her, I hold her to me. "But you don't leave my side," I growl into her hair. "Promise me, Sara. You don't leave my side." I feel her nod against my neck and huff in frustration.

I have a bad feeling about this, but Sara is the most stubborn woman I've ever met, and I know I've lost this argument. *Trust my magic, the same way I trust yours*. She's not wrong about that. From the beginning, she has always trusted my magic.

Shaking my head in resignation, I frown at her, ignoring her mischievous smile. She knows she's won this argument. "Come then, my soldiers are waiting, and you'll need a horse if you're joining us."

"Already done," she says, surprising me again. "I asked your steward to take care of it."

"And he listened to you?" I ask skeptically— not to insult her authority, but I've noticed how my staff treat Sara. That's something else I will have to address. She doesn't take offense to my question. She only laughs.

"The story of you groping me in the passage has trickled down through the ranks. If I'm good enough for their King, then it seems I am good enough for them. They bow and curtsy and jump to my every command. It's a little unnerving," she adds with a frown. I tug her back into my arms and kiss her until her frown is smoothed away.

"You're not just good enough, Sara. You're better than all of us and deserve every bow they give you. You are Queen of Rohn." That frown flickers back uncertainly, but I do my best to kiss it away along with any doubts she might have about my feelings for her.

SARA

When I spot the ship tied to the wooden jetty, I admit I breathe a little sigh of relief. Lachlan's right that I know nothing about the Mer Kingdom. I imagined we had to swim there. Grow tails, breathe underwater—that sort of thing.

I was trying to convince myself it would be an adventure, but I was terrified. My visions are still too fresh in my mind. The Elves trapped under the ocean, so cold their hearts are slowing down... I don't want to think about that right now.

Tipping my head up to the sun, I sigh happily when the wind whips across my face. It's that simple. I might have fallen in love with my husband, but that home of his is a different story.

Glancing up at it now, I can't help but reflect on how much the castle resembles a terrifying bird of prey. The castle's east and west sections extend in both directions like a bird's wings. The round tower in the middle is its neck, and the crenelated walls on the top of that tower are like a beady-eyed head glaring down at us.

I shiver and wrap my arms around my waist, watching dark magic roll like a black mist down the mountain, coming closer. No, I push the magic back, refusing to let my visions take over. But I still can't shake the sense that the castle is watching our departure, and I imagine dark eyes following us through the fjord.

I hate that castle, I realize. It's not just that it's old and dark. I hate it, and it hates me. I start shivering again, cold seeping into me. Lachlan folds his arms around me and pulls me close, warming and grounding me instantly. He kisses my temple gently.

"Try to control your visions on this trip." His voice is low, a whisper only. He doesn't want his soldiers to hear us. I nod, but only because I know he's afraid.

"I'll try." It's the best I can offer. His arms squeeze tight for a minute, and then he's gone, striding up the deck. As sure-footed on the water as he is on land. It makes me smile to watch him, and it's the perfect distraction from that brooding castle and its dark eyes.

I can still feel them on my back, but the further we sail, the lighter we feel. All of us. I sense it in the soldiers, and even Lachlan looks happier— he jokes with his soldiers, and although the words are indistinct, their laughter floats back to me on the wind.

And then a flash image: the castle tower, taken apart stone by stone, and a light that shoots straight up from deep within the mountain. A surge of power blasts the castle to dust, leaving nothing behind. Nothing— and the joy that sweeps through me is akin to the feeling I had on the boulder outside the castle gates. It is the spirit of the mountain begging to be released.

I tip my head back and smile up at those cliffs, thanking the Etain for my magic and that message; for telling me what I must do to fix our home. The Etain are the spirits of nature and the source of all our magic. Without them, we would be lost.

After that message from them, I feel alive in a way I've never felt before. I'm sizzling with electricity. It's crackling from my fingers, charging up my limbs, radiating from my chest. I feel invincible. More alive than I've ever been before. The mountain spirit is flowing through me. Her power is mine now. *Home*, it whispers.

And for all of my aunt's evil machinations, I send up a prayer of gratitude that Luneda sent me here to Rohn. To Lachlan.

It takes us all day to reach Aescheles, but the journey is so beautiful that I revel in every moment. I've never seen a landscape more inspiring, and I've worked in some of the most beautiful areas of the human world, so that's saying a lot.

But it's different here. The air is softer, but the colors are brighter. The cliffs above us are lush and green with plants, the waterfalls that cascade from the mountains sparkle with turquoise and silver water, and the waters we're sailing through are the purest, cleanest blue I've ever seen.

Once we enter the ocean's open waters, the wind picks up, and the waters shift from turquoise to navy blue, dark and a little forbidding. I watch Lachlan surveying the seas with a frown. He's nervous about the welcome we will receive, but for once, I'm calm. I trust my magic, and it's telling me that I have to be here with Lachlan.

He paces to the back of the boat and stands beside me, his hand reaching for mine and holding on tight. He keeps me at his side while his gaze travels restlessly over the waters, scanning for movement.

"Sssh, relax. King Muir wants to kill me himself. He's given orders that I'm to arrive unharmed." I laugh as I say it, intending to lighten the atmosphere, but the fear that shines from Lachlan's eyes makes me regret my ill-timed joke. "I will not leave your side," I promise again and lean in, brushing my shoulder against his.

"Your magic told you this?" he asks eventually.

"We will return to Rohn. Both of us," I add firmly when that worry still mars his face. He only nods, his features set into such stern lines he could be carved out of those cliffs we've been sailing past all day.

The sun is beating down on us, and it feels so good to be warm again that I tip my head up and close my eyes, soaking it in. Lachlan's hand tightening on mine is the only warning I get. I open my eyes to a fog so dense I can't see beyond the end of my nose. It shrouds the boat, and an eerie, unnatural hush descends before my hand is ripped from Lachlan's, and I'm tossed to the other side of the deck.

"Sara." I hear his anguished shout, but I can't reply. Something wet is wrapping around my mouth, gagging me. The smell of it...ocean, fish, seaweed... is in my nostrils, and my stomach heaves. A harsh laugh comes from behind me, and then hands are on my arms, binding them behind my back.

"Hold your breath, little human, if you want to survive." The voice is slippery and cool against my ear. That's all the warning I get before I'm dragged from the boat and into the water. The icy cold hits me in the face, and the shock of it is a stinging lash against my skin, but I'm held firmly in someone's arms. The cold doesn't touch me, not really.

It's seconds only, maybe as long as one minute, and I'm tossed out of the water. Gasping, I tug at the seaweed wrapped around my mouth. Hands bat mine away and calmly unwrap the seaweed first from my mouth and then my wrists.

"Go." The mermaid laughs at my panic and points toward the beach. When she smiles, her teeth are sharp incisors, and her smile is terrifying. She laughs again at the look on my face and dives below the water, disappearing into its depths. I drag myself to my feet and stumble toward the beach. The fog has cleared, and the soft golden sand beneath my feet is soft and warm. The waters lap gently here, the same gentle turquoise as the sky.

"Sara!"

I hear Lachlan's shout and turn to scan the beach for him. He's on the cliff above me, a small figure out of reach, until I notice a flight of steps carved into the cliff.

Behind Lachlan, a large crowd stands watching my unceremonious arrival here in Aescheles. There is delight on the faces of the Mer, a delicious sort of joy that is both cruel and careless,

When I look for Lachlan again, he is halfway down the steps, and I walk slowly toward him. My legs are still shaking. In fact, every bit of me is trembling, and I collapse against him when he reaches me.

"What happened to you arriving unharmed?" he growls and wraps his arms around me to hold me upright. I tip my head up, and the shock of what just happened leaves me feeling tipsy. I'm unsure if I want to laugh or cry.

"I am unharmed," I whisper. "My visions aren't perfect," I add defensively, but Lachlan's only shaking his head in frustration as he pulls me against him and holds me tightly.

"Fucking Mer." I hear him mutter furiously to himself, and I start to laugh. He stares down at me, and at last, I see a slight twitch of his lips as he almost smiles, but before I can say anything, he gathers me tight, and in front of the whole Mer welcoming committee, he kisses me. Claims me—a clear message to King Muir.

Chapter 14

L*ACHLAN*
    By the time we reach the top of the cliff, my rage is simmering too close to the surface. It takes only one look from me for the crowd to part, and the tittering and cruel smiles peter away to a loaded silence.

The court emissary is waiting for us at the entrance to the palace. I level him with a look that has brought others to tears, but he only regards me with polite deference. Clearly, their behavior has the support of their King. If I'm not mistaken, Muir himself ordered it.

Walking beside me, Sara resembles a wet, bedraggled girl at my side, nothing like the Queen she is. She is still trembling, but she's slowly managing to control it, and I'm nearly sure I'm the only one who can see it. Her clothes are stuck to her like a second skin, and as we walk along the marble colonnade, her boots squelch with every step, and the titters start again. I hear the stifled laughs, and my hands bunch into fists again, ready to attack anyone who comes near her. I glance at Sara, and everything inside me contracts with fear.

She's alive, she's unharmed...

But those reassuring sentiments don't work. My beast is snarling for revenge. It takes Sara turning her head and looking me straight in the eye for me to unclench my fists, but that rage is still there.

Fire flashes in her gaze and amazingly mirth. How can she be amused by this? She nearly died. She gives a tiny, almost imperceptible shake of her head and reaches for my hand. Anyone watching would think she needs my comfort.

The truth is the very opposite— her touch is soothing my beast, placating him. I am holding onto my rage only because she is touching me.

As we pass through the imposing silver arch that leads from the colonnade to the ballroom, she releases my hand and raises her head to peer down her nose at the Mer waiting for us inside.

Sara is royal and beautiful, even as she leaves a trail of water behind her with every step. Her skin still glistens, and I resist the urge to brush my fingers along her neck and wipe the water away. If I want to keep her alive, I must show only strength before King Muir.

Once inside the ballroom, one thing is evident immediately – as though I needed further proof – Muir is in the mood for playing games. There is a suppressed excitement in the crowd, an anticipation of danger.

Stemming my frustration, I wipe my face void of all expression. Muir may not be a friend, but since I assumed the throne, he has always been a loyal ally. Our meetings in the past have been peaceful... on occasion, even enjoyable. But I can already tell this will not be one of those times.

The ballroom is packed with Mer, but a narrow path through the crowd allows us to approach the King.

At the start of the colonnade, my soldiers were barred from entering. That means Sara and I are alone as we approach King Muir. I have never before been treated with such disrespect by the Mer court.

I should have trusted my instincts back in Rohn. This visit is a mistake.

The few Mer who dare to meet my gaze do so with a contempt that is concerning. I thought my position as King of Rohn would be enough to protect Sara, but I am no longer sure of this.

A loaded silence surrounds us as we walk forward, and as we step through the crowd into the empty space in front of the royal family, the crowd closes ranks behind us, blocking our retreat. Muir sits before us with his Queen to his left, both resplendent in jewels. Their large, silver thrones are designed to impress. To the right of the King stands his daughter, the crown princess, Kira.

Sara stands beside me, dripping water onto the marble floor. Like me, she waits, taking her measure of the room and the Mer within it. My beast is growling low in my head, warning me...the energy in this room is prickly, fraught with danger, and I know Sara can feel it too.

The lack of respect the Mer show for life has long been a subject of contention in my relationship with Muir. Too many times, we've clashed over his treatment of the other races in our realm. And now I'm here with Sara...

"Welcome," Muir intones, no smile on his face as he glances dismissively at Sara before turning his attention to me. This is worse than I feared. "We have a gift for you, King Lachlan of Rohn. As our neighbor and close friend, it seemed only fitting." When I raise my eyebrows in question, he continues. "Why, since you gift us with the presence of this human." He waves his hand in Sara's direction without looking at her. "We thought we would give you something in return."

A young Mer girl appears through the crowd carrying a silver platter. She stops before me and bows low. On the platter lies the Rohn red-tailed hawk, an arrow through its breast and my letter still attached to its leg.

I school my face to betray none of the anger I feel. Sara stiffens at my side; I know how she feels about hunting for sport and how much she loves the Rohn hawks that are abundant around our home. Fortunately, she remains silent as I reach forward and remove the missive from the hawk's leg.

"This is all the gift I require," I say to the Mer girl. "I thank you." She bows awkwardly and slips back through the crowd. The air in the room is charged, expectation humming through the court. Blood sports and games, these are the things the Mer thrive on. Entertainment is all they care about, and Sara and I are nothing now but entertainment for them.

Sara, I'm sorry. I let my magic whisper to her.

At your side is where I'm supposed to be, is all the response she gives me, not so much as a flicker of emotion crosses her face.

"One gift deserves another. Do you not agree, Lachlan?" Muir's voice has lost its impersonal tone, and his rage boils to the surface— as tempestuous as any storm.

"You should have read the letter." I keep my voice steady, unwilling to engage in this fight.

"After the way you insulted my family— I will hear nothing more from you."

"Insult?" I ask, a deceptively light ring to my question.

Muir's hand slams down onto the arm of his throne, the thud echoing in the hall as all hold their breath. "You dare to bring this woman. This human," he adds with a disgusted hiss. "Here. To my home. Here. To parade her before us. Before my daughter, whose heart you've broken with this betrayal." My gaze flickers to Kira, who remains at her father's side, her face impassive, devoid of emotion.

"I have brought my wife to your court—"

"A role you promised to my daughter," he interrupts me with a roar, his face turning a mottled red with the effort.

"I never offered marriage to your daughter." My voice is still calm— how, I don't know, when all I want to do is give in to my rage. "Not once," I add. "In all the years we've known each other. You've alluded to the union twice, but I never agreed to it. I never so much as indicated an interest in your daughter," I add harshly, and I see Kira flinch and then lower her head quickly.

"The contracts were drawn up," Muir shouts, refusing to acknowledge anything I just said.

"Not by me." I see uncertainty flicker in Muir's eyes for the first time.

"Your signature is all over them," he blusters and slams his hand against the armrest again. His anger lacks conviction, though.

"*My* signature?" I ask steadily. "The Master Tracker signature I use on all correspondence? The one that can't be forged and leaves a magic trace?" I pause and let my question sink in. "That signature, Muir?"

His eyes narrow, and I see him trying to backpedal. "It has the royal crest and the stamp of Rohn on it. It was negotiated with your most trusted advisor and hand-delivered by him." Muir is seething with anger, still not ready to back down. "This union has cost me months of negotiations, and, in the end, you tossed it aside with no regard for the years of friendship between our two kingdoms." He's building up into another rage. "I have turned suitors away because I believed you would honor this union with my daughter. Even when I heard the stories of how you lusted after this human woman, I never believed you would insult us by actually marrying her."

With every added insult that slips from his mouth, I can feel my beast stirring, fur rising, ready to tear this Mer King apart.

"And then you did marry her." Disgust drips from his words. "That, at least, is a problem easily resolved. Now that you've had her and your lust is sated, I will do us both a favor and clean up your mess. I will kill this human for you and free you once more for my daughter."

Before he's finished speaking, the Mer dagger, sharp and deadly, is already in the air.

SARA

Without my magic, I would be dead, a crumpled heap on the marble floor. The prickling feeling at the base of my skull warned me, but I was so preoccupied with the argument between Lachlan and Muir that it took the flash of silver out of the corner of my eye to finally wake me up to the danger I was in.

Stopping the blade with only an inch to spare, I watch as it hovers before my neck. The tip is so close if I exhale, it will surely nick my skin, and the poison on its surface will finish me as surely as if it had pierced my neck.

With a flick of my finger, I spin the blade away from me so that it points now into the center of the room. It hovers in the air, held there by my magic. In my first months in Emuria, before I was willing to admit I was a Seer, the palace in Soraya trained me in telekinesis. I can lift objects up to five times my weight, so stopping this little dagger is no strain on my magic.

I exhale slowly and concentrate on holding that knife where I want it. The ballroom is quiet, and the only sound I hear is my own shuddering breath, and then gently, I give another tap of my magic and send the dagger away from me.

There are loud gasps from the crowd behind me, and I tug on my magic, freezing the knife in mid-flight. I let it hover there for a few seconds, celebrating the shock I see on the King's face. Like all the other Fae I've met in this realm, he has underestimated me, and I can't help the satisfied smile that slips across my face.

With another flick of my wrist, the blade begins to spin faster and faster. Every eye in the room is on it, waiting to see what I will do next.

The blade is only two feet from the throne, but I leave it spinning there for a few more seconds before I flick my wrist again, and the blade flies toward Kira, the crown princess of Aescheles. A cry goes up behind me, and I smile but pull back on my magic at the last minute, halting the dagger's path.

Taking a step forward, I hold Kira's gaze as the blade hovers before her porcelain throat. A flare of panic in her eyes is quickly suppressed. That is the first bit of emotion I've seen on her face since our arrival. She's sucking in her breath and straining back without actually stepping back. Her eyes fly to mine, imploring me.

I can't kill the crown princess of Aescheles. I know that.

I release the dagger from my magic. In the tense silence that follows, the only sound in the ballroom is the clang of the dagger as it hits the marble floor. Nobody bends to retrieve it. Nobody moves at all.

Tearing my gaze from the beautiful Mer Princess, I look at her father, King Muir. "These games are wasting time," I tell him. "We have seven Elves in Rohn Castle who are close to death, and we need your help to save them."

"Human." Muir's lip curls in disdain. "You are in no position to even talk to me, let alone ask anything of me." He stares at me sullenly, and I see unease flicker through his eyes as he reflects on my words. "Tell me why you think I should be the one to help you with this Rohn problem?"

"Because if they die, you'll be the one responsible for killing them."

Silence greets my statement before the Mer court erupts behind me. I hear the fury behind their insults. How dare a human speak like this to the King? How dare a human threaten the princess? How dare I live and breathe when I am a walking insult to all that is Mer.

It seems I've said the wrong thing.

Again.

LACHLAN

"Seize her."

Muir's roar finally unlocks my frozen limbs, and as a Mer guard rushes at Sara, I toss him effortlessly across the ballroom. He crashes into a huddled group of Mer, and they all tumble to the ground. Another guard attempts to grab Sara, but she sends him flying with only a flick of her wrist. Six guards rush toward us, circling us cautiously.

Sara raises her eyebrows at me in a silent question, and when I nod, she uses both hands this time, and all six Mer find themselves lying in a heap on the other side of the ballroom. More guards rush at us, and my patience finally breaks.

"Muir, enough," I roar above the deafening volume of the court. Muir has gone still, and he's surveying Sara in a new light, one I'm not comfortable with, but he holds up his hand, and the ballroom falls quiet. The cold slits of his grey eyes swivel back to me.

My rage is leashed by a thin, fragile cord.

"Since our arrival here in Aescheles, you have insulted me with stories of fabricated contracts. You have insulted my wife." I let the growl rumble up my throat. "You have attempted to kill my wife."

"She is only human. There are plenty more where she came from," Muir says dismissively, still not heeding the anger in my voice.

"Enough." I cut him short. "Whatever your thoughts on humans. Sara is my wife and the Queen of Rohn. I expected her to be treated with the same dignity and respect you would treat all visiting royalty instead—"

"Bringing her here as your Queen is an insult to my daughter. It is Kira who should be Queen of Rohn."

"Enough," I roar again. "You *know* I never signed a marriage contract with you. Just like you *know*, because of our long friendship, I would never sign anything this important without meeting with you first. Without meeting with Kira first and establishing her wishes in this."

I glance at Kira and find her staring at her feet, a blush staining her cheeks. Muir has fallen silent, but his jaw is clenched as he considers my words, and his hands are balled into fists.

"But she is human," he hisses in frustration now, more than anger. "Human," he repeats. "You know how I feel about humans. What they did to my people. They hunted us for hundreds of years until we were forced to flee the human realm. Now you bring one of their kind here into my home."

"Sara is Queen of Rohn," I repeat, my voice low and steady. "She is also the daughter of Queen Aisleen of Soraya." I see him start at that. "Consider yourself lucky that Sara stopped your blade, or you would have had two kingdoms at your borders preparing for war." I wait for the tumult in the room to die down before continuing. "Muir, hear me now. If Sara so much as slips and falls while she's here, I will tear your palace apart stone by stone. What happened to your people in the human realm will seem like a fairy tale compared to what I will do to you. Sara is not only my wife. She is my bonded mate."

Muir knows what this means. Every Fae in Emuria does.

"There will never be another Queen for me. Kira will never be my Queen. Now, tell me, Muir. Do you still wish to destroy the peace our two kingdoms share?"

Silence follows, and the rage seeps out of Muir. One minute he's determined to kill my wife, and the next, he's leaning back on his throne and reaching for his own wife's hand and pressing a kiss to her palm. The affection between them is genuine. I have been witness to it too many times to doubt it now. But the switch in his personality is as unnerving as it always is. He flips from brutal tyrant to paternal mentor so quickly it hurts my head.

"You allowed the bonding ceremony?" Muir asks suddenly, a sharp glint in his eyes while he looks between Sara and me.

I can't say the question surprises me. I always swore I would never permit a bonding ceremony. It was not something I ever wanted for myself... or my bride. Binding a wife to my beast seemed like the cruelest thing I could do. But Sara came into my life and changed everything.

"I did. The signs told me I must."

Muir accepts my answer. In Emuria, we do not ignore the signs. He turns his attention to Sara then and studies her with a narrow-eyed look, a ponderous expression on his face.

"Sara, Queen of Rohn, welcome to my home. You will be safe here with us. I give you my word."

I release a small sigh, letting myself finally relax. Sara has been accepted by the Mer royal family. They might never like her, but they have accepted her.

Chapter 15

L*ACHLAN*

Muir grants us permission to inspect his labs and ask all the questions we want, but he does not join us. Instead, he waves away my suggestion that we should discuss this matter.

"Those Elves were healthy when they left here. If they are dead now, that is a Rohn problem," he says bluntly, with his usual callousness.

I feel Sara stiffen at my side, but she remains silent, her expression carefully blank. In my short marriage to Sara, I have despaired at her impulsiveness, what I perceived as recklessness.

But there has been no sign of those traits during this visit. If I discount her insistence on accompanying me in the first place. But she was following the signs, and that is something I can never argue against.

Maybe every impulsive decision she's ever made can be justified with this excuse. It's possible, I now realize, that Sara has never been reckless. I just didn't understand. I didn't believe in her magic.

As we walk through the Mor Palace, I reach for her hand, needing to feel her skin against mine. We're following in the wake of a palace courtier, but I need to touch her, and I ignore the servant. I'd be lying if I said my heart wasn't still beating out of my chest with fear. I don't know if I've ever been as scared as I was in that ballroom when Muir threw that dagger. Another inch, and Sara would be dead now. That old, familiar rage—

Sara squeezes my hand firmly, and the rage simmers down. I glance at her from the corner of my eye, but she catches me looking and sends me a quick wink. We're not behaving in a way befitting royalty. I feel like a kid. What am I thinking? I have no idea how a kid feels. Even when I was a kid, I never felt like this. Almost happy, I realize. How does she manage to do that? How does she turn my rage into happiness with only a look?

"Are you sure you wouldn't rather change first?" I ask her now, glancing at the wet clothes still clinging to her body.

Sara shakes her head impatiently. "No. I want to see these labs. After all the visions, I want to know what's going on. How it all started... why it started. We have to find a way to help them, Lachlan." She's silent for a minute, and then she adds, "And if Muir is telling the truth and the Elves were healthy when they left here, then... what happened?"

I squeeze her hand, trying to comfort her. I know how much her visions have frightened her. Sara acts tough, but she feels everything deeply, and on top of these new fears, her old nightmares have not abated. It was arrogance on my part, but I believed that having me beside her in bed would protect her from her nightmares. I was wrong, and when Sara began to cry in her sleep, there was nothing I could do but hold her. She didn't mention her dreams when she woke up this morning, so neither did I.

"What are you thinking about?" she asks me now, snagging my attention, a slight frown on her face as she senses my worry.

"You and everything that just happened. When I saw Muir throw that dagger." I shake my head to clear the image from my mind. "How did you know to do that? Where did you learn telekinesis?"

"Soraya. I didn't want my aunt to know I was a Seer, so I agreed to telekinesis training. A little diversionary tactic so she wouldn't discover my real magic. I still have a lot to learn," she admits quietly. "I can only do it if I'm focussed. If I let my fear take over, then it doesn't work."

"Well, I'm glad it worked today. You were incredible in there." When she laughs, I wrap my arm around her. Palace etiquette be damned. I want to feel my wife at my side. She grins and rests her head on my shoulder.

"Look at you breaking all the rules," she teases light-heartedly. "Where do you think he's taking us," she whispers, nodding towards the courtier. "How much further is it, do you think?"

"The Mer Palace stretches across most of the island." At the confusion on her face, I add, "Well, along the coastline. The center of the island is still wild and open, with forests and mountains. It's beautiful here. One day I will bring you back and show you around properly."

Sara arches an eyebrow at me in surprise. "I thought you didn't want me anywhere near Aescheles."

"You've been accepted now."

"As simple as that?" I nod. "Huh, okay. Then tell me more. Why did I think the Mer lived underwater? Aren't they supposed to have beautiful underwater cities hidden away from the outside world?"

"They do. All around the palace, you will find rock pools leading to the ocean. Deep beneath the sea is the real city of Aescheles. This palace, as beautiful as it is, is only for show. A place to entertain visiting Fae."

"Have you been there? To the real Aescheles." I nod. Her eyes grow wide, her curiosity lighting her up, and I long to show her everything about this realm. I want to impress her, I realize suddenly, show her that Emuria can be her home if she just gives it a chance, gives me a chance.

Her grin slips away quickly, and then she frowns at me. "Lars signed that treaty, didn't he? He arranged the marriage behind your back and signed it. That's why he tried to kill me when I returned to Rohn. He needed me out of the way."

I tug her closer and press a kiss to her temple. She's right. I'm only sorry it's taken me so long to see what Lars was doing. It frustrates me to realize how blind I've been all these years.

The courtier stops suddenly, and I catch myself quickly, removing my arm from Sara's shoulders and putting some distance between us. She smirks at me but then smooths her face clean before the courtier turns around. He bows to us, indicates a door on our left, then slips quietly away, no doubt off, to report our conversation to Muir.

We step into a quiet and dimly lit room. To the left of us are a wall of computer screens, and to our right are three sleeping pods, each one dimly lit and containing a sleeping

Elf. Only one of the Elves is hooked up to the monitors, and his pod glows with a green light. It illuminates the shadowed room.

At first, I think we're alone, but then another Mer man steps out from behind the panel of computers and bows his head.

"King Lachlan, Queen Sara. Welcome. I'm honored that you've requested a tour of our facilities. This work is special to all of us here in Aescheles. A breakthrough in technology." He stops, barely able to conceal his excitement. He is a small, narrow-faced Fae with short black hair and wire-rimmed spectacles balanced on his nose. That surprises me. Fae usually have excellent vision.

He notices my curiosity and shakes his head with a chuckle. "Oh no, these are not regular glasses." He grins and pulls them from his face holding them out to me. "I developed the technology myself. Here. Try them." Holding them in my hand, I wait for him to explain. "I've developed a lens that can pick up on the colors in the energy field. It helps with my studies here in the lab. Using these glasses, I can detect from the colors whether an Elf has donated enough energy in any one sitting. Try," he insists again, looking pointedly at the glasses in my hand.

I slip the glasses on and turn to look at the Elf hooked up to the machines. Color surrounds him in such vibrant detail I catch my breath. I sense Sara twitching restlessly at my side, and I know she wants to try the glasses herself. Before removing them, though, I turn to look at my wife. She is awash with green and lavender. So beautiful... so soft. Not the colors I would have expected from her. They are gentle, loving colors, and her words come back to me.

I love you so much.

And she does. I see it now. Her heart is open when she looks at me, and there is so much love in her eyes. My own heart contracts with fear. I can't lose her love.

Snatching the glasses from my face, I hand them to her. My hand shakes as I pass the glasses over, and she frowns at me. I see her open her mouth to question my mood and shake my head quickly. This is not the place to discuss this. Her mouth snaps shut and stretches thin in a disapproving line that morphs into an instant smile as soon as the glasses are on her face.

"Oh, Lachlan. This is incredible. This must be what Lilly sees when she uses her magic."

Sara swivels her head, looking at the Elves, the Mer doctor, before finally settling on me. She scans me quickly, and if I hadn't been watching her so closely, I would have missed the little frown that crosses her face. She covers it with a bright smile as she hands the glasses back to the doctor.

"Fascinating. Can you tell us more about your experiments with the Elves?"

"With pleasure, My Lady. But first, I would like to clear up some confusion. I need to state quite emphatically that the Elves volunteered for this experiment." His face has become stern now, a defensive straightening of his shoulders as he frowns at us.

Sara smiles, and I watch as the Mer man blinks, mesmerized by her beauty. "We know they came here willingly. We are more concerned about what happened after they left Aescheles."

The doctor's stance softens, and he nods, a concerned look crossing his face. "I heard they are not well," he says quietly. "All I can tell you is that they were well and excited to return home when they left me."

"Can you talk us through what is happening here?" I ask. The doctor drags his eyes away from my wife long enough to look at me, and noticing my scowl, he quickly explains.

"These are the last of the volunteers. We staggered the experiments for their safety. We only extract energy from one Elf at a time. For one hour a day. Never more than that. They need time each day to recuperate.

"And the purpose of the experiment?"

The doctor's face lights up again. "Imagine if we could become our own energy source. That is the ultimate goal. I want to find a way for each of us to generate our own energy. But for now, I am experimenting on creatures of the highest and purest vibration— Elves, as you see." He indicates the pods. "But I would also be interested in working with other mythical creatures... dragons, unicorns." At my frown, he nods. "I know. I realize there are ethical considerations that must be taken into account. So, for now, the experiments have been conducted with Elves only."

As the doctor talks, he moves over to the bank of monitors and starts inputting codes. I see a sequence of letters and numbers flash across the screen, and the green light from within the active pod gently dims.

"This Elf is finished for today. He must rest now, but he will be awake in a few hours if you wish to speak with him."

"That won't be necessary." I shake my head and notice his surprise. "These Elves are not in danger. I can see that." Turning to Sara. "Is there anything more you would like to ask?"

She frowns at my question and turns a considering gaze on the doctor. "Tell me, at any point during these experiments were the Elves held underwater?"

The doctor shakes his head firmly. "No. Definitely not. That would be counterproductive to our experiment. Being held underwater would be too stressful for them. They would grow weak. Elves need sunlight and nature. Trees in particular." He waves his hand toward a bank of windows at the back of the room. Through the glass, I see a forest of pine trees. "When the Elves wake, the first thing they do is go out into the wood. They even sleep out there." He smiles. "Please, believe me, we wish these Elves no harm."

SARA

Stepping out of the lab, we find two courtiers waiting for us with a request that Lachlan join King Muir in his study. I'm not included in this invitation and promptly escorted to the room where we will be staying tonight. The word luxurious can't even come close to describing the room. And the bath alone nearly convinces me to live in Aescheles forever. Well, that might be an exaggeration. I don't forgive quite that quickly, and King Muir did try to kill me after all.

After a long soak in the bath, I dress in warm, dry clothes, and I'm trying to figure out what to do while I wait for Lachlan to return when there's a knock on the door, and the next thing I know, the royal princess is sticking her head around the door with a mischievous grin on her face.

"Queen Sara, I've come to ask if you will join me for a tour of the island."

"Are you going to throw me to the sharks?"

She laughs and shakes her head as though her family didn't just try to kill me only hours earlier. "I'm sorry about my father," she says now. "But you handled him very well, I have to say. There aren't many who can. He's so...passionate," she concludes.

I would have used the word violent, and though I keep the thought to myself, I wonder if she can read my mind because her mouth twitches again in amusement.

"Will you come? I promise to behave, and I will tell you a little secret just between us." When I raise my eyebrows and wait, she sighs. "I am sorry, sincerely. The truth is I never wanted to marry Lachlan. He's always scared me a little bit. He's so stern. I'm not sure I've ever seen him smile." She cocks her head to the side and studies me. "Does he even know how?"

There is a mischievousness to this princess that is endearing— if I can get past the fact that her father tried to kill me. She is beautiful too. Far more beautiful than me, I experience an unexpected pinch of jealousy as I look at her. She has porcelain skin and oriental-shaped eyes with ebony black hair. She's exotic and lovely. And here was me imagining that all mermaids are buxom blondes luring sailors to their deaths. She's the opposite of all those clichés. Although... she's probably still deadly.

"Say you'll come. I would like to make up for what happened earlier."

I give in with a sigh, and she grins, revealing her sharp canines. She catches me looking at them and quickly closes her mouth. "I know. They're a little scary to outsiders."

"They remind me of vampire's teeth," I say, and she blinks at that and blushes a pretty pink color. Bowing her head, she then looks up at me from beneath her lashes.

"Closer to the truth than you think," she says then, surprising me. "But that is one of our many secrets, and I shouldn't be telling you any of those. Not on your first visit here. Come. You've seen the worst of us. Let me now show you some of the good."

I follow her out of the room and down a series of passages until we reach a marble courtyard. In the center of the courtyard is a square pond with steps leading down into it.

"That is one of the many ways to reach the real Aescheles. I might take you there one day."

She will. A vision flashes across my mind, so brief I can't hold on to it for long enough to understand. Water surrounds us, pinpricks of light in the distance, and this woman beside me with a large tail shimmering pinks and purples. Is it even me with her or someone else...The vision is gone so quickly I don't get a chance to explore it. When I glance back at Kira, she's watching me cautiously.

"You're a Seer?"

"And you're a mind reader." She nods and keeps walking. "Do you have other magical abilities?"

"Some," she admits and then grins again, lightening the mood. "But you must understand that technology is the real magic for the Mer. We will change Emuria with this technology. Magicians will no longer hold all the power." She grins wickedly. "Does that scare you, Queen Sara? Your family is one of the most powerful families in Emuria. Does the idea of losing that power scare you?"

"I wouldn't say Lachlan and Arlen are among the most powerful unless you're talking about their royal status?"

"Not Lachlan. *Your* family. I did some research while you were in the labs. Your mother and all of your siblings. I'm surprised my father did not know who you are. In truth, I'm surprised he allowed himself to be so led in this matter. It's not like him." She's frowning as she says it.

"Lars can be persuasive." The whole situation does seem odd and smells of Influencer magic, something powerful and dark.

"Mmm, I think you're right," Kira says from beside me, and she's frowning again. "I will need to look into this some more. I will talk to my mother. Maybe from this side, we can uncover what is going on. If I learn anything, I will send news, I promise. Now. Enough of all this depressing talk."

We spend the next two hours exploring the island, its pine forests, and perfect coves. It's a beach lovers paradise, a honeymoon destination I can't help thinking, and Kira suddenly claps her hands and grins.

"Yes. You and Lachlan must come back here for a holiday. I bet he hasn't taken you anywhere yet, has he?" The way she says that makes me feel a little defensive of Lachlan, but... she's right. We never did have a honeymoon, and the idea of spending a few days here, lying on a beach, far away from cold and depressing Rohn castle, is so tempting.

"Maybe after all this Elf business is worked out, we'll come back."

"I'm glad," she says. "And this time, we won't try to kill you." She laughs as she says this.

The platters are being cleared, and Mer are starting to leave the table, making their excuses and bowing low to the royal family. Muir waves them off with paternal affection; tonight, he's almost likable. A father figure. Playing with the gold wedding bands around my neck, I watch as the night slows down. I'd be lying if I said I wasn't tired. So much happened today that it's hard to believe we left Rohn castle only this morning.

Out of the corner of my eye, I see Lachlan stand, and when I turn my head to look at him, he holds out his hand to me. Smiling, I take it and let him pull me to my feet. He bows to the royal family, and I catch the mischievous twinkle in Kira's eyes and grin back at her. Muir's eyes flick between us, and he releases a booming laugh.

"Well, Lachlan, your wife has made an ally in my court. Fast work, Queen Sara." He raises his wine glass in salute. Lachlan squeezes my hand, so I smile at Muir and, like him, bow my head. We leave the ballroom together, still holding hands, and little titters and whispered laughter follows us. I look at Lachlan.

"Ignore it," he says with a smile. "That is how they are. Everything amuses the Mer."

I yawn and smother it quickly with the back of my hand. "I'll excuse them anything if I can just go to bed. I am exhausted. How was your meeting with Muir?"

"Lars has been spending time here in Aescheles, as we thought. Negotiating the treaty and working in the labs with the doctor. He is also the one who brought the Elves to Aescheles in the first place and the one who organized their return journey home." His voice sounds heavy as he says this.

"This is not your fault, Lachlan."

"Yes, it is. It's taken me too long to see Lars for who he is. If I could have seen earlier, maybe I could have stopped it."

I swallow back the instant objection that comes to my lips. Lachlan is a King, and he feels that responsibility keenly. It's easy for me, as a human, to say we're responsible for our own actions only but it's different for a King.

I understand why this weighs so heavily on him, and I wish there was a way for me to take some of the burdens from him. It worries me that I will never be able to help him with his workload. I haven't even told him about my dyslexia and how I struggle with all the correspondence that comes to the castle.

We had so many fights about it before I left for Cork. He couldn't understand why I wasn't responding to the letters I received from the other royal families and I was too proud to tell him about my dyslexia. Too embarrassed to admit that my clumsy handwriting and poor spelling were the reason I didn't respond to any of the letters.

I glance at him from the corner of my eye. Would now be a good time to have that conversation? No, I'm not ready.

It's humiliating, and I prefer to have that conversation when we've got time to ourselves.

Excuse after excuse. And I know that's all they are. I will have to tell Lachlan the truth... but not tonight. It's been a long day and an even longer night. Lachlan wasn't exaggerating when he said the Mer are tempestuous – wild. Unpredictable would be my word of choice.

At the dinner table, the conversations around us jumped from subject to subject with lightning speed. The witty observations were cutting and cruel, as sharp as those pointy canines in their mouths. I try to imagine how I would even kiss a Mer man without getting my tongue cut up. Lachlan squeezes my hand firmly enough to get my attention.

"The only Fae I want you to think about kissing is me," he says quietly, and I chuckle softly before batting my eyelashes at him.

"Yes, My Lord."

He frowns at me then his eyes dip lower, skimming over my dress, the amber in his gaze flaring bright. The evidence of his desire quickens my heart and squeezing his hand impatiently, I tug him along, walking faster. He chuckles at that and drags me back, slowing me down again.

"A Queen never runs," he says with a smirk and then laughs when I glare at him. I hate it when he's this controlled... while I feel like I'm about to crawl out of my skin, I want him so bad. Stepping into our room, I hear Lachlan close and lock the door as I walk toward the bed.

When I turn back, that frown is still on his face, and I don't know how to read it. Or maybe I'm simply too tired to read it. Too much has happened today, and it will take me time to process everything. Time to understand the Mer... understand my husband. He is not stoic and cold. Lachlan is vulnerable and loyal and –

"Sara." He's standing beside the door, still frowning. "Come here."

I don't move, but the intense way he's looking at me is all beast, and although excitement flares inside me, I only raise my eyebrows at his commanding tone.

"Come here," he repeats, a low growl in his voice now, and I can't help but notice the flare of amber in his eyes. Lachlan's not even trying to control his beast tonight, and that makes me smile. His frown deepens at the look on my face. "I swear you like him more than me," he mutters, shaking his head, and the note of vulnerability I hear in that statement wipes the smile from my face.

"Lachlan." I walk toward him, and his eyes fall to my hips. They move up, grazing over my breasts before stopping on my lips, and I smile again. "Lachlan," I repeat his name, and his eyes find mine. "There is no choice. Your beast is you," I say, tugging his face down to mine so I can kiss him.

He growls deep in his throat. "Sara, you've been driving me crazy all night. All I could think about was getting you back to this room."

"And now we're here. What are you going to do with me?" I tease him as I nibble on his jaw and kiss his neck. His hands are palm down on the door behind him as though he's scared to touch me.

"Sara." The seriousness in his voice stops me, and I take a step back. He still hasn't moved his hands away from the door. "I want to fuck you," he says quietly, watching me. "Is that okay?" I gulp and nod— the only answer I manage. But he doesn't move. "Take off your dress."

I look from him to the large king-sized bed behind us. "Here?"

He nods. I take another step back and slip the straps from my shoulders, and the soft fabric pools around my waist, exposing my breasts. His eyes flare brightly, but still, he doesn't. I'm shaking with desire, biting down on my lip. Tugging the dress over my hips, I let it drop to the floor and step out of it.

"Shoes," he says next. I kick the heels off and wait. So does he. I'm standing in front of him, wearing nothing but a little green thong and a whole lot of nervous anticipation. "Take off your panties," he says gruffly and watches me hook my fingers in the fabric and tug them down.

Lachlan has me squashed to his chest and pressed against the door before I've even drawn breath. His Tracker magic is swirling around us as his arms wrap tightly around me, his mouth close to my ear. "I can't be gentle. Not tonight." I don't believe him for a minute. Lachlan is always gentle with me. "Sara, tell me you understand."

I press my mouth to his and wish I'd asked him to remove his clothes, too, but he's already parting me, his fingers slipping inside, preparing me for him. "You're so wet," he moans into my hair, and I'm shaking and panting, so close to release, when he pulls his hand away. I hear his trousers drop to the floor, and then he's lifting me up, positioning himself before he surges inside me. My orgasm explodes around him instantly— just like that.

"Sara. More, baby, come again for me. Let me hear you scream my name." He's pounding into me, deeper and harder, and the tension begins to coil inside me again. It builds tighter and tighter even as Lachlan loses control and roars my name, and I fling my head back, knocking it off the door with every thrust from his powerful hips. A second orgasm explodes behind my closed lids.

"Lachlan," I weep, my arms wrapping tightly around his neck as I bury my face in his neck, clinging to him.

We're both breathing heavily, our breaths shuddering. I'm fully naked and wrapped around Lachlan like a clinging vine while he's still clothed. He lifts me off him and lowers me to the floor but doesn't let me go. I'm grateful. My legs are shaking so badly I might fall over if he lets me go.

When I've caught my breath, I step out of his arms and lean against the door for support. I watch as he toes off his shoes and steps out of his trousers. With a quick yank, he pulls his shirt over his head and drops it on the floor. Only when he's naked does he look at me again.

The amber in his gaze has receded, and I stare into chocolate brown eyes that hold a hint of uncertainty as they watch me. I reach up and cup his cheek, smile. I want to tell him I love him, but I don't want to scare him away.

"Bed?" I ask instead.

"Wait." He hesitates. "I didn't—"

"You didn't hurt me," I say firmly and watch the uncertainty recede, but it leaves an ache inside me. I wish he didn't fear himself like this.

Chapter 16

L *ACHLAN*
    My beast is sniffing at the air before we even cross the threshold into Rohn castle. Reaching out with my arm, I block Sara and push her behind my back. Izod notices and cuts across me.

"Izod, out of my way."

He ignores my growling command and steps into the foyer before me, his sword drawn, his magic scanning for danger. There are three more soldiers behind us. I am King, I must be protected, but my beast is not impressed. I hear him snarling deep inside me, longing to push all these men aside. He's sniffing the air again, scenting danger...

"Lars." My voice is a rumbling growl from deep in my chest. Sara places her hand on my back, and her magic sizzles against my skin, amplifying my magic. My senses sharpen, and my hearing is amplified in a way I've never experienced before. I can hear voices in the kitchen on the other side of the castle, but it's not those sounds that have me growling low. "Lars," I say again. His scent is strong. I would have recognized that sharp disinfectant smell anywhere— even without my beast.

"Stay with me," I say quietly. Izod nods to the other three soldiers, and together, they form a shield around us. Sara remains at my back, but I feel her magic rubbing against mine.

"Ice room," she murmurs suddenly, fear in her voice.

Yes. My beast is tracking Lars in that direction, toward the kitchen, down the passage alongside it, and down the spiral stairs. There's more than one scent here in this closed space. More than one Fae has been down here recently, but underneath it all, I can still detect that distinct disinfectant smell that always lingers when Lars is near.

We stop before the closed and locked door. Izod has been with me a long time, and with a smirk, he stands to one side, waiting for me to tear the door from its hinges. But a discreet tap on my shoulder stops me. When I turn, Sara is biting back a smile and holding something out to me.

"Master Key," she mouths dramatically with a mischievous glint in her eye. "Conserve your strength." *You might want it tonight*, she adds telepathically, just for me.

Even now, amidst all this, she manages to bring humor into this castle. That is her gift, her real magic. Sara floods my life with joy.

Taking the key from her, I cup one hand around her neck and tug her close, pressing a quick kiss to her lips. She looks so startled it drags a choked laugh out of me. My soldiers wisely avert their eyes, but I catch the amusement on Izod's face when I turn back to the door.

Holding the key card in front of the lock, I wait for the green light before pushing it open. I'm almost afraid of what we will find here. What brought Lars back to the castle? Why would he risk it?

And then I have my answer. The room is empty.

Lars came back for the Elves. And the other scents I can still detect in the air... he needed help to move the bodies. Slamming my hand into the door frame, I curse loudly. Everyone is silent, our shock a tangible thing.

"Upstairs." No one questions my command, and single file, we retreat to the foyer. My beast is restless, hackles rising.

Sniffing the air, I begin down one passage and then another, always tracking. It takes another four hallways before Izod finally stops me.

"My Lord." His hand lands on my shoulder, halting me. He drops his hand instantly, but he doesn't look away. "I will send soldiers to search the castle. May I suggest you wait in the library until we deem the castle safe?"

Izod doesn't back down from my hard stare; eventually, I relent. Reaching for Sara, I tug her to my side, and we follow Izod toward the library. Once he ensures the room is safe, he leaves us there. I close the door after him, locking us in.

Immediately, Sara is beside me, wrapping her arms around my waist and holding me. When I don't immediately return her hug, she squeezes tight and mutters impatiently. "Put your arms around me, Lachlan."

Huffing out a laugh, I do as she asks, and, of course, she's right. This is precisely what I need. Sara in my arms. Her warmth holding me close. She tangles her fingers in my hair, tugging on it sharply.

"We'll find him, Lachlan," she says fiercely.

"Your magic?"

She starts laughing and shakes her head. "No. I just refuse to let that bastard win."

She pulls back and paces over to the fire, which I'm relieved to see has been lit. I join her beside the warmth, and we stand there in silence, our hands stretched out toward the flames.

"I had a vision about this castle," she says suddenly. "I know how to fix it."

"Blow it up?" I ask, only half-joking, but the look on her face makes me laugh out loud. "Seriously? Your vision showed us blowing up the castle?"

She's grinning at me. "Maybe not all of it," she says with a cryptic smile, but my eyes snag on a glass of whiskey sitting on the stone hearth beside the fire.

"That's not mine."

Sara stares at it for a minute before crouching down and stretching out her hand for the glass. Her fingers don't even touch it before she snatches her hand back, gasping. I recognize the flare of magic around her just before her head falls forward onto her chest, and she slips into a trance.

Kneeling behind her, I place my hands on her shoulders and anchor her to me. It's only a minute before she's leaning back. Her breathing is erratic and loud in the quiet room. The fire crackles in front of us, throwing orange light over her face. Her eyes are pinched closed as though she's in pain, and tears leak from her eyes.

Lowering myself to the floor, I tug her into my arms and hold her close. She burrows into me for a second before popping back up with a frantic urgency. "Arlen. He's got Arlen."

"Arlen is in Soraya. Who's got him?"

Sara is shaking her head, tears still falling down her cheeks.

"No, Lachlan. He's not in Soraya. He was here last night. When Lars came back. Arlen was here. He was asleep in this chair. Lars took him. Drugged him while he slept." She's scrambling to her feet and staring down at me with wide, terrified eyes. "Lars hates Arlen. Why would he take him?"

A loud knock on the door distracts me, and I stand quickly. Lars has Arlen? Lars has... Striding across the room, I yank open the door and stare blindly at Izod.

Lars has Arlen is the only thought in my mind.

My bodyguard opens his mouth to speak but pauses when he sees my expression. His gaze slips past me, and I know he's looking at Sara's tear-streaked face.

"Izod," I bark out his name. His eyes return to me, and he nods, confirming what we already know.

"Arlen was here last night. No one has seen him today."

"Lars has him," Sara says from within the library. She's pacing, not looking at either of us.

Izod does not look surprised by Sara's news. He accepts it with a nod. "My Lord, what do you want to do?"

"Is the castle secure? Everyone else accounted for?"

"A few soldiers are missing, but we can assume they went willingly with Lars. There were a few loyal to him."

I stare at him blankly and then nod, accepting the truth of this disloyalty. Of course, Lars had soldiers and members of this court who would side with him. Lars could not have done all this alone.

I turn to watch Sara pacing, and Izod does the same. Both of us are waiting for her guidance. As she becomes aware of us looking at her, she stops abruptly.

"What?" She blinks at us in confusion.

"Where should we start to look?" I ask her quietly, relying on her magic to guide us.

Sara snaps her eyes closed, and I watch as she pulls her magic back in, and then she mutters, "Torin."

Opening her eyes, they're clear now, and her voice has a new clarity and strength. "Torin. We need to go to Aaronn and Lilly. And I need to send word to the twins. We need them." She shivers as she says this, her eyes slipping back, exposing the whites of her eyes... but only for a few seconds. She shakes it off and slaps herself hard across the face.

"Sara!"

"I'm allowed to do that to myself," she explains, and then before I can stop her, she does it again. "There. I'm back," she says firmly as I reach her side and pinion her arms to her side.

"Sara, will you stop hurting yourself?"

She ignores my glare and presses a kiss to my lips. "I'm okay, Lachlan. That's the quickest way to push the visions back."

Sighing, I tug her into my arms and turn her so I can talk to Izod over her head.

"Send word to Queen Aisleen, request that she fetch Sara's sisters in Cork."

"Not necessary," Sara interrupts, popping her head up to look at me. "Aoife and Clodagh can cross the veil on their own. We all can." That's news to me. "How do you think I left the last time I returned to Cork? You'd already sent Arlen away."

I file that information away for later and turn back to Izod. "Will you go for them?"

I feel Sara's surprise, and she turns to my bodyguard with a frown.

"You can cross the veil on your own?" I see him trying to hide his amusement at her question, and I have to bite back my own smile. Sara has no idea how powerful Izod is.

"Yes, My Lady," he says. "With your permission, I will travel to Cork and bring the twins back. I can escort them to Torin. I think we will all feel better if they have some protection with them for the journey."

Sara smirks. "Word of warning, don't tell Clodagh you're there for her protection. She won't take that well."

SARA

Lachlan had the foresight to send a missive to Torin before we left, so by the time we arrived, Aaronn and his uncle had done the necessary work in calling for a meeting of all the tribes.

Aaronn's uncle's house was full, so we spent our first night on the plains camping under the stars, the long grass waving around us. By the time morning came not only were the tribal elders gathered, but Izod had arrived with the twins. They traveled through the night to make the meeting in time. But I took one look at my sisters' exhausted faces and sent them straight to bed. I need them both strong for what's about to come.

When the meeting is due to start, we all gather in the largest barn in the village. I slip into the back of the room and find a seat next to Lilly. Reaching for her hand, I squeeze it and hold on, needing her comfort. A moment of frustration pulses through me. Why do we only spend time together during times of crisis?

Lilly cocks her head to the side, studying me. "Are you okay?"

"Of course not," I answer flippantly. "When would I ever be something as boring as okay?"

She rolls her eyes and squeezes my hand back before pulling hers away. Breanna and my brother, Cian, push past us to take the seats on the other side of Lilly.

Watching them, I feel that warning shiver from my magic, but I nudge it away. I can't let my fear distract me. Nobody will let anything happen to Cian— the others heard the warning too. All of us will be watching him. Whether he wants the attention or not.

I smirk as he finds my gaze and frowns at me.

"What?" He mouths.

Shaking my head, I smile and turn my attention to the proceedings, only half-listening. I'm not here for this meeting.

No, my magic is nudging me in a different direction, and as I scan the room slowly, a sudden sharp tingling on my neck makes me pause, and I glance back toward the entrance where a small group of Elves has gathered.

Yes, my magic whispers, and following the nudge, I crouch low and slip from the building, heading for the door and the Elves gathered around it. I can feel Lachlan's eyes on my back as I leave.

I won't go far.

Stay close.

Our messages bounce off each other simultaneously, and I smile to myself.

Slipping through the group of Elves, I walk a few steps away from the barn and find a wooden bench to sit on. The sun is hot, even early in the morning, and I tip my head up, soaking it in. My eyes are still closed when I feel a tingling on my skin, and blinking them open, I see a young Elf woman standing in front of me.

She has an ethereal quality to her. Her long blonde hair is tucked behind her pointy Elvin ears, and she is biting her lip, shifting awkwardly where she stands. She points at the empty space beside me. When I nod, she perches on the bench. She's holding something in her hand. It looks like a wooden toy.

"You're the Seer, aren't you?" Her question forces me to drag my eyes away from the toy in her hand. I look up.

"Yes." I'm a little cautious in admitting this. The last thing I want is to turn into the entertainment at this gathering. Nothing like a Seer to attract a crowd wanting to know their future. But these people are Fae, I remind myself.

The woman looks down at the toy in her hand, suddenly holding it out to me. My magic is humming so loudly that I nearly don't hear her words.

"My brother made this for me."

Looking back down at her outstretched hand, I see the toy is a detailed carving of a bird.

"It's a robin," she says. "They're my favorite bird. My brother made it for me last year."

I'm still reluctant to take it from her, but my magic is nudging at me insistently, and I find myself opening up my hand.

"Who is your brother?" As I ask this, I see the image of an Elf boy of about sixteen. He's crouched in the wood with a small knife and this little wooden bird in his hand. He's carving it, smiling as he does. He's thinking about his sister. I want to smile with him; he has a contagious smile.

"My brother is one of the missing Elves." The image of the boy in the wood vanishes. "You're a Seer. I thought maybe something he made might help you... find him." She shrugs uncertainly. "It can only help, I think," she trails off, needing my encouragement to continue.

The little bird is nearly burning my hand. The magic pouring off it is so powerful.

"Yes, you're right." I finally smile at her and pull her in for a hug, startling her. "Thank you. I'll bring this back, I promise."

She nods, and I see her eyes flicker over my shoulder before she jumps to her feet quickly. She smiles nervously at someone behind me. I don't need to look around to know who it is. Lachlan's hands land on my shoulders and squeeze hard. Both a warning and a caress.

Reaching up, I place my hand over his. "Thank you," I say again to the Elvin girl. She nods and leaves quickly. "I think you scared her off," I tease, craning my head to look up at him. He frowns at me. "Yep, that look would do it, for sure. You could scare just about anyone with that frown."

"Not you," he grumbles, moving around the bench to sit beside me. "You should know better than to allow your visions when you're alone."

"It was only a teeny, tiny vision," I tease him and then open my hand so he can see what I'm holding. "Her brother is one of the missing Elves. He made this for her last year."

His eyes narrow in concentration. "Do you think you can find him?"

I answer his question with one of my own. "Will you be able to put a trace on him if I do?"

"Work together?" he muses softly. "I've never done that before," he continues uncertainly, but then he wraps his arm around my shoulders and pulls me close. "We have to try." After a tight squeeze, he stands and holds his hand to me. "Come, let's get the others and find a quiet place to do this."

Aaronn asks his uncle if we can use his home after the meeting, and we're gathered on the porch, sitting and perching on every available surface while we debate our next steps. They all know that Lars has Arlen and the sleeping Elves. I've explained to them about my meeting with the Elvin girl and the bird carving. Is it mad that I believe we can use it to find the Elves? Wishful thinking... But Aaronn's nodding along as Lachlan explains our plan... so maybe it's not completely mad.

"What do you want us to do?" Lilly asks. Lachlan and I look at each other and shrug. We hadn't got as far as working out the hows of this plan.

"If intention is the most important rule in using magic. Why don't we start with that?" Clodagh, my youngest sister, surprises us all by taking charge. "Let's go outside where there's more space." When no one moves, she rolls her eyes. "Seriously, you're not going to listen to me because I'm the youngest here?"

My brother barks out a laugh and heads for the door. We all grin and follow him. Clodagh is still shaking her head irritably, and I watch her twin, Aoife, biting back a smile and ducking her head to avoid looking at her sister. They're born only seventeen minutes apart, but Clodagh has always hated being the baby of the family.

Once we're outside, we turn back to face her, and she glares at all of us. But she's hurt that we didn't take her seriously right away. Cian breaks the tension. "Where do you want us, Clo?"

"In a circle," she says gruffly, smiling gratefully at Cian. "Sara and Lachlan stand in the middle. I'm going to place a ring of fire around the circle." She warns us all.

I see Lachlan's bodyguards standing nervously to one side and watch my husband give Izod a discreet shake of his head. The Fae soldier takes a step back, but as I watch him, he scans the group before settling his gaze on Clodagh. He's watching her with laser-like attention –

"Sara." Lachlan snaps his fingers in front of my face. I bring my gaze back to him but I'm not ready to let this go.

"Who is Izod?" I ask Lachlan, watching him closely.

His eyes narrow. "My bodyguard."

"No." I shake my head and glance toward the Fae man once more. "No. He's not."

Impatience streaks across Lachlan's face. "Sara. You want to talk about Izod now?" he asks quietly.

Startled, I shake my head and almost laugh. "No. Sorry. I was getting distracted – again." He laughs and pulls me close, pressing a kiss to my forehead.

"Focus, wife. While you were eyeing up my bodyguard, Clodagh told us what she wanted us to do."

I grin up at him. "Where do you want me?"

He turns me around and places his hands on my shoulders, standing behind me, but then he leans in close and whispers in my ear. "When all of this is over... in my bed. And we're not leaving it for a week."

I feel the smile that spreads across my face, and even Clodagh's impatient glare can't dent it. "Are you two finished?" she snaps, and I hear Lachlan's snort as he tries not to laugh.

"Sorry, Clo. We're ready now," I tell my sister, trying to smooth out my smile.

"I will build a fire circle around all of you. This will concentrate your magic; contain it." Her eyes flit over us. She seems to be making this up as she goes. "Sara and Lachlan stand in the middle with everyone else in a circle around you. The rest of you, focus your magic into the center. Your job is to act as amplifiers for Sara and Lachlan. Okay?" When nobody says anything, she snaps. "Well, does anyone have a better idea?"

We all grin at each other, and Clodagh rolls her eyes.

Lachlan swallows back his amusement and takes charge. "Silence now and follow Clodagh's lead." He looks back at my younger sister and gives her a nod.

He only met the twins for the first time today, but he seems to like them, which is a relief... I could never stay with someone who didn't like my mad family. I feel him squeeze my shoulders, a gentle reminder that I need to focus.

Letting my eyes drop closed, I slip into my magic, knowing I'm safe. Lachlan won't let anything happen to me. The little wooden bird hums with the life of its creator, and I find him quickly. Images flash through my mind. Aescheles. Rohn castle. Duana Mountains. The ocean. And then suddenly, it all stops, and I'm inside a dimly lit room. It looks a little like the lab in Aescheles but bigger.

A glass pod is encasing me. I hold onto that image and pulse it to Lachlan, using our bonding magic to send it to him. I feel him there with me, inside the pod— his magic tangling with mine. His beast is sniffing the air, listening, straining against the confines of the pod, and then I feel him tugging on me. Lachlan is pulling his magic back, slowly, slowly, as though he's unwinding a ball of string. He's creating a trace, a way for us to find our way back to the Elf and that hushed lab that holds him.

Chapter 17

L*ACHLAN*

Our journey across the grass plains takes two days. We sleep a few hours at night, but that is the only delay I allow. I'm worried I'm pushing the women too hard, but it's a needless worry. The O'Driscoll women have the strength of their Celtic ancestors in their blood. Resilient and determined, they are as eager to get there as the rest of us.

Sara has gone strangely quiet, and I fear she has seen something...

I'm too scared to ask.

The trace is leading us toward the coast, and by the second day, I can smell the salt in the air, and the breeze picks up, fresh and wild. It's a relief after the heavy heat on the plains. Standing on the wide beach, they're all waiting for me to lead them, but for now... I'm lost. The beach stretches for miles in either direction, wild and open. To our backs are sand dunes. There's no sign of life anywhere— no sign of a lab. A structure of that size should be visible from a distance, but I can't see anything along this stretch of coastline.

Sara comes to my side and slips her arm through mine. She stands there in silence, placing her head on my shoulder, amplifying my magic. It makes me smile. Having a mate who supports you is such a simple thing. Turning my head, I press a kiss to the top of her head.

"Thank you," I murmur. Sara squeezes my arm in response, but she doesn't say anything. There is a heaviness to her today. A sadness in her scent, it's leaching off her skin. I can smell it, and it makes my heart clench in fear.

Arlen.

She loves my brother too.

What has she seen?

"Sssh, focus, Lachlan," she murmurs now. How have our roles reversed? That's usually my line. Huffing out a tired laugh, I pull in a deep breath, exhale loudly and let myself drop into my magic. I release my beast. I am no longer afraid. With Sara at my side, he will not hurt anyone. He listens to her, and he loves her, just like Aaronn said he would.

I'm dropping, releasing control, letting my magic come to the foreground. My beast is now in charge. Monosyllabic at best, he points across the water.

Sara keeps her hand firmly wrapped around my arm, and I can feel her magic brushing against mine, amplifying my Tracker senses. Sniffing the wind, I catch their scent. Lars and Arlen. It's no longer the Elf trace I'm following. It's my brother's scent.

"We need a boat." I hear Sara say. "They're on one of the islands."

I want to prowl, move, and Sara steps back instantly, releasing my arm. I didn't need to say a word. I look at her now, standing beside the ocean, tall and proud, so damn beautiful, even after days of traveling, her clothes creased and dirty, dark smudges under her eyes. But all I can think about is pulling her close. Claiming her. She's mine, I want to shout to all of Emuria. Mine. The possessive growl is low and quiet, and she chuckles and steps closer.

"Hi, my beautiful beast." She strokes her fingers through my beard and cups my jaw. "I'm so relieved you're here with us. I always feel safer when you're near." She's whispering comforting words to my beast, but I hear her, and I know these words are for me too.

Sara's loving my beast, accepting him, and I feel him growing more powerful with every loving word she rains down on me. His pride, his power, his magic swells. I can feel the magic gathering— concentrated in him. In me, I realize this with startling clarity. Sara smiles suddenly, wide and big.

"Yes, Lachlan. It's all you. Your beast is you. Love him, baby, please. Love him, trust him." She presses her mouth to mine in a soft kiss. The wind is whipping around us, it's cold, and I tug her closer. The tang of the ocean catches in my nostrils, and beneath that, Arlen's scent is tugging at my magic, calling to me.

"We found a boat." Cian's voice drags my attention back to the beach, and I hear Aaronn's voice rising above the wind as he directs the others.

I squeeze Sara to my chest, holding her tightly in my arms for a few seconds before we break apart and rejoin the others. The knowing looks from Sara's family would have annoyed me in the past, but now...they don't. I feel accepted and safe for the first time in my life. They accept me as I am.

Sara joins me at the front of the small sailboat. It's only just big enough to hold our party of twelve. She squeezes in next to me on the narrow wooden bench, and reaching up beneath the fall of my hair, she wraps her hand around my neck. Her warm fingers tingle against my skin, and instantly I receive a flash of knowing that combines with my Tracker senses.

The rolling of the ocean buffets us gently as we crest and dip over each swell. The fresh breeze fills our sail, and although it's dark, my Tracker magic guides us across the inky water. The islands are quiet, with no sign of life as we approach, but my senses are so sharp now that I don't need lights to tell me which one holds my brother.

I'm coming, I send that whisper on the wind, hoping he can sense my magic approaching. *Arlen, I'm coming.*

Well, hurry up, brother. Darling Larry is about to fry me like an egg. His usual dry wit in my head shocks me.

"Hurry. We must hurry." The urgency in my voice prompts Sara to tighten her hold on my neck. Please, I'm praying to all the gods, don't let Sara's sadness be about Arlen. I can't lose him. "Can we not go any faster?" I shout to be heard above the wind.

My bodyguards are manning the sails, and when I turn impatiently, Izod's stoic expression makes me growl. He says nothing, as is typical of him in times like this. Izod is the quietest Fae I know. I look again, sharply this time. He is decidedly green, and as I watch, he leans over the boat's edge and vomits into the water.

I avert my eyes so as not to embarrass him, and suddenly we pick up the pace, our boat sailing through the water faster than should be possible. Grabbing hold of the wooden seat, I turn to see everyone else sharing the same look of amazement.

Sara taps me on the arm and points to the water, and I see what has her smiling. A flash of silver and pink scales, barely visible in the dark water.

"Kira," she murmurs, worry creasing her brow.

"She won't hurt us," I say to reassure her, but she's shaking her head, still frowning as she stares into the water.

"That's not—"

"We're here." Cian's urgent whisper cuts her off, and she throws a look toward the beach.

"No sign of life," Aaronn says quietly. "Are you sure this is the right island?"

"Yes."

Nobody questions that simple answer, not that it would have done them any good. I'm already leaping out of the boat. I land in the shallow water and shiver as the cold water soaks through my boots. By the time I reach for the boat, Aaronn is at my side, and together we pull it ashore.

When we're all on the beach, Sara pitches her voice loud enough to get our attention.

"Lars has warriors with him. Everyone, please be careful." Her eyes linger on Cian, and I watch Breanna's gaze sharpen and then flick between Sara and Cian, a frown now crossing her face.

And just like that, Sara's fear makes sense. This isn't about Arlen. This is about Cian and the vision she had of his death. Breanna is a mind reader— she would have picked up on Sara's thoughts. Good. Breanna is sensible; she will keep Cian out of trouble.

Reaching for Sara's hand, I pull her to my side, and we set off across the beach with me leading the way. Arlen's scent is strong and easy to trace.

Leaving the beach, we enter a wood. It feels darker here, shadows looming over the paths as we slip amongst the trees. We seem to be walking up, and as we break free of the trees, I see a gently sloping hill. Arlen's scent pulls me toward it, but a movement, a shadow above us, halts my march. Nudging us all back into the shadows, I study the hill again.

Yes. Two warriors are guarding it.

"Okay. Cian and Aoife, you're up." Aaronn takes charge, issuing commands. "Do not engage," he says sternly, looking at Cian. Breanna has gone stiff at his side but doesn't dare argue with Aaronn.

Cian and Aoife look at each other, grin, and suddenly, Aoife disappears. Cian winks at all of us, a shimmer of blue smoke clouds our vision, and when it clears, he's gone too. I just have time to detect the shimmer of scales as he slips off through the grass in snake form.

"I didn't know Sorayans could shapeshift," I say quietly to Aaronn.

Aaronn offers me a tight smile. "Cian is the only Sorayan I know who can."

"And Aoife?" I ask, thinking I might have missed the animal she shifted into, but Aaronn shakes his head.

"Not a shape-shifter. Aoife has invisibility." He grins. "They're a useful family to have around." He winces then as Lilly elbows him in the ribs.

"Ssh, something's happening up there," she whispers.

Breanna looks like she's about to step forward, but Sara stops her quickly. "Cian's okay. On the water, Breanna. It's on the water we must watch him." Sara's voice is low and toneless, and I recognize the signs of a vision coming through her. There's no time to ask, though, as Lilly's right. There's trouble on the hill.

One of the warriors has fallen over, and then a wisp of blue smoke appears, and Cian is standing behind the second warrior. All we can see from the tree line is the second warrior falling to the ground. For Sara's sake, I'm glad that's all we see.

"Right." Aaronn's voice is grim in the sudden silence. "Let's go." And we're all sprinting up the small hill to reach Cian.

He's crouched low in the grass and waves us all down as we approach. Crawling forward on our knees, we lower ourselves onto our bellies and look down into the valley below. A glass dome rises out of the earth.

We've found Lars' lab. As I realize this, a shimmer of magic reveals Aoife's location beside the glass dome, but then she disappears again, and a few minutes later, we see a door into the lab slide open.

"For once, I would really love it if you all listened to me," Aaronn grumbles under his breath and then glares at Cian. Sara's brother only rolls his eyes.

"It had to be done," he says unrepentantly.

I hear Izod snort as he swallows back a laugh, and I know my other three bodyguards are equally amused by this crazy family I've married into. They never had this much fun when on patrol with me in the past.

"Aoife's gone inside." Aaronn sighs as he says this and exchanges a worried look with Lilly.

"Come on then." Cian hops up. "We can't let her do it all on her own," he says over his shoulder, already running down the hill. I hear Aaronn grumbling beside me, but he's the first to follow Cian down the hill.

SARA

Watching the lab door swallow up my little sister is terrifying. I don't have time to get stuck in the fear, though. Lachlan has my hand, and he's pulling me down the hill after Aaronn. His bodyguards are behind us. Lilly and Clodagh are on my right, with Izod on the outside, protecting my sisters. Breanna is already halfway down the hill.

Cian and Aaronn are waiting for us at the bottom of the hill, their daggers drawn. Lachlan and his bodyguards have swords. Looking to my right, I notice even Breanna, Lilly, and Clodagh have blades.

"Why am I the only one without a weapon?" I hiss, and they all turn to look at me.

"You're dangerous enough without one," Cian says smoothly, but his lips twitch as he suppresses a laugh.

"You say the sweetest things to me." I bat my eyelashes at him, and he winks. I'm laughing at my brother when I feel Lachlan press something into my hand. Looking down, I see it's his own dagger. He takes my hand and wraps my fingers around the hilt.

"Stay close." The smile slips from my face when I see the grim look on his face. Arlen is in this lab, and Lachlan's fear reaches out and wraps around me.

I nod, wishing I could hold him instead. *I love you,* the message slips out too quickly for me to stop it. Lachlan looks unblinkingly back at me, his eyes glowing amber in the dark, and I want to apologize and pull my words back, but the door slides open, and both Aaronn and Cian raise their weapons.

The doorway is empty, and then it's not. Aoife shimmers into form before us. She places a finger to her lips and beckons us to follow her. In single file, we pass into the tunnel, which leads to a set of stairs. Three floors down and deep into the earth Aoife stops before a set of double doors. They slide open at the touch of a button, and we follow her inside, crowding around her when she stops.

The lab is dark inside. Only the soft glow from the pods illuminates the room. Horror is a pit in my stomach.

I start to count the pods, getting to seven, eight, and nine, when I hear Lilly's strangled gasp and see her fly across the room to the largest pod. And then I understand. Her unicorn, Majesty, is asleep inside the glass container. There are wires attached to him, just like with the Elves.

Looking closer, I study each pod in turn, and the Mer doctor's words come back to me: *I would like to study the mythical creatures, but of course, that poses ethical considerations.* But somebody is doing it. One pod holds what looks like a baby dragon. His scales are a dull red. I look at the pod beside it, and my breath catches in my chest. The white hawk of Rohn. My hawk. Lachlan's hawk.

"No." I rush across to the pod and press my hands to the glass, feeling a helpless rage. The hawk that brought Lachlan and me together. Tears are running down my cheeks as I look at the beautiful bird lying in the glass case, wires attached to its body.

But then Lachlan's fear reaches me, and I look up sharply. He's prowling around the room, looking inside every pod. Arlen's not here.

Lachlan's eyes are more amber than I've ever seen, with no brown trace when they meet mine in the dark. Fear is rolling off him. It nearly knocks me back.

"His scent is here," he mutters, ignoring the rest of us. "It's here."

"Trace it, Lachlan." I move to his side, wishing I had some way to soothe his fears. I scan the room. Arlen has to be here somewhere.

I spot the door at the same time Lachlan strides toward it. Another, smaller chamber lies behind the door, and within it is a single pod and the doctor we met in Aescheles.

Lachlan lets out a roar; his rage is powerful, and the doctor flinches. He's frozen to the spot, his eyes flicking beyond us and his mouth open to say something, but before he gets a chance, Lachlan has him pinned to the wall.

"My Lord, it was with their consent. All the participants in this trial volunteered," he sputters.

"My brother is in that pod." Lachlan's voice is a low growl, his beast is fully present, and I watch as the doctor's face pales, and he begins to shake.

"The crown prince of Rohn?" He gasps out his question as Lachlan's hand tightens around his neck. "I didn't know."

"Lachlan, no." Rushing to his side, I grab his arm, the one choking the life out of the doctor. "We need his help."

I'm not sure Lachlan can even hear me. His fist tightens around the doctor's neck, and the man's eyes bulge with panic.

"Lachlan, you can kill him later. For now, you have to let him go." I keep my tone firm but calm, and suddenly his arm drops to his side. The doctor slumps against the wall, his face ashen.

"Reverse the charge," I tell him.

The doctor's blinking at me, unresponsive.

"Hurry up, doctor. And you better pray that Arlen's alive, otherwise, nothing will save you from Lachlan's beast."

The doctor's eyes skitter nervously to Lachlan, who has retreated to the far side of the small room. He's holding himself pressed to the wall, his arms behind his back, his breathing labored.

"Now, doctor," I snap, beginning to lose patience. I can't even bring myself to look at the pod. I'm scared of what I'll see. We can't lose Arlen. Not now.

The doctor is fumbling at the monitors when Izod appears in the doorway, an anxious frown on his face. I see him sigh when he spots Lachlan, but his jaw clenches when he sees Arlen in the pod. He's the only one who's been brave enough to look. Lachlan and I have been studiously keeping our eyes away, but what Izod sees there makes his face pale, and I spin around quickly. Arlen is as white as the sheet he's lying on. Anaemic and frail.

"How could you do this?" I murmur the question, not expecting an answer, but the doctor takes my question literally.

"It's been a fascinating experiment, actually. This particular Fae is a powerful magician. His vibration is not as pure as the Elves but powerful nonetheless. Tapping into his energy has yielded fascinating—" He doesn't get any further than that.

Izod has his hand wrapped around the doctor's throat, and he's lifting him up. The doctor's feet are now dangling off the ground, his face turning a mottled purple.

"Shut up," Izod says calmly. So calmly, a shiver passes through me. "You're a monster," he adds quietly before lowering the doctor to the floor. The man stumbles. He would have fallen if Izod wasn't still holding him by the throat. "Not another word."

The doctor grabs at his neck and nods. His throat has an angry red hand print on it. I doubt he could talk now, even if he was brave enough to attempt it.

Izod stands at his back, only two inches of air between them, looming over the doctor, watching him work the monitors, and an idea occurs to me.

"Cian, get in here," I call quietly from the doorway. I see my brother beside the central monitor, a frown on his face as he scans the screens. He looks up at the urgency in my voice. "Come in here," I repeat. "Watch what the doctor's doing."

Cian is beside me so quickly I feel dizzy. Tracker magic. Shaking my head, I point Cian toward the monitor. My brother is already peering over the doctor's shoulder, watching intently. His eyes scan the screen, blinking at the flashing codes that mean nothing to me. But I watch him nod.

He asks a series of low questions and then snaps loudly, "Just nod or shake your head. And you better be telling me the truth, or I'll come back in here and cut out your tongue. You'll be permanently mute when I'm finished with you."

The doctor's hands are shaking as he types code into the computer. Cian asks more questions, his eyes glued to the screen, and then he's gone. Glancing over my shoulder I see he's already at the control console, working confidently, reversing the charge.

I watch the doctor step back from the monitor. The glass lid on the pod pops up, and we all turn to look at Arlen. Color has returned to his face, but he still looks frail, too thin.

Izod glances between us, nods, and exits the room, but I watch Lachlan. He hasn't moved from the wall and his eyes are trained on his brother.

Looking back at the doctor, I point toward the door. "Out," I tell him. He stumbles to the doorway but halts when he sees Lachlan's bodyguards waiting for him.

"Doctor, you are under arrest for the attempted murder of the Crown Prince of Rohn."

I watch as they bind his arms behind his back. The doctor blinks back at them as if he doesn't understand what's happening, doesn't understand what he's being charged with.

Turning back into the room, I see Arlen stir in his bed, his eyelids flicker, and I rush over to his side. "Arlen." Reaching for his hand, I squeeze it gently.

"Hey, sweetheart," he murmurs. His voice is whisper-thin, and he forces his eyes open to look at me. "I wasn't sure you'd get here in time."

I blink at him through my tears and lean over him to kiss his forehead, lingering there, not wanting to let him go.

"Sweetheart, you better move. Your breasts are in my face, and your husband is growling at me."

A laugh bursts out of me and I press another quick kiss to his cheek and turn to Lachlan.

"He's all yours," I say with a smile.

There's a softness to his gaze when he looks at me. His eyes, a warm brown, hold mine for a minute before he nods. I leave them alone and step back into the main chamber, stopping in surprise when I see all the activity.

"Fast work," I mutter under my breath, but Breanna hears me and grins.

"Your brother has serious skills."

"I know," I say and roll my eyes. "You've told me that before."

Breanna laughs softly. "Not those skills, although he has those too," she adds mischievously, teasing me.

"No, Breanna. Just no. I do not want to hear about my brother's skills in the bedroom," I say firmly. She laughs again and walks off.

Looking around the room, I see the glass pods are open, and the Elves beginning to stir. Lilly has her arms wrapped around Majesty's neck, and Aoife is pumping healing energy into both the white hawk and the baby dragon.

Everyone is so busy helping revive the prisoners that nobody notices the doors sliding open until Aoife gives a strangled gasp. Looking up, I see a warrior standing in the doorway with an arm around Aoife's neck and a knife to her throat.

Her eyes are wide, startled. But before I can even blink, two daggers slice through the darkness. One lands in the warrior's hand, and, surprised, he drops the dagger he's holding. The second buries itself deep into his jugular vein.

The man's eyes bulge in shock as he stumbles back, clutching at the dagger in his neck. He yanks it out, and blood pumps from the wound, splattering all over Aoife's silver hair. She screams and dodges out of the way while the warrior drops to the ground. Clodagh and Izod stare at each other before both step forward to retrieve their daggers.

"You're a bloodthirsty family, aren't you?" I hear Izod mutter as he yanks his dagger from the man's hand. Clodagh ignores him, her eyes on her twin.

Chapter 18

L *ACHLAN*
The scene that greets us in the main chamber locks my feet to the floor. Arlen is beside me, holding onto the wall for support, and we turn to look at each other. The pods are empty, and the seven Elves are no longer in the lab. The mythical creatures are dazed and weak, but Aoife is the sight snagging my attention.

She is standing wide-eyed and trembling beside the door, her silver hair covered in blood, red splatters across one cheek. A body is lying in the doorway, and Izod and Clodagh are dragging it out of the way.

I flick my gaze around the room again. Aaronn is helping Lilly guide the unicorn out of its pod, but there's no sign of Cian, Breanna, or my wife. Where are they?

"Aoife, sweetheart, are you okay?" Arlen's quiet question brings my attention back to the scene at the door. Aoife's gaze flies to my brother, and she gives him a shaky smile.

"It's not my blood." She shivers as she says it and scrubs at her face with a frown.

Lilly's eyes widen, and she hurries across the room.

"Sorry, here, let me help," she says, tugging Aoife over to the side so she can help wipe her face clean. "I should have done that straight away," she's chiding herself even though she's talking to Aoife.

"I'll forgive you this time," Aoife says with another shaky smile. "There's sort of a lot going on in here."

Lilly rolls her eyes. "There's always a lot going on when we're all together. There. That's better. Your face is clean, at least. I'm afraid there's not much I can do about your hair. Unless you feel like swimming alongside the boat on the way back." Lilly grins suddenly, and Aoife is rolling her eyes now, but fear is clawing at me. Too much time has passed.

"Where is Sara?"

Lilly blinks over at me in confusion and then shakes her head suddenly as she understands. "She went with Breanna and Cian. They're helping the Elves down to the beach. Some of them are too weak to walk on their own."

"What—" I don't even get the question out.

A large Mer warrior is standing in the doorway. He's a large Fae, even bigger than me, and he has one hand wrapped in Sara's braids as he tugs her into the room beside him. Her right eye is already swelling where the Mer clearly punched her. It is the only explanation for how he managed to subdue Sara in the first place.

He has a dagger pressed close to her throat, the point digging into her skin, leaving a pinprick of bright red blood. It runs down to her collarbone, and my vision goes black. When it clears, the Mer warrior is looking directly at me.

"Your wife, King Lachlan. Will I gut her for you? Here in front of you, or would you prefer not to watch?" The menace in the man's voice is all I hear; the words are indistinct, a rushing noise in my ears.

I watch the man's arm shift as he adjusts his hold. One flick of his wrist, and he will split her throat open.

But I also see Izod wink out of sight at the same time. Even if Izod drives a dagger through him, the Mer warrior will still have time to plunge that knife into Sara's throat unless...

Tracking to her side, my hand lands on the warrior's wrist at the exact moment Izod slices his blade across the Mer's throat. The warrior's hand jerks, but I grab the blade, yanking it back before it pierces Sara's skin. The Mer falls back, crashing to the floor, his hand still tangled in Sara's braids. She falls with him, and a scream rips from her throat as she lands on top of him.

Izod slices through her braids, freeing her as I lift her to her feet. I run my hands over Sara's face and hair, searching frantically for the source of the bleeding. There is blood all over her.

"Where are you hurt? Sara. You're bleeding. Where are you hurt?" I'm frantic with worry, so scared.

"Lachlan, sssh, stop. Lachlan, baby. Stop. Look at me." She cups my jaw and forces me to look her in the eyes. "Your hand, Lachlan. Your hand is cut. It's your blood on me."

Staring at her blankly, it takes long, fraught seconds for me to understand her words, but looking down, I see she's right. I have a deep gash across my left palm— bright red drops leach onto the grey floor at my feet. I stumble back a step just as Aoife reaches for my arm. She holds my hand palm up and then places her left hand over it, holding it only an inch from mine. The tingling sensation is warm and soothing, and my dizziness passes immediately. My palm is warming up until it's burning with an intense heat.

"We need to leave." I hear Aaronn's low-voiced command. "Can everyone walk?" I don't hear the response, but I'm aware of movement behind my back. Sara's at my side. She hasn't left me. Her arm is wrapped around my waist, and her head is pressed to my chest.

I wrap my good arm around her and squeeze. Over my head, I see Izod wiping down his blade. "Thank you."

He nods and turns away. Sara is trembling, and I hold on tight, pressing a kiss to the top of her bowed head. I touch the patch of short braids sticking up from the top of her head and kiss her again.

"I'm cutting these fucking braids off," I hear her mutter into my chest, and the frustration I hear in her voice makes me laugh. Hearing her sister's comment, Aoife giggles too, and soon the three of us are laughing so hard we're crying.

The others stare at us in confusion, but Aaronn's sharp "let's go" is enough to silence our laughter.

Looking down, I see my hand is completely healed. "Aoife, thank you. You have an incredible gift." She smiles sweetly at me and turns away quickly, hurrying after the others. Sara and I are the last to leave the lab.

"Where is Lars, do you think?" she asks as we climb the stairs. "He must know we're here."

As we climb, I scan the stairwell, sniffing out Lars' scent. I can detect it, but it's faint.

"He's running away. He knows he's no match for our combined magic."

"I don't like it, Lachlan. We need to catch him."

"Sssh." I squeeze her close. "Let's get everyone to safety first. We'll find Lars, I promise. I'll track him down." She's silent after that, but she holds tight to my hand as we run through the forest.

When we reach the beach, we see a second boat has been found, and Aaronn is directing the Elves and mythical creatures onto one. Lilly is leading Majesty onto the vessel, and Aaronn joins her.

With a nod at Izod, I gesture for two bodyguards to join them. Aaronn will need help sailing the boat. Izod frowns at my request, but he barks out the order anyway before turning and making his way to the second boat.

He takes his place at the back and begins unfurling the sails. Drum, my other bodyguard, has one oar in his hand, and Cian has the other. Breanna hops into the space between them and places her hand on Cian's thigh.

I watch as he smiles at her, but Sara stiffens suddenly, and a look of terror flashes across her face. "No," she says, shaking her head, refusing to budge. "No."

"Sara, we have to get in the boat." A bright flare from the forest behind us only emphasizes what I'm saying, and I turn to see a band of warriors emerge from the trees. "Now," I shout and lift her, dumping her in the boat before shoving it forward off the sand until I'm waist-deep in the water, and then I drag myself in.

Cian and Drum are already rowing through the shallow waters. The wind picks up as we leave the bay, and the sail fills out, but it's not fast enough. I look over my shoulder to see that while most of the warriors have stopped on the beach, four don't hesitate. They throw themselves into the surf, disappearing under the water. Mer. We can't outsail the Mer; no vessel can.

The water is as dark as the night sky, the waves buffeting us as we dip and crest over the swells. I have no idea where the Mer are. Which boat are they targeting? Both? My answer is a sudden bump against the keel, and the boat shudders and rocks dangerously to the side. They're going to tip us into the water. Drown us all.

I find Sara in the dark. She's crouched on the deck, her lips pressed tight together, her eyes glowing green and terrified, and I follow her gaze to Cian. Water. He's in danger on the water... her vision.

She's shaking, trembling so hard she has to wrap her arms around herself. What have I done? We had a better chance of surviving on land. We should have stayed on the beach and fought them there.

I'm scanning the boat now, assessing. Izod meets my gaze from his position at the wheel and nods sharply. In front of him sit the twins with Arlen between them. I haul Arlen out of his seat and drop him down beside Sara.

"Hold her," I shout, the wind carrying my words away. "Don't let her go."

Arlen's eyes narrow, but for once in his life, he doesn't argue. He wraps his arms around Sara, and I hear him whispering to her.

Exchanging a look with Breanna, I place myself in front of Cian. She nods and shifts in her seat, so she's a little closer to him, too.

Cian looks up sharply, his eyes narrow as he looks at Breanna and then back to me. "What's going on?" He's straining at the oars but doesn't break his rhythm, keeping up with Drum on the other side of the boat.

Before I can answer him, a large tail rises out of the water and swipes toward Cian's head. I grab him out of the way and toss him to the deck as I knock the tail back into the water, slicing at it with my sword.

"Lachlan," Sara's scream rips through me, and I turn to see a Mer man reaching into the boat, his long white fingers wrapping around Cian's ankle. Breanna is there before me, leaping across Cian's back, her dagger slicing at the Mer's face.

The Mer hisses at Breanna and drops back into the water to avoid her blade, but with a sudden swipe of his long arm, he wraps his white fingers around Breanna's wrist and hauls her into the water. I'm scrambling across the deck to get to her when Cian roars and dives in after them, disappearing beneath the surface.

The boat goes eerily quiet. Everyone stares at the dark water until Sara gives a choked gasp and starts to rock back and forth, keening quietly. I hear Arlen's whispers resume.

Aoife is crying, silent tears falling down her cheeks, her eyes glued to the spot on the boat where Cian and Breanna went over. Clodagh is staring at the water, her eyes wide and unblinking. She starts to shake, though, the trembling taking over her whole body. Aoife reaches across and takes her twin's hand.

I'm watching all this as if from a long way off—

Water crashes over the boat, and a loud thud makes us all jump until we see Cian sprawled across the deck. He pushes himself to his knees, choking and coughing up water, but he's already scrambling to the side of the boat.

I grab him and hold him down. He's screaming Breanna's name, his voice growing more hoarse with every scream until it's so faint we can barely hear it over the sound of the wind and the crashing of the waves against the boat. We are so focused on Cian that we don't see the Mer warrior clambering over the side.

"Lachlan." Arlen's shout, laced with panic, is the only warning I have. When I turn around, the blade is already arcing through the air above me. Arlen leaps forward, intercepting the sword.

"No." Sara's scream cuts through the night, and Arlen falls across me.

I'm aware of Izod fighting the warrior, driving his sword through the Fae's chest and pushing his body overboard. Beneath me, Cian has stopped struggling and is staring at Arlen in horror.

Sara is bent over us, weeping uncontrollably.

"Aoife," she says suddenly and loudly, and then she shrieks her sister's name again. "Aoife, help. You have to help him."

Aoife is already beside us, crouching on the deck as I manage to lift Arlen off me and lay him carefully down. His breathing is erratic, his eyes rolling into the back of his head. There is blood everywhere, pooling onto the wooden deck. Aoife nudges Sara to the side and bends over Arlen, placing her two hands above the deep gash.

Sara is shaking so hard I pull her into my arms, but I'm shaking too. We are both covered in Arlen's blood, and I don't know what to do. I don't know how to save him.

"I don't know, I don't know," Aoife mutters, tears on her cheeks.

"Intention is everything." I hear Clodagh murmur, and suddenly she's in the middle of our small group. "Cian, channel your magic into Aoife. Sara. Focus. Channel your magic into Aoife. Lachlan, you too." She reaches for Cian's hand and places her other hand on Aoife's shoulder. "Izod and Drum, get us back to the beach."

Sara grabs Cian's other hand. He stares at her woodenly, but he doesn't push her away. She reaches for my hand then. Holding it tight in mine, I complete the circle, placing my free hand on Aoife's shoulder. Clodagh looks at me with a tight worried frown.

"Now, everybody. Focus."

It's a relief to have something to do. Something we can do.

SARA

The boat bumps against the sand, and I'm aware of Izod and Drum leaping into the shallow water and dragging the vessel up the beach. I blink myself back to the present and look down at Arlen and Aoife. He's no longer bleeding, and the wound is knitting back together, but he's lost consciousness... and after everything else he's already suffered, I don't know if he's strong enough to survive this.

I look around our small circle; all of us are dazed and numb. We're not looking at each other, though, not meeting each other's gaze.

Breanna.

I can't bring myself to say her name. Cian is staring out to sea, his face ashen, twisted with grief as though he's waiting for her to return.

Lachlan scoops Arlen up into his arms and carries him ashore. Aoife follows behind him. She stumbles, climbing down, but Izod is there to help her. He scoops her up and takes her up the beach towards the sand dunes.

Lachlan places his brother on the sand and kneels beside him, reluctant to leave his side. I notice how he keeps touching him, a hand on his shoulder, a squeeze to his hand.

Lilly and Aaronn rush up the beach toward them, and I see them asking questions, and then they're working together, building a protective shield around Arlen and Aoife. It will be enough to keep out the wind and the cold for now.

At last, I can't delay any longer. I look back at my brother. "Cian, are you coming?" He ignores me, and I glance at Clodagh in desperation. She shakes her head at me and gestures for me to go on. My legs are shaking so badly I think I might fall over, but Izod is there to help me down, and gratefully I take his hand and let him help me to the beach.

Lachlan is pacing the area outside the protection shield, his eyes locked on his brother as Aoife continues to heal him. I look back and see Cian standing on the boat still. He seems stuck up there, unable to climb down.

Clodagh hops down, ignoring Izod's outstretched hand. She turns and shouts something back to Cian. He doesn't appear to hear her, but his chin drops to his chest, and he clambers over the side.

Clodagh grasps his hand and tugs him up the beach. She's talking to him. I can't hear the words. I'm not sure if Cian can either, his expression doesn't change, and he doesn't look up. The pain pierces me again, and I turn to look back out to sea. And that's when I see a flicker of silver in the water, and a head pops up.

Kira. Her long black hair wraps around her shoulders, and tears run down her face. Hurrying into the water, it's not until I'm closer that I understand.

Kira has Breanna cradled in her arms, but she's lifeless, her eyes unseeing as they stare up at the sky. The wind whips at my face, and the water is cold as it drags at my legs, but I keep wading out, deeper and deeper.

"I'm sorry," Kira whispers. "I tried to save her. I'm so sorry, Sara."

I hear shouts from the beach, and Kira looks past me. She stares for a heartbeat before the tears start to fall again. She shoves Breanna into my arms and turns and dives into the water. I watch the shimmer of pink and silver getting further away.

Cian is at my side now, frantic, grabbing at Breanna, squeezing her lifeless body to his as he rushes back up the beach.

"Aoife," he roars. "Aoife," his cry is anguished. Hopeless.

"Breanna's dead," I whisper to his retreating back. There's nothing Aoife can do.

I don't even make it back to the beach before my legs give way, and I'm kneeling in the shallow waters, sobbing. My pain is so deep I don't know how to get it out. I'm crying and gasping, my legs turning numb in the cold water when

I feel Lachlan scoop me up and carry me onto the dry sand. He doesn't let go, and I cling to him while I cry for Breanna. I loved her like a sister.

"She sacrificed herself for Cian." I'm sobbing into his chest. "She sacrificed herself. I didn't... she should never..." Lachlan holds me tighter, his one hand stroking up and down my back.

"What do you mean she sacrificed herself for me?" Cian's shocked question cuts through my grief, and I gulp and look up. My brother is staring at me. Fury simmering beneath his gaze, and I can see him replaying every moment in that boat. "Tell me the truth."

But I can't. My mouth won't form the words.

"Sara had a vision— she saw your death," Lachlan says quietly, and Cian's gaze turns to him. "We all knew. We were all protecting you."

"You sacrificed Breanna to save me?" He turns his gaze to me, and the anger in his voice makes me flinch. Lachlan's arms pull tight around me.

"Of course not," he snaps at Cian. "We didn't tell Breanna. We didn't want her to know. We didn't want either of you to know. Breanna was a mind-reader, Cian," he says in exasperation, and then his voice cracks. "Nobody wanted Breanna to jump in between you and the Mer warrior. No one. That was never supposed—" but Cian is already walking away, and Lachlan falls silent. Pulling out of his arms, I look up at his face. He looks shaken from that exchange, almost broken. "We should never have got on that boat. I should have listened to you."

"We don't know what would have happened had we stayed on the beach." Reaching up, I cup his jaw. "We don't know...." I don't finish the thought. Tears are running down my cheeks again. I feel them falling and scrub my cheeks dry. "Come, let's check on Arlen." I take his hand and pull him up the beach.

I see Aaronn and Lilly kneeling beside Breanna's body, tears streaming down their faces. Breanna was Aaronn's youngest cousin and more like a sister to him than a cousin. His grief is painful to watch, and I turn away.

That moment on the boat when she threw herself between Cian and the Mer warrior... I can't get that moment out of my head. There was no fear on her face. No regret. Determination flashed in her eyes and love. She loved my brother so much, and now she's gone, and I'm not sure he will ever recover from this.

Lachlan squeezes my hand and drags my attention to Arlen. Aoife has returned to his side, and under her careful attention, he is awake now. I hear Lachlan's rough exhale and tug him forward. Nudging him forward into the protective shield, I remain outside.

For the first time since landing on this beach, I take a good look around us. The seven Elves have found shelter up the beach, amongst the sand dunes. I can see Majesty and the white hawk are with them. The animals are still sleeping. It will take Aoife's magic to revive them fully, but Aoife also needs to rest.

As I'm standing there, Izod and Clodagh walk over. She has the baby dragon curled up in her arms. "We've been talking," she starts, glancing once at Izod. "We must get everyone back to the Elvin forest and the Mya." I nod and wonder where she's going with this. "But this little dragon needs to be returned to the desert. Her mother, if we can find her."

I'm waiting, but when she doesn't go on, I glance at Izod. His face is carefully blank.

"I'm going to take the dragon," Clodagh says suddenly.

"What?" I stare from one to the other. "Wait. Why you? We can find someone else to take the dragon home."

"I want to do it," Clodagh says stubbornly, cradling the dragon gently in her arms.

"The dragon has bonded with Clodagh," Izod says quietly.

"Bonded bonded?" I ask in amazement and watch Izod blush. He holds up a hand quickly.

"I can't say for sure."

"Izod said he will go with me," Clodagh adds.

"Is that wise?" Lachlan's voice cuts through our conversation, and when I turn, he's staring at Izod with a concerned frown. "Will you be safe?"

"I was thinking more of Clodagh's safety," I interrupt, but both men ignore me, and Lachlan's frown only deepens. I can feel his fear.

Eventually, Izod sighs and offers us a fatalistic shrug. "Who else can take her?"

"Her is standing right here, excuse me, and I can take myself. I don't need a bodyguard." Clodagh's frustrated statement is heard without comment while the men stare at each other.

"Maybe it's time," Izod says quietly, and this time it is Lachlan who sighs.

"If you feel that way, then, of course, you have my blessing." I have no idea what he's talking about, but Lachlan doesn't give me a chance to ask. "Sara, Arlen wants you." Frowning at Lachlan, I'm about to demand an explanation when he pulls me close and presses a kiss to my temple. "Later," he whispers against my skin.

Chapter 19

L*ACHLAN*
  The funeral procession winds its way through the dark forest, guided by the light of a thousand lanterns strung from tree to tree. We left the Elvin village, Antil, an hour ago. It is the birthplace of Breanna's mom and the home of the Elves we rescued from Lars' lab.

Arlen is on my left, and my four bodyguards walk behind us. The last weeks have shaken all of us, and they are reluctant to leave my side. I glance over my shoulder to check on them and shake my head when I see Izod carrying the baby dragon. Clodagh is with Breanna's family, and Izod offered to look after the dragon during the funeral. The way the two of them are carrying on about that dragon, you'd think they were sharing custody of a child.

Walking on my right is Queen Aisleen of Soraya, Sara's mother. We have only met once before, and to say I'm a little intimidated is an understatement. Her magic pulses powerfully with every step she takes. It builds a bubble of light around her. She is fierce but stoic, her face devoid of emotion. As we reach the sacred grove and see Cian step forward with Breanna's family, her façade cracks, and I glimpse the pain beneath. It makes me realize she's grieving as much for her son as she is for Breanna's death.

Cian is pale, his steps wooden as he shoulders his corner of the funeral pyre. Aaronn and Breanna's two older brothers are stationed at the other three corners. Cian is the only dry-eyed one in the group. His pain is still too raw for him to show it. Since learning of Sara's vision, Cian has not spoken a word. It's been two days, and Sara is aching, blaming herself.

The procession fans out to form a circle around the grove. I step closer, searching the faces for Sara, and find her at the front beside her sisters and Breanna's parents. I long to push through the crowd and go to her. Tears run down her cheeks, and I watch her wipe them away. Her throat bobs as she swallows and tries to stop her tears. She feels guilty crying, as though she has no right to grieve. I know this from the little she told me last night before we fell asleep.

But they are all crying— openly sharing their grief, letting it connect them all at this time. It is the Elvin way. On the far side of the clearing, I see the Elvin initiates we rescued from Lars' lab. Their faces are wet with tears also— they would all have known Breanna. Everyone knew Breanna; loved Breanna. She was a free spirit, never happy to settle in one place for long, that is, until she met Cian. Her four months in Cork was the longest time she'd ever spent in one place.

My eyes are drawn inevitably to Cian once more. How do we make this better for him? How can I help him carry this grief? He's only twenty-two, too young to lose the woman he loves. A brush of movement against my arm drags my attention to my right, and I look down to see Aisleen leaning closer as she cranes her neck to see through the crowd. Her face is pale, and her lips tremble as she pushes them together.

"My Lady, how can I help?" She blinks at me, her lashes wet with tears, and her lips tremble again as she tries to speak. "Lean on me," I say, slipping her hand through my arm. I shift a little to the left as I do. She will have a better view of the funeral now. She squeezes my arm gratefully.

Sara looks so much like her mother, the only striking difference is the color of their skin. Aisleen's skin is a dark ebony, while Sara's is a softer brown. But both of them carry themselves with regal authority.

Sara doesn't even know she does that. I didn't realize that at first. During the first few months of my marriage, I was so frustrated with this woman who seemed to think she was better than us.

I could never make sense of my feelings for her; I didn't know if I loved or despised her. But I realize now Sara never thought she was better than us. Sara holds herself at her most regal and disdainful when she's afraid...when she's vulnerable.

It breaks my heart to think how she spent months as my wife feeling – not that she was better than the Rohn Fae as I believed – but that they would never like or accept her. That I would never want her. She felt unloved by me.

And now? Does she still feel this way? Her words in my bedroom come back to me now. *What does it matter if I tell you I love you? I'm not asking you to love me back.* And she hasn't. Not once.

I can't stop looking at her. Can she not feel how much I love her? She doesn't have to ask for my love. She's always had it. She's *always* had it. I've loved Sara from the first moment I saw her...and longer than that— if possible.

Arlen is standing to my left, and I turn to check on him, worried that the walk through the forest was too much for him. He would not be dissuaded, though, and I understand...none of us could stay away.

I can't erase the image of Breanna leaping between Cian and the Mer warrior. I see those final moments in my dreams, over and over. I keep trying to rewrite the ending and change the dream's outcome. And then I wake up and realize we're all too late. Breanna's gone.

Arlen feels my gaze on him and turns to look at me. He's still too pale, his cheeks sunken, his cheekbones even sharper than usual. He inclines his head, just the tiniest nod, acknowledging my concern, and turns his attention back to the grove. I do the same.

I am unfamiliar with Elvin funeral rites and cannot join in the chanting that starts softly around the pyre. The family steps back into the crowd, and the Mya twins are standing beside the pyre now. They were waiting in the sacred grove for us.

I have never seen these ethereal beings before. Few have. They are not of our realm, but they are the guardians of it. Genderless, beautiful— they are surrounded by a soft glowing light. One stands at Breanna's head, the other at her feet.

The lilting chant increases in volume, and I watch the grove glow with light so vibrant that I have to shield my eyes... then it's gone, and the grove is dark once more but for the flickering lanterns. The Mya and Breanna's funeral pyre are gone too.

The crowd is silent. Nobody moves, and then an anguished cry is heard, and I see Cian fall onto his knees. He's broken, at last. The crowd disperses quickly, giving him space to grieve, but I can't tear my eyes away from the sight of Cian on his knees. His tears are silent as he stares at the spot where the funeral pyre lay.

"Lachlan, go to Sara." The urgency in Aisleen's voice snaps my attention back to my wife. She's crying as she tries to push past Aaronn to get to her brother. She's frantic now, her voice rising as she argues with him. She's not even making any sense; her words are jumbled and incoherent.

"Let me, please, let me. I need, oh my god." She starts sobbing again as I reach her and pull her into my arms. She's fighting me now instead of Aaronn, but I barely feel the punches she lands on my chest as she pushes to get free of my arms. Her fight only lasts a few seconds before she collapses against me. I scoop her up into my arms and carry her away from the crowd, away from her brother.

Cian needs time to grieve— alone. Sara can't help him now. She wraps her arms around my neck, burrowing her head into my chest. "I know," she's mumbling into my shirt. "I know, but—" She starts crying again.

When we're alone, I lower her feet to the ground and wrap my arms tightly around her. She clings to me and cries for so long that a sense of helplessness begins to creep in, and I feel my own eyes moisten with tears. I can't fix this for her.

My wife is hurting, and there's nothing I can do. I squeeze her closer and press my face into her hair.

Her crying subsides eventually, but she's still trembling. Others might not see it, but it's only because I'm holding her so close that I feel the tremors passing through her. Scooping her into my arms, I carry her back to the village.

She's asleep before we reach the tree house we've been assigned. Climbing the stairs slowly, I'm being extra careful not to bump her legs against the wooden rail, and I manage to ease her into the small room without waking her.

Laying her on the bed, I remove her boots and pull the covers over her. I toe off my own boots and climb in behind her, gathering her close. She tugs her arm free and moves it over mine, holding me to her, but when I lean over her shoulder to check, I see she's still asleep. Pressing a kiss to her temple, I let my eyes close too.

Footsteps pounding up the wooden stairs jerk me awake, and I sit up, staring blearily at the early morning light. I'm blinking in confusion, trying to work out where I am, when Clodagh bursts into the tree house.

"Cian's gone. He's gone."

Sara's out of bed instantly, scrubbing at her face. "What do you mean he's gone?" Her eyes are wide with fear, and she reaches for me, her fingers biting into my arm. "He wouldn't go to Aescheles, would he? He's angry and not thinking straight. He wouldn't go after the Mer, would he? Lachlan." Her nails dig into my skin as I remain silent, thinking, trying to put myself in Cian's shoes. If Sara were dead...if the Mer killed Sara...Yes, I would want revenge.

I don't even bother answering her. I race past Clodagh and down the stairs, leaping the last few. I hear Sara and Clodagh following, but I don't stop until I reach the fourth cabin. I know this is where Aaronn and Lilly are staying, and I burst into their room much like Clodagh burst into ours.

"Cian's gone," I announce loudly enough to wake them both up. They stare at me in horrified silence. I don't need to spell it out for them to know what I'm afraid of. I spin around as I hear steps behind me. Clodagh and Sara have followed, and behind them, I see Aoife and Izod running toward us.

"Would he be so foolish?" Lilly's quiet question draws my attention back to the room.

"Yes." Aaronn and Clodagh answer simultaneously. Cian's more dangerous than ever before. He was always reckless, but now he's fearless too. He doesn't care if he lives or dies...and I can't even fault him for it. I know I would be the same way if I lost Sara.

SARA

It was easy to put a trace on Cian. My connection to my brother led my magic straight to him, and then, like before, Lachlan tracked him back to us so we could follow him. He had maybe a five-hour head start on us and was already at the coast.

The walk from the Elvin forest to the sea takes half a day, but with his Tracker magic, Cian could cover that distance in half the time. The rest of us are not so lucky, and although I urge Lachlan to use his magic to go ahead, he refuses. Izod is no longer here to protect us and Lachlan won't leave my side.

Clodagh and Izod left the Elvin Forest with us, heading straight for Rohn. From there, they will use the Rohn portal to reach the Desert kingdom and return the Dragon to its home. It didn't make any sense dragging that dragon around with us while we searched for Cian, and Clodagh could not be persuaded to leave it behind.

My mother was distraught when she heard the news about Cian. I know she was hoping he would return with her to Soraya, but we convinced her to go on home without him, citing Arlen's need for rest as our excuse that they both return to Soraya.

The rest of us set off immediately, traveling through the forest without stopping, reaching the sea by lunchtime. Lachlan was leading us, following the trace he put on Cian.

Our fear is tangible, and I know we are all thinking the same thing...my vision. It's not like the messages come with a date and time. Cian's death at the hands of the Mer— what if it was never meant to happen the night Breanna died.

My arrogance was in believing I could alter fate— that I had some control. Tonight Cian will be on the ocean again, but this time he'll be alone— and angry. And reckless.

On the beach, we find one boat, pulled ashore where we left it. Cian has taken the other, confirming all our worst fears. My heart is hurting. I'm so scared for him. For myself, too, I don't want to live in a world without my brother. I need him too much.

Please, Etain, please, Mya, help us now...my prayers float up around me, and I'm using my magic to push them out into the realm so all the spirits can hear them.

We have no choice but to follow Cian back onto the water, even Lachlan looks scared, and I have never seen him afraid. But I know his fear is for all of us, not himself. We climb aboard the boat, and Lachlan's bodyguards take the oars while he unfurls the sails and sets our course. From the concentrated look on his face, I see that he's still tracking my brother, letting his magic guide us.

Looking across the deck at Lilly, I can see she's praying, just like me. Her head is tipped back, her eyes closed, but her lips are moving as she prays to the Etain. Lilly, more than any of us, knows how important it is to ask the Etain for help. She nearly lost Aaronn because she didn't ask the nature spirits to help her find him. They can hinder or help— it's all up to us. All we have to do is ask. Right now, I'm begging.

We're not alone in this realm; countless nature spirits are waiting to help us, and I'm calling on them now. The sails swell with the wind, and our small boat bounces over the waves with the wind at our backs.

Yes. Thank you, I whisper.

Lilly moves to stand beside me and takes my hand. "Together," she whispers. "Our prayers will be more powerful together."

Aoife and Clodagh join us at the front of the boat, combining their magic with ours as we link our arms and pray for Cian's safety. I never would have thought it possible, but the vessel picks up speed, the elementals taking charge of our journey, taking us where we need to be.

Please let us not be too late; I send out one last prayer just as the wind drops and an unnatural hush descends. A shiver passes over me... Mer magic.

"Look," Aaronn shouts, pointing to the right of our boat. I move to the side to see what he's pointing at, but Lachlan's hand clamps around my arm, keeping me away from the edge.

A small upturned boat lies in the water, and what looks like blood swirls with the waves. So much blood. I can't... my stomach heaves, and ignoring Lachlan's warning, I rush to the side and vomit over the side.

I don't want to look, but I can't seem to drag my eyes away from the upturned boat and the blood, and then I see them...the fins surfacing from the deep, circling the vessel. Lachlan wraps his arm around my waist, dragging me back from the edge.

The shark-infested waters of Aescheles. Shivering tremors wrack my body as I imagine those sharks feeding on Cian's body.

From some distant part of my mind, I hear Aaronn issuing orders, trying to get the boat turned around, but we are becalmed, not one knot of wind to help us now.

Etain, where are you? But I'm screaming it in my head, too scared to break the silence.

A large wave splashes over the edge, drenching all of us in cold water, and a loud thud follows, making us jump. Lachlan has his sword drawn, ready to attack, when a choking cough and a moan comes from the body lying on the deck.

My brother is lying there, still coughing up water as we crowd around him.

"Give him space." Aaronn's voice is calm and steady as he reaches through us, hauls Cian to his feet, and slaps him a couple times hard across the back.

Cian coughs, bends double, and throws up more water. When he's finished heaving, Aaronn pulls him in for a hug and growls something low in his ear that I cannot hear, but I see Cian nod once and close his eyes in resignation.

"He seems determined to kill himself," a cold voice cuts through our questions, and we all spin around to see Kira perched on the boat's edge. She frowns as her eyes roam over us. Her eyes settle on Cian, and her frown deepens. "I might not be around the next time you decide to throw yourself into shark-infested waters."

"I never asked for your help," Cian mutters, but I can tell the fight has left him, and he's not even looking at Kira; he's staring at his feet.

Lilly pulls Cian over to a bench. Aaronn takes off his coat, and she wraps it around Cian. He's shaking now, and she holds it around him, rubbing his arms vigorously.

"Aoife," Lilly murmurs, turning to look for our younger sister.

Aoife is staring at Kira, her eyes wide with amazement, but she blinks suddenly upon hearing her name.

"Sorry," she mumbles and hurries over to Cian and Lilly. I watch my sister lay her hands on Cian's back and see the trembling stop almost instantly.

I still can't believe Cian is alive. And we have Kira to thank for that again. She's still perched on the boat rail, her tail dangling into the water and her long black hair falling across her chest, covering her naked breasts.

She's beautiful on land, but as a mermaid, she is mesmerizing. She glows with ethereal light, and her eyes shine a bright turquoise blue. She scans the boat again until she finds me, and then her frown softens into a smile.

"Sara, I told you I would investigate the Elves' disappearance."

Nodding, I step closer. Lachlan follows, and then Aaronn steps forward until we form a small huddle on one side of the boat.

"I'm sorry." She looks away for a moment, the frown returning. "I have to tell you that my father definitely knew more than he was telling us. He's been involved in this plan to siphon energy from the elves...and other Fae...from the beginning." She glances at Lachlan. "You know my father's distrust of the other kingdoms— other Fae. It always surprised me how much he liked you, to be honest. This plan was not quite the altruistic one they were telling you it was." She stares out to sea, and a blush stains her neck and cheeks a soft pink color.

"They were targeting the magic other Fae hold— to study it," she says, turning back to us. "To reproduce in a lab. Replicate." She stops to see if we follow, and I remember then the glasses the doctor showed us. The glasses that could do what Lilly's magic does. "My father hoped to use this technology to become the most powerful race here in Emuria. You know how he fears for our people's safety. Our persecution in the human realm has left him suspicious of everyone," her voice trails off. She doesn't need to say more. We know what King Muir is like.

"What are you telling us, Kira? Did your father build the lab where we found the elves?" Lachlan's steady voice soothes not just me. I see Kira's shoulders relax just a little, and I'm grateful to my husband for his calm.

"Lars had Mer working with him on the island. They could not have been there without my father's consent."

Aaronn had already said as much, but confirming it does not comfort us. King Muir is a powerful enemy.

"But there is more." Kira hesitates before continuing. "When I questioned my father about this and... our engagement." Her eyes flick to Lachlan. "He seemed confused, unsure of himself. My father is one of the sharpest Fae I know. He doesn't get confused or mix up his stories."

"Influencer magic," Aaronn says quietly, his face creasing with worry lines. "Lars?" He asks, turning to us.

"There has never been any sign of Influencer magic about him," Lachlan says.

"But you said he always smells of disinfectant. That's how you tracked him," Aoife says from behind us. I wasn't even aware she was there. We all turn to stare at her, and she blushes under our scrutiny. "Disinfectant solution can mask a magician's magic, neutralize it temporarily." When we all continue to stare at her, she adds, "Disguise it. A disinfectant solution can act as a disguise. It's such a strong, overpowering scent that it masks the magic. The smell is distracting. We all know how important our scent is in detecting magic and especially for a Tracker." She looks at Lachlan now.

Turning to him, I see the shock on his face as he pieces everything together. Aoife shrugs and then smiles shyly.

"Anyway, that's my guess." She turns away, returning to Cian's side to check on him.

Kira nods. "It does make sense. Lars has made repeated visits to Aescheles in the last year."

"We need to find him." Aaronn's voice is low, almost like he's talking to himself.

"Sorry to interrupt." Lachlan's bodyguard, Drum, is at my side now. "We need to get going. I'd like to be off the water before nightfall."

"Of course. Yes." Aaronn nods his head and looks around us. We are still becalmed, though. "We will have to row our way out of this weather."

Kira laughs at that, and it's like a spell is broken— the wind picks up, the waters rise and fall, and our boat rocks from side to side. Kira looks at Cian before saying softly to us, "try to keep him away from the water."

"Kira, what happened here? The blood in the water?" I ask her, studiously avoiding the sight of the upturned boat.

"I'm sorry. My people attacked Cian. I don't know why... on whose orders."

"You killed your own people to protect Cian?" There's an urgency to Lachlan's voice. "Your father, Kira. What will he do to you when he finds out about this?"

"Let me worry about my father, Lachlan. You need to find Lars."

Our boat is already bouncing over the waves, the wind behind us again as we set sail for Rohn. Without another word, Kira dives from the rail into the sea. The flash of pink scales is visible for seconds only before the deep water swallows her up.

Chapter 20

LACHLAN

By the time we reach Rohn, it's mid-morning. After hours of sailing and a night spent camping on the banks of the Schoenberg Fjord, we're all more than tired. Worse than that— we're defeated. I trace the pattern of the city's crenelated walls ahead of us before I let myself look up at the castle that sits high above it.

A growling from deep within my chest halts my steps. Sara's hand is on my back, and like my beast's growl, her magic is loud this morning. It's a warning sizzle against my skin. Her palm leaves a magic imprint on my magic. It's full of images, too many to make sense of them all. Is that what her magic is like for her?

"Lars is here," she whispers, her eyes wide as she looks at me. Wide and a little scared, so I pull her close. She wraps her arms around my waist, and her magic continues to tattoo messages into my skin.

Looking at the others over the top of Sara's head, I say for their benefit, "Lars is here." Not one of them is surprised by my announcement. It almost makes me laugh. This family is extraordinary. No wonder Lars was so afraid of them. Did Aisleen know the power her children would possess? Is that why she hid them in the human realm for so long? For their own protection?

She must have known that they would become targets once they showed themselves. Their combined magic is a threat to those in power. A single, powerful family— I would fear them myself if they weren't all so good.

Sara's arms tighten around my waist. Is she reading my thoughts? The O'Driscolls are not something separate from me. I'm one of them now. *This is my family. Mine to protect.* A new sense of calm washes over me with that thought. A warmth suffusing through my body. This is *my* family.

"Are you ready to face him?" Aaronn finally breaks the silence— asking the only question that really matters. Lars has been a part of Rohn castle for as long as I've been alive. I never liked the Fae, but I always respected him and valued his input during council meetings. He was the voice of reason when other council members opposed my changes. But the whole time...

"Lachlan?" Sara's questioning look makes me realize I've been quiet too long. Pressing a quick kiss to her temple, I step back from her and turn to face the city walls again. The darkness feels heavier than usual. Was it Lars' dark magic I was sensing all along? Not mine, like I had believed all these years.

"Be on your guard," I warn the others before we set off again. The city gates are closed when we reach them but remain so for seconds only as the guard on duty recognizes me. I cannot read the expression on his face. Shock, perhaps.

By the time he opens the gates, another five soldiers are standing on the sidelines, staring at us with their mouths hanging open. With a start, they remember themselves, drop to their knees, and prostrate themselves before me. And suddenly, I can't stand this anymore.

"Get up," I roar at them. "Get up... and you." I point to the nearest soldier. "Explain what has happened in my absence."

He's staring at me in fear which only (irrationally) increases my anger. Fifteen years of trying to be nothing like my father, and yet they still fear me the same way they did him.

"My Lord, you died." He seems to realize the ridiculousness of his statement and blushes scarlet. "That is, you didn't...Councilor Lars told the city you are dead. He announced it only last night and declared a twenty-four-hour period of mourning. No one is allowed to leave their homes."

And that's when I notice how quiet the town is— an unnatural silence hangs over the deserted streets. "Where is Councilor Lars?" I hear the growl in my voice; the soldier standing before me hears it, too, and pales. The Fae standing behind him grins widely.

"It really is you, My Lord. Councilor Lars warned the patrols to block all gates. He said to watch out for anyone claiming to be you."

"Claiming to be me?"

"Yes, My Lord." His eyes rake over our small group, and he grins again, recognizing my three bodyguards. "But I cannot imagine there's a magician alive strong enough to impersonate all of you." His eyes land on Sara, and he bows his head. "My Lady, welcome home."

I sense Sara's amusement before she inclines her head to the soldiers. She's dying to laugh but holding it back for my sake. And just like that, my anger settles down.

"Is Lars in the castle?"

"Yes, My Lord," the first soldier speaks up again.

"He sent everyone home." Another soldier adds, and then another voice joins the group.

"He cleared out the castle. Even Mae was sent down to the city, and she's lived up in the castle for fifty years. My mother took her in, My Lord. She's safe," he adds when I frown at him.

"Lars said he was doing it for the city. He said the castle wasn't safe. But," this soldier goes suddenly quiet, reluctant to continue.

"But?"

"He has his own warriors with him. They are not from Rohn."

I've heard enough. Holding up my hand, I wait for the soldiers to quiet down.

"Close the gates," I tell the first one. "You and you." I point at two others. "Come with me. We will be leaving the city through the northern gates. Once we leave, I want you to seal the gates. No one is to come up to the castle."

We're currently running as I continue to issue commands to the soldiers. They keep up, running at our sides.

"Keep our arrival as quiet as you can. I want everyone to remain indoors."

They nod, and I fall quiet, tapping into my magic. I'm not sure why, but suddenly it seems vital that we hurry. My magic is growling, urging me on, tracking Lars but also...another scent catches my nostrils. Mer. The warriors Lars brought back with him are Mer. Flashing Cian a look out of the corner of my eye, I keep this news to myself for now.

It takes only twenty minutes to cross the city to the northern gate, thanks partly to the empty streets. Once there, I herd everyone through, issuing final instructions to the soldiers and ensuring they lock the gates behind us.

"Whatever happens up on the mountain, you keep these gates locked." The soldiers look at each other nervously but are too scared to argue with me.

"Lachlan, we must hurry." Sara's voice at my side forces me to turn away from the gates. I'm already climbing the hill but turn back and wait for her. "We will keep him safe." I hear her promise the soldiers and notice the relief on their faces as she reassures them.

The fear I witnessed on their faces: they were not scared of me. They're scared for me. The realization is enough to freeze me in place. I stare at my soldiers before my eyes snap back to Sara. She cocks her head and studies my face, then reaches up and kisses me.

"Of course, they love you, you fool. Now, come on." She grabs my hand and tugs me away from the gate. The road we're on winds up the mountain, banked on both sides by boulders and wild grass. The castle hunkers above us. A dark, menacing presence even now in the middle of the day. The sky is a typical summer blue, not a cloud in the sky.

As we approach the castle gates, I nudge my way through the group to reach the front. Sara is at my side as I stride forward. I sense the dark force field as I step closer. It forces me to stop. The others are silent behind me, and I feel our magic, like tentacles reaching out, probing at the dark shield.

"It's strong," Aaronn mutters at my shoulder.

"Drum, announce my arrival to the warrior on the gate."

I hear Drum demanding the gates be opened. The warrior looks through the metal grill, and his eyes find mine. It's the Mer who attacked us – the same one who dragged Breanna from the boat. His cruel face haunts me every night. Cian stiffens at my side, and I fling my hand out, grabbing his arm.

"Lachlan." There is no deference or respect in the Mer's voice. "You have been stripped of your crown and are no longer King of Rohn."

"Who made that decision?"

"The council has voted. Your close association with the Sorayans has distracted you from the needs of the Rohn Fae. You no longer deserve their loyalty and have been deemed unfit to rule."

I'm so focussed on keeping Cian at my side that his words bounce off me.

"Don't," I growl at Cian now. My eyes are still on the Mer, so I see when his eyes turn to Cian and his mouth slides into a cruel smile, his incisors showing.

"Cian." Sara's voice is low, and I know he can't hear her. He can't hear or see anything but the mocking look on the Mer's face.

Sara must realize this because she leaves my side and steps in front of her brother, cupping his jaw and forcing his face to hers.

"Listen to me, Cian. You will kill him. Today. You will kill him. My magic showed me. But not now."

Cian's arm relaxes under my hand. "Your magic told you?"

"Yes. Today, Cian. But not now. Step back. Everyone." She glances at me then. "All of us. Step back from the gate." She places a hand on my chest. "We have other ways to fight them," she whispers.

SARA

"I could shape-shift," Cian says, and the excitement in his voice has a strange electrifying effect on me. My magic is sizzling, sparking. Almost dangerously so. I'm trying to tamp it down when Aaronn speaks up.

"No, Cian. The magic is too dark." His quiet, steady voice is always our group's calming force, and I smile gratefully at him. We've retreated down the hill to discuss our plans. Not all the way down but far enough away so the warriors on the gate cannot see us.

"Sara, what was your vision for this castle?" Lachlan is staring at me intently. There's a sharpness to his gaze that tells me his beast is close to the surface. His eyes flare amber as if to confirm it, and he grins at me.

Lachlan's ready to fight. I get lost in his amber eyes; the connection between us is so strong I can feel his beast inside me, ready, waiting.

"Sara?" Lachlan's voice is more amused than impatient as I continue to stare at him. "What was your vision for fixing this castle?" he asks again. And I know now he's asking for my sake. He remembers. He knows what we have to do.

"We blow it up," I whisper and turn back to look at the castle. Its dark presence behind me makes me shiver even on this hot summer's day. "We need to blow up the castle," I say more firmly, turning to the others. At the shock on their faces, I almost laugh. "I had a vision about blowing up the castle," I explain. The vision was so much more than that simple statement, but now isn't the time to go into it. "The tower," I add, turning back to Lachlan. "The tower needs to come down."

"And then?"

"And then the mountain will do the rest." My cryptic answer is met with silence, but I see Lachlan smile.

I trust your magic. The same way you trust mine.

I hear his voice in my head, and instead of answering him, I reach for his hand and squeeze it hard. His belief in me means more than he can know.

I know – again, inside my head, and after a stunned moment, I laugh. Lachlan hates communicating like this, yet he's doing it for me.

He pulls me closer and whispers into my hair. "Sara, I trust you. What do you want us to do?"

Reaching up, I press a kiss to his lips. "Do you think everyone is really out of the castle?"

"The only ones left inside have chosen to be there." He sounds so sure, but I have a feeling he's saying that to reassure me. We can't know for sure everyone is out.

"We need to bring down the tower," I say, turning back to the others, and a smile spreads across my face as an idea comes to me. "Lilly, can you paint us some rockets?"

Lilly grins. "How many?"

"Paint four," Aaronn answers, and his gaze is filled with amusement.

"Paint?" Lachlan's bemused question only makes me smile wider.

"You'll see." I feel nearly giddy with excitement. This could work. This plan could actually work.

Lilly's not wasting any time, and I see Lachlan's eyes widen as the colors pour from her fingers, and she begins to paint a rocket in the air. She glances up at me, our eyes meet, and she laughs.

"I'm painting them, but then what?"

"You paint them. I'll throw them."

She nods once more and gets back to work. "Aaronn, you're our weapons expert," Lilly teases her husband. "Give me a hand here. Tell me if I'm painting these right."

Turning to look at the castle, I'm aware that Cian is watching me.

"You were telling me the truth? You didn't just say that to stop me shifting?" he asks suddenly.

"You will fight him."

When Cian continues to watch me, suspicion in his gaze, I squeeze my eyes shut. I don't want to see that look in his eyes. He's never looked at me like that before, and it hurts so much.

Why did I have to get involved? I should have kept my mouth shut.... I should have... Shaking my head to clear those images of Breanna, I force myself to look at my brother when I speak again.

"I'm *not* trying to protect you, Cian. You can fight your own battles."

"That's obviously not what you thought a few days ago. A few days ago, when it might have made a difference. When it might have saved Breanna." He's not even trying to disguise his anger.

"Cian, I will never not be sorry that I kept that vision from you. I didn't know how to tell you." I shake my head. "No, that's not true." I sigh and feel my eyes prickling with tears again, but I don't want to cry. Cian will hate me even more if I do. "I thought I could stop it from happening. I thought... since the vision came to me, it was a sign that I could change it." My voice cracks, and I stop.

Cian is still staring at me with that cold, angry look. He blames me, and he's right. He's right. Of all of us that night, I'm the one who made mistakes. I'm the one who can't work my magic correctly. My siblings are amazing.

I act confident, but the truth is, I have no idea what I'm doing. My magic is powerful, but I have no idea how to use it.

"Cian, I make a lot of mistakes. You know this about me. I'm the one who jumps into things without looking first. The one always getting into trouble at school. Look at you. You're brilliant. So smart, you scare me... and I couldn't even finish school. I was too stupid to finish school," I say quietly.

Cian blinks at me in surprise. I don't know why. He knows all of this about me. My siblings know me, yet they still love me, and I don't know why... I don't understand how they can love someone like me.

"I was too selfish to come home when dad got sick. I didn't want to be at home. I didn't want to see him die."

"You weren't selfish, Sara. You were grieving. You'd just lost Josh." Lilly's voice is quiet, but it carries across to us, and Cian and I turn to look at her.

"Josh?" It's Cian who's confused now.

"Sara lost her boyfriend a month before dad died. He died in a climbing accident... in front of her," she adds, glancing at Cian sternly before returning her gaze to the rockets she's painting.

"Sara," Cian's voice cracks with emotion, but it's too much for me. I can't take his sympathy.

"Don't. Don't do that. It's not the same thing. I was never in love with Josh. I... what you're going through.... It's not the same thing. Please don't look at me like that. This is all my fault. You have every right to be angry. I'm saying sorry, Cian. I'm saying I fucked up, and I'm sorry. I'm sorry, I thought I could control fate. I'm sorry I wasn't there when dad was sick. I'm a coward... I run away when I'm scared. I ran away from school because it was too hard. I ran when dad got cancer. I ran from my marriage too." I look sideways at Lachlan as I admit this last bit, and I see he's frowning at me, listening to every word.

For the first time in our marriage, I'm telling the truth. This is the real me. All the parts of me that I hate. Now, at last, Lachlan will know his wife— the woman he's chosen to rule this Kingdom with him...I didn't even finish school.

The shame hits me hard, as it does every time I let myself think about it. I'm desperate to take back my words, already regretting the impulse to admit this to him...to talk about any of it.

I trust you. Lachlan can't know what those words mean to me. I've been making a mess of things my whole life.

Turning back to Cian, I frown at the look on his face. I don't know what he's got to be shocked about. It's not like he didn't know any of this about me. It's Lachlan's reaction to my words that I'm worried about.

I shake my head impatiently and remind myself I'm talking to Cian, not Lachlan. It's Cian who needs to hear this. It's Cian I need to apologize to first.

"The point is. I fucked up when I told the others about my vision of you. I was scared. That's not unusual, my visions often scare me, but this one felt...too real," I finish lamely.

Tears are running down my cheeks, but I ignore them. I need to say this now before I lose my nerve.

"Sometimes it's hard to distinguish between a vision and something I'm scared of. Maybe I was too scared to read the signs right. I don't know. I thought that having these visions meant I could control the future. That I could save you."

"You did." His voice is quiet.

"I didn't do anything that night, Cian. Breanna saved you. And yesterday, Kira saved you."

"But if you didn't have your vision," his voice trails off uncertainly as he begins to understand what I'm saying.

I shrug and smile sadly.

"We can't know for sure how it was all meant to work out. I'm only sorry that I interfered. I'm sorry, Cian."

He's staring at me, unblinking.

"From now on, I'm not interpreting my visions. I promise to tell you everything I see and nothing more."

My chest tightens on a choked laugh as I realize they're all staring at me and my face heats up.

"The point I was trying to make." I suck in an agitated breath. "I fucked up. I do that a lot, but I also learn from my mistakes, so... no, I didn't tell you that stuff earlier to protect you. You don't need my protection. You are a powerful magician. You will fight the Mer. You will kill him." I offer him a conciliatory smile and then huff out an embarrassed breath. Everyone is still looking at me.

"Lilly, how are those rockets coming?" I ask her pointedly, and she blinks at me in confusion before looking back at the rocket she's manifesting.

"Right," she mutters under her breath and starts painting again.

"Sara." Lachlan's voice is rough when he says my name, almost as if it hurts him to say it. I blink back my tears and force myself to look at him. He deserves to know the truth about me before it's too late. Now he can still walk away. He can find a wife better suited to be his Queen. Someone who deserves him...because Lachlan is the best Fae I know.

Arlen said that to me back in Cork, but I didn't believe him. I've never known someone with more integrity, loyalty, and strength.

Lifting my eyes to his, I swallow nervously when I see the expression in them. He's angry with me. Pressing my lips tight together, I try to swallow back my tears, but it doesn't help. I'm crying all over again. Lachlan's looking at me with that hard stare that I hate so much, and I can't stand it. It makes me sob harder. I'm losing him.

"Sara." He repeats my name, and his voice is hoarse, barely above a whisper this time.

"I can do better," I promise him in a low voice. "I know I can. I will be the Queen you need— you just have to give me time to learn. I promise I will stop being so impulsive. I'll stop talking all the time."

Lachlan reaches for my arm and tugs me away from the others.

"I'll learn to shut up and listen more, and I promise I'll stop running away." I'm babbling now, my sobs getting louder. "I can learn," I whisper as he continues leading me away. "Lachlan, please talk to me. I can take anything, just not that look. Please don't hate me."

I don't get a chance to say more. Lachlan cups my face, firmly pressing his thumbs over my lips to silence me. He still hasn't said a word though and I need to know what he's thinking.

He sighs loudly and pulls me against him, wrapping his arms around me. "Ssh, Sara. It's okay." His voice is a low murmur as he rubs my back. "Take a breath. There you go. Okay, breathe in again. Let it go." His hand continues to rub steadily up and down my back. "It's been a long week. You're tired, Sara... and grieving. Everything's going to be okay."

I feel him press a kiss to my head, and my breath shudders as I release it.

"I'm sorry," I mumble into his chest, too scared to see the look in his eyes. "I should have been more honest with you...about everything. My dyslexia... I didn't finish school. I'm not book-smart. I'm just not, and I can't change that. I will never be able to change that and I'm so ashamed because

I never went home when my dad got sick. I wasn't there when my family needed me. And then I wasn't there when you needed me. I run away. I know I do that. I don't want to do that anymore."

"Sara, you ran away from Rohn because your life was in danger. I don't blame you for that."

"But I should have come to you. I should have been honest about my fears. I should have told you why I wasn't doing the work you assigned me. It's not that I didn't want to. I..." my voice falters. "I want to do better... if you'll have me. I know I should step aside and let you find a better Queen. Lars was right about that. I hate that Fae, but I always knew he was right. I'm not the right Queen for you."

"You are the Queen I want." His hand resumes its gentle path up and down my spine as though he senses how much I need that. "The *wife* I want," he continues quietly. "Not because the signs told me to marry you but because I love you. I've always loved you, Sara." He cups my face and tilts it up, forcing me to look him in the eyes. The anger is still there in his gaze, so fierce it hurts me to see it.

"You don't have to earn my love, Sara. You are my Queen." His eyes squeeze shut, and he drops his forehead to mine. "It hurts me to hear you doubt yourself. It hurts me to hear you fighting to stay with me. It's my fault you're questioning my feelings for you, Sara. You are everything to me. Everything." His mouth presses firmly to mine, kissing me hard. "Baby, tell me you hear me. Tell me you know how much I love you."

Chapter 21

L *ACHLAN*
    I have Sara in my arms; her lips are soft and warm. Blinking down at her, I see the same dazed expression on her face that I'm sure is on mine. Fortunately, the despair is gone. I never want to see that look on her face again.

"Sara. Lachlan. Come quick. I can't hold these here much longer," Lilly shouts to get our attention.

I squeeze Sara tight and turn her around. She's pliant in my arms, still shaken from her emotional outpouring. Slipping my arm over her shoulders, I lead her back to the others.

But I needn't have worried; by the time we reach them, she is already steady, her gaze focussed. She pulls away from me and examines the rockets closer.

"Do you think it will work?" Sara directs her question at Aaronn, who only shrugs.

The four rockets are floating in the air side by side and three feet off the ground. My three bodyguards are standing in a row, a makeshift wall to conceal the rockets from the warriors at the gate. We need the element of surprise— especially as we have no idea how powerful Lars is.

Standing to one side, I watch Sara use magic to raise one rocket above the others. She lifts her gaze to mine, and I feel her hesitant question. This is my home she's blowing up, after all. I nod once, and she offers me a small smile.

With only a flick of her wrist, the rocket flies over our heads, picking up speed as it approaches the castle, only to slam into the dark force field and explode on impact. All of us are thrown back by the blast.

"Now we know they work," Cian mutters, picking himself up and dusting himself down. Sara's frowning at the rockets, but Lilly speaks up.

"Aaronn, can you break through the shield? Just enough for the rocket to get through."

Aaronn frowns at his wife, and his gaze flicks to Sara. "Are you ready?" he asks her. She positions herself beside him, watching as Aaronn fires his magic through the force field with just enough power to create a tear in the shield. "I can't hold this for long," he mutters under his breath, already straining to keep the hole open.

We all watch as Sara flings one rocket toward the gap. When it shoots through, she follows quickly with the next two. Aaronn pulls back his magic. The hole seals closed just as the first explosion rips through the air, followed by two more. We hear a scream, followed by shouting, and then an ominous silence before the tower topples. It crashes into the front courtyard, large stones smashing against the ground.

The force field stutters and disappears, but before we can charge the castle, the gates swing open. A line of twenty warriors forms a barricade between us and the castle. All of them Mer. All large and armed with the long, curving blade the Mer prefer.

"Aoife, disappear. Lilly and Sara, stay behind us," Aaronn commands without taking his gaze from the Mer warriors. His voice is cold and stiff with fear.

Glancing at Sara, I catch the amused smirk she tosses Aaronn's way. Clearly, my friend has never seen Sara in action. But even knowing her strength, I catch her eye and shoot her a warning look. She opens her mouth to make a smart retort but then snaps it closed and nods.

Her compliance makes me laugh. "Give the rest of us a chance to do something."

Her wicked grin slips out then, and she winks at me and takes a few steps back, tugging Lilly with her. "We'll be watching from over here," she says innocently. I don't believe her for a minute, but I laugh and return to the gate.

The Mer warriors are waiting for us to charge them, but for a full minute, nothing happens. Nothing. And then a tendril of blue smoke wafts beside me, and Cian is gone. A roar goes up from the Mer warriors, and they leap forward, blades flashing in the sun.

The fighting is intense, and the bit of ground we make is hard-won. I have three warriors around me now, three blades slashing at me. I parry one with the sword in my right hand and stab at another with the dagger in my left. I feel it slice across flesh and hear the angry hiss of the wounded warrior. He redoubles his effort, pushing me back.

"Sara," I roar over my shoulder. "This would be a perfect time to do something." I hear her laughter and the warrior on my left flies through the air. He lands with a sickening crunch against a boulder, and I feel Sara's wince inside me.

It doesn't stop her, though; the other two warriors are tripped up and tossed back. Their eyes are wide when they scramble to their knees, and darting looks at their dwindling number, they leap to their feet and take off down the mountain.

I watch them go. There's no point in pursuing them. With luck, they will be back in Aescheles by tomorrow.

Taking stock, I count another ten warriors. They're retreating, backing through the castle gates, but the last thing I want is a game of hide and seek through the castle.

Pursuing them, I engage one after the other, using my Tracker magic to fight them quickly. They don't stand a chance when I use my magic, and soon only one Mer warrior remains.

The largest one of all.

Cian is fighting him, their blades grinding together, sparking with the force of the blows.

Cian is faster and more agile, but the Mer is stronger...and Cian hasn't slept in days.

Before I can step forward, Aaronn stops me. "No. This is Cian's fight. Wait."

We follow them through the castle gates. The courtyard is strewn with rubble, giving Cian an advantage at last. Lighter on his feet, he dances through the wreckage parrying each hammer blow of the Mer's blade until the warrior trips over a pile of rubble and lands with a grunt, stumbling to get back to his feet.

Cian doesn't give him a chance. He drives the blade through the Mer's heart and stumbles back, panting with the effort.

Even from here, I can see the tears on Cian's face. The Mer is saying something to him, a sneer on his lips. I can't hear the words but see Cian pale and watch as his legs buckle. Reaching him just in time, I pull him upright.

Aaronn is with me, and we help Cian out of the castle gates. Leaving Cian with the others, I return to the dying Mer. He's gasping his last breaths, that cruel sneer still on his lips, but then he looks past my shoulder.

Turning, I see Lars stepping out of the castle doorway. He seems confused by the chaos outside, and then I notice the bloody gash on his head and the way he stumbles unsteadily. He ignores me, making his way over to the wreckage of the tower, clambering shakily over the fallen debris.

"What are you doing, Lars?"

He's turning over stones, searching, his movements becoming frantic. But then Sara's voice in my head is louder than anything else.

Get out of the castle. Run, Lachlan. Get out now.

The ground beneath my feet begins to shake, and for a minute, I'm frozen. Large cracks snake across the castle walls, tearing the castle apart. The trembling beneath my feet is increasing.

Lachlan, Sara's desperate cry finally pushes me forward. Everything is falling, the walls breaking. Glass smashing. I'm only feet away from the gates when a bright light shoots up from deep within the mountain. What's left of the tower is blasted into dust as the light escapes. Chunks of masonry bounce off my back as I run. The castle is coming down around me. It feels like it's trying to swallow me up into it.

SARA

It all happens too quickly.

Lachlan is running toward us, the ground shaking with the force of the eruption, and then it starts to tip. Even from here, I can see the confusion on his face as he turns away from me. He's slipping on the loose stones, being dragged back.

The eastern wing of the castle has broken loose from the mountain and is tipping precariously into the valley below. Nothing happens for one horrible long minute, and then a roar bellows from the mountain beneath us. The castle slides from its perch, disappearing from sight, and the courtyard walls crash in on themselves.

"I can't see Lachlan," my voice is only a whisper compared to the noise and chaos around us. The thud of the castle hitting the valley floor reverberates beneath our feet. Aaronn's arm clamps around my chest, holding me to him. Not letting me run. Not letting me go. "I can't see him. I can't see him. Aaronn, please."

Where the castle stood is a cloud of dust. Debris is strewn across the mountaintop, blown in every direction by the blast. The only movement is the shifting dust as it slowly drifts down the mountain.

Sunlight beats down on us from a clear blue sky, and the mountain is...singing. I can hear it. I can feel it in my blood.

"Where is he?"

Nobody will answer me. Aaronn still has me locked in place, and I'm desperate now. Clawing at his arm, trying to pull it off me. Terrified that the castle took Lachlan with it back into the earth.

"No, Etain, he didn't deserve that. No, please tell me you haven't taken him," I whimper.

The only answer I receive is a soft breeze blowing over us, and finally, Aaronn releases me. I stumble forward, running to the last spot I saw Lachlan.

I pick my way across the piles of fallen stone. I'm so scared of what I'll find. I don't want to see his body crushed beneath these rocks, but this is worse.

Where is he? I can't lose him now. Please, no, not another person. Not him.

"Sara." Aaronn's shout spins me around. Aaronn stands at the mountain's edge, his gaze trained on the valley below.

The castle lies broken like a child's lego blocks dropped on the floor. Please don't let him be down there, I pray silently, unable to tear my eyes away from the scene, searching frantically for any sign of life.

"Sara." Aaronn's fingers dig into my shoulders as he turns me in another direction. "Look. Not in the valley. Look over there."

And then I see what's caught his attention. On the mountain's edge, a short climb down is the most enormous white leopard I have ever seen. It's watching us, a low growl rumbling from its chest. But it's the Fae he's standing over that makes my heart beat faster.

Lachlan. But he's so still. From here, all I can see are his jean-clad legs covered in dust and dirt. It looks like he fell onto a stone overhang...or was pulled.

"Wait." Aaronn cautions me as I tug to get free from his hold. He steps in front of me and starts climbing down the mountain. He's walking so slowly I want to scream at him, but the leopard hasn't ceased its growling, and as we approach, it hunkers low over Lachlan's body...protecting him.

Aaronn stops six feet away from the leopard. The growling sounds louder up close, and the cat's eyes narrow as he assesses us, limbs poised to attack.

"Wait." I touch Aaron's arm lightly, not wanting to make big gestures that will unsettle the leopard. "Let me," I whisper, already stepping out from behind him.

Taking a careful step forward, I see those amber eyes latch on me, staring unblinkingly. Another step, and the growling falls quiet. The leopard steps across Lachlan's body and approaches me.

"It's okay," I croon softly, unsure which of us I'm reassuring— the tense warrior at my back, the leopard, or myself. "It's okay," I whisper again and reach out slowly to lay a hand on the leopard's head. A loud purr rumbles from its chest as my fingers rub through its fur. I keep my gestures slow and gentle, and when his amber eyes slide closed, I finally let myself smile.

Withdrawing my hand slowly, I take another step toward Lachlan. The leopard follows me but stops and waits while I kneel beside him. I'm holding my breath, too scared to find out if he's alive, and then I detect the gentle motion of his chest and shove my fist in my mouth to stifle my sob.

Lachlan's eyes blink open, and I see his face scrunch in confusion as he stares at the sky and then turns to scan his surroundings. He finds me and stills for a split second, but I stop him quickly as he tries to lift his head.

"Don't. I want Aoife to look at you first." He grimaces and blinks his eyes as a nod. A sure sign that he's in pain. "Aaronn?" I call back to him.

"On it," Aaronn shouts over his shoulder, already climbing the mountain.

"What happened?" Lachlan's voice is hoarse, and he coughs as he tries to speak, wincing when he does.

"Sssh," I murmur, reaching for his hand and squeezing his fingers. I'm scared to touch him in case I hurt him, but I need to feel his skin against mine.

"Sara." His eyes close, but when they blink open again, he looks at something over my shoulder. "Sara, why is there a leopard sitting with us?" I hear the bemusement in his voice and something else...fear, nerves.

He's remembering the leopard his father killed. The angry beast that is still such a massive part of his childhood. His nightmares.

Lachlan has gone rigid beside me. I squeeze his hand and wait for him to look at me. It takes a long agonizing minute for him to drag his eyes away from the leopard.

"He saved you, Lachlan. When we found you, he was standing over you, protecting you."

I watch as Lachlan looks back at the leopard, three lines creasing his brow. "He saved me? Me? Are you sure?" I want to laugh at the disbelief on his face.

"Yes."

I feel hot breath on my neck and see Lachlan's eyes widen in fright. Turning, I find the leopard standing at my shoulder. His head is a foot above my own, and his amber eyes are trained on Lachlan. Fear passes through Lachlan's gaze and then something else that looks like grief to me.

The leopard lowers his head and in the next instant a large pink tongue swipes out and licks Lachlan across the cheek. Lachlan goes rigid, his eyes opening in shock.

The leopard does it again, and Lachlan's mouth twitches as he tries to hold back a laugh. His eyes, full of amusement, find mine as the leopard bows his head and rubs it against his chest.

"I think you're forgiven, baby," I whisper, trying not to cry again. Hearing voices from above, I turn to see Aaronn and Aoife climbing carefully down to us.

The leopard lifts its head and sniffs the air, then leaps across Lachlan. It scrambles up the nearest boulder and jumps down the other side of it. I try to follow the leopard with my eyes but soon lose it as it blends into the mountain rocks, slinking away and out of sight.

Chapter 22

L*ACHLAN*
  Cork, Ireland

My first time in the human world, and I haven't so much as set foot outside this house. I've barely left the room. The O'Driscoll women have become my jailors— bed rest, they declared, and nothing will change their minds.

Having Sara in bed with me is the only thing that's made it bearable. She seems reluctant to leave me, and no matter how often I tell her to go— she won't. It amuses me, though. She's so restless she's nearly tearing the hair out of her head, but her stubborn streak is winning, and she remains glued to my side.

The door opens as if I've conjured her with my thoughts, and she comes in holding two mugs. She nudges the door closed with her bum, then climbs into the bed beside me, offering me one of the mugs.

"Camomile tea for the patient. Aoife's orders," she says and waits for me to sit up. She's already taking small sips of her coffee as though she can't get it into her fast enough. "You'll have to buy me a new coffee machine."

And I have a sudden image of her new Nespresso coffee machine lying smashed into tiny pieces in the valley below Rohn.

"You could always switch to camomile tea," I suggest, taking a sip from my mug.

Sara's nose wrinkles in disgust. "Not a chance. The chamomile tea is all yours." She crosses her long legs and turns to face me. She's now sitting cross-legged on the covers, wearing tiny cotton shorts and an even tinier tank top.

I admit I'm a little distracted, my eyes roving all over her, hungry. Starved. We're not allowed to have sex until my ribs are better. Aoife's been giving me daily healing sessions, but even she can't fix the damage overnight.

Another two days, she promised yesterday, and I grimace at the thought of waiting that long. I want to pull Sara onto my lap now. Bury myself inside her and stay there – forever.

"Are you in pain?" Sara asks, noticing my grimace.

She has no idea. I'm so hard it's a throbbing ache between my thighs. She tilts her head to the side, still studying me, lines etching her brow as she frowns. I brush my thumb across those lines, smoothing them away. The braids are gone, and her orange hair is once more its natural afro.

"I like your hair like this."

The worry lines smooth away, and she grins. "Arlen will be furious. It took him forever to put those braids in."

"He'll get over it." I don't want to talk about my brother now.

"Lachlan." Her hand stretches across the covers and touches mine lightly. Her touch is almost shy. "I wanted." She stops and licks her lips, her gaze slipping away.

"Sara?"

She huffs an embarrassed laugh and looks back at me, now meeting my gaze. "I wanted to talk to you about us. But only if you're feeling up to it," she adds quickly, almost apologetically.

"I've got nowhere else to be, Sara." She grins at the sardonic tone in my voice.

"It's only two more days, you big baby. And then I promise I'll take you out and show you everything Cork has to offer."

"It's not Cork I want to explore." I trail my hand up her naked thigh. She bats my hand away with a grin.

"No sex. Doctor's orders."

Wrapping my hand around the back of her neck, I tug her closer and kiss her. "Aoife's not a doctor. We might need a second opinion." And then I'm forced to take a breath at the sharp pain that pierces my side. Flopping back against the pillows, I glare at her. "Fine. Doctor's orders. I'll drink my chamomile tea and be good."

She laughs at me. "I love you," she says, still laughing, but then she looks stricken, and her laughter dries up. "I'm sorry. I know you don't like it when I say that."

"Sara?" How can she even think that? Now? After everything else that's happened between us.

"Are you sure?" she asks suddenly. I have no idea what she's talking about. "About us. Me, I mean. Are you sure you want to stay married to me?" My heart pinches at the look on her face. It's almost as if we're back on the mountain. Those same old doubts are there, still.

"Firstly, there's nothing to decide. We're bonded. That's unbreakable." I try the logical approach first.

"So you're stuck with me whether you want to be or not," she says with a frown. Okaaay, the logical approach didn't work as planned.

"With you, on you, under you, pressed up against you." I remember our night in Aescheles, and the flare in her eyes tells me she's thinking of the same thing. That's better.

"Lachlan." Her frown returns. I place my mug on the floor beside the bed and reach for her hand.

"Tell me what's worrying you about being my wife."

She looks down at our clasped hands. "I want to be your wife," she starts slowly. "But...I don't want to embarrass you or mess up. I see the amount of correspondence you get from the other Kingdoms. I should be able to help you with your work, but I can't even do that."

I rub my thumb lightly across the back of her hand. "You can help me in other ways. You do help me." When she frowns again, I chuckle. "No, I'm not talking about sex."

Her sigh is despondent. "I don't know, Lachlan. I make so many mistakes. You know I do. I'm always saying the wrong thing. I find it impossible to hide what I'm thinking or feeling," she trails off and bites her lip, a nervous tic. "I don't want you to be ashamed of me. Ever."

"Come here." I hold out my arm, and she shifts around and tucks herself underneath it. Her movements are slow and careful as she eases in next to me. I tug her head down, so it rests on my shoulder. She notices my wince and frowns up at me.

"Lachlan—"

"Sssh, I'll live." Her shoulder beneath my palm is silky smooth, and I can't stop trailing my fingers along her skin. "Sara, you keep pointing out all the ways in which you're not suited to a royal life." She's quiet, her breath tickles my neck, and I rest my head against hers. "But what about everything that makes you perfect for this life?"

"Like?"

"You love me, for a start." She laughs, and I squeeze her shoulder. Why can't she see how amazing she is? "You're brave. That's vital for a Queen— especially a Queen in Rohn. You know we're not an easy bunch."

Her head pops up, and slowly I pull my arm back, lowering it to my side.

"You're compassionate— again, an important quality in a ruler. And, as far as I'm concerned, you don't say the wrong things. You tell the truth, and that's not always a comfortable thing to hear, but you never lie, you never mislead."

"I think you should nominate me for sainthood," she says, rolling her eyes.

"No. I like your wicked side too much."

And I love seeing the grin that slips across her face when I say that.

"But your councilors hate me." She raises another objection.

"I hate to tell you this, but I think they're all dead— problem solved."

Sara rolls her eyes and grimaces. "That's not something to joke about, Lachlan. We have no idea who was in the castle that day."

"It was your vision that showed us the way, Sara. Your magic freed us from the darkness. What more proof do you want that you are the Queen Rohn needs? You are the Queen the Rohn Fae want," I add deliberately.

Aaronn and Cian have been back to Rohn every day since the explosion. They've been supervising the clean-up of the castle while I've been stuck here in bed.

"Have I mentioned how perfect it is that you have a Portal in your house?"

Sara rolls her eyes at me. "Only about three hundred times in the last five days."

"So you will know already that Aaronn returns daily with news from Rohn. With requests for our return. Our," I emphasize and enjoy watching the embarrassed flush that darkens her cheeks. "The Rohn Fae want you, Sara. You. And more importantly, I want you."

SARA

Rohn Kingdom, 3 weeks later

As we approach the gate, my heart beats faster. From outside the city walls, I can hear the raised voices, and I pull in a nervous breath...hoping. This is our first time returning since the explosion, and I was so worried last night I couldn't sleep.

The Rohn Fae have been waiting for news of their King for three long weeks, but selfishly I made them wait. Our time in Cork is Lachlan's first holiday in fifteen years. I didn't want him to rush back before he was ready. We both know the amount of work that waits for us here.

We step through the gate, and both of us stop in amazement. While we knew they were eager for our return, I don't think we expected a welcome like this.

The main street is lined with Fae. Children are running in and out amongst the adults. From somewhere, I can hear music playing, and as I sniff the air, I catch the scent of smoke and...I can't place it, but it smells delicious. My stomach grumbles, and Lachlan looks over at me and grins.

"You should have eaten breakfast."

"I was too nervous," I admit. The look in his eyes is like a giant hug, and I will never know how I ever thought this Fae King was cold and distant.

We declared our weeks in Ireland an unofficial honeymoon and spent our time exploring and having sex in every conceivable position...and location. The memory of our run from the security guard at Trinity College is something I will never forget; even thinking about it now makes my face heat in embarrassment.

Lachlan tilts his head, studying my face, and then lowers his voice. "As much as I would love to know what's caused that blush on your cheeks, I think we have too many witnesses to start that conversation."

The devil.

He knows exactly what I'm thinking about. His sudden laughter when I glare at him confirms it.

But a line of soldiers has stopped before us. They bow low. They no longer prostrate themselves on the ground. One more good thing that's come from the changes in Rohn.

The music ceases, and the soldiers swivel neatly and proceed up the main street, signaling the start of the parade.

"Time to greet everybody. Are you ready?"

Not really. I try to keep the grimace off my face. "What do I do?"

"Smile. Say hello. Be you." Lachlan gives me a reassuring smile. "You take that side of the street, and I'll take this one," he says, pointing to the right." He winks at me, then. "Let's see who gets the biggest crowd." Lachlan's laughing at me again. Teasing me out of my anxiety. He's good at that.

So many Fae are lining the streets, crowding down, pushing to get a place on Main Street. I find myself blinking back tears as I greet everyone on the left side of the street. I knew the Rohn Fae wanted *our* return, but a part of me still believed it was only a figure of speech. It was Lachlan they longed to see. He is their King and the Fae they all look up to and admire. Admire, not fear. I hope, at last, he's learned that lesson.

It doesn't take me long to realize that he's right. Gone are the sideways looks and suspicious glares. The Fae are eager to talk to me, their children pushing close to give me small bunches of flowers. So many that I'm forced to hand them to the soldiers walking behind us.

And that sight makes me want to giggle. These burly, gruff soldiers with their long hair and bushy beards carrying bunches of flowers as they follow in our wake. I can't help thinking that there's something poetic about it. A symbol of the new Rohn, perhaps. Soldiers carrying flowers instead of swords.

Our parade through the streets of Rohn takes over an hour, but we do not want to rush this. These Fae have been through too much in recent weeks. Too much uncertainty and fear...and change. Yes, that most dreadful thing that the Rohn Fae fear so much.

Lachlan did warn me— the Rohn Fae hate change. And the rebuilding of the castle is no exception. I'm losing count of the times I've been asked about the changes. The new castle looks nothing like the old one. Once it's finished, it will be modern and light. Dare I say, elegant? I bite back a smile at this thought.

Lachlan catches my eye and raises an eyebrow in question. We are on opposite sides of the street, both doing our share of greetings. I'm gratified to see my side of the road is as busy as his. Maybe he's right after all. The Rohn Fae have finally accepted me as one of their own. I hope so— because this Kingdom feels more like home with every day that passes.

We've reached the northern gate, and Lachlan holds out his hand for mine.

"What happened to no PDA for royals?" I tease him.

He grins and tugs me close, planting a quick kiss on my lips, much to the shock of the Fae around us. He doesn't seem to care, and even though a startled silence follows the kiss, his eyes burn with mischief. Placing a hand on my lower back, he nudges me through the gate, and a cheer erupts behind us.

"You see?" he murmurs to me. "They just need time." I can't help laughing at him. He's so arrogant in his confidence.

"And what do you need?" I tease him.

His eyes flare amber when he looks my way. He's still holding my hand firmly clasped in his. *You, Sara. Tonight, tomorrow, forever.*

I thought you didn't like communicating like this.

No.

Yes, I argue stubbornly. *You said you didn't want me inside you.*

Well, it's true that I'd rather be inside you. Lachlan grins wickedly and laughs when I roll my eyes. *It's not that I didn't want you inside me. I was protecting you. I thought the only way to keep you safe was to keep you far away from my beast.*

But I love your beast. It still makes me laugh to say things like that. He's laughing now, too, shaking his head at me. But he leans in and brushes a kiss to my neck.

"He loves you too."

Epilogue

C *LODAGH*
  The city of Shiam, The Desert Kingdom

I would say this is just bloody typical, but that sounds too much like whining, and if there's one thing I hate, it's whining.

This trip seemed like a good idea back in the Elvin Forest. Well, a straightforward idea anyway. If not necessarily a good one. Use the Rohn Portal to reach the desert on the other side of Soraya. Find the dragons and return the baby dragon to its mother. Return to Portal. Return to Cork. Get back to work. Simple. Straightforward. Achievable goals.

I look around at the dark prison walls and then glare at Izod.

This is all his fault.

"You might have mentioned you were wanted for treason before you offered to escort me here." He turns his dark eyes in my direction but says nothing as usual. If I hadn't heard it with my own ears, I'd swear this Fae doesn't have a voice. He hasn't said more than three words since we left the forest, and those three words in chronological order were—

OH. NO. FUCK.

That's it, and it's not like he's offered an explanation for our imprisonment in the days since then. I only know what the douchebag general spat at us when he caught us.

"Izod, son of Malik, you are under arrest. Charged with the murder of the King and high treason."

Murder. Treason. And not any old treason. High treason, whatever that means.

Murder. And Izod had the gall to call me bloodthirsty.

I glance sideways at him again. His head is tipped back against the wall now, his eyes closed. His body looks relaxed, his legs stretched out in front of him and his hands resting loosely on his thighs. He looks like he's taking a nap.

I wish I could sleep. I haven't slept in days, not properly, anyway. I'm too wired, too anxious. I have no idea if the others found Cian. Is my brother still alive?

I'm having a difficult time sitting still and wriggle again on the hard floor. I've spent most of our time here pacing this small room. My legs are restless with the forced inactivity.

Oh my god, I want to run. I can't stand this confinement. I run every day when I'm at home. I need to run. I get twitchy if I don't.

Leaping to my feet, I resume my pacing. It's a small room. Six steps one way, and I'm forced to turn around. Another six steps back to the other side. Fuck I'm going crazy.

"How much longer will they keep us in here?" Izod ignores both my pacing and my question, but his closed eyelids flicker, so I know he's heard me. "Fuck," I growl and punch the wall, moaning at the pain that shoots through my hand.

Still, Izod says nothing, but his right hand jerks in his lap, and his mouth turns down in what appears to be a frown. I can't believe he's just ignoring me. He seemed like a nice guy when we were with the others.

Nice— for a Fae, that is. I'm revising my good opinion of him when his eyes snap open, and he looks at me. His eyes flick down to my hand.

"That was a stupid thing to do," he says calmly, silently pushing himself up.

Everything about this Fae is silent and graceful. It's one of the first things I noticed about him. When he moves, it appears weightless, a gliding through space.

He's at my side now, reaching for my hand. He traps it between his own two, and when I try to tug it free, his eyes flick up to mine. "Be still," he says quietly.

Izod makes a cupping shape of his two hands with mine in the center. He leans forward, bringing his mouth to the top of our hands, and blows hot air onto my aching knuckles. I feel his breath against my skin— dry, hot, and soothing. He does it again, and my hand tingles.

"There," he says, releasing my hand. He doesn't step back, though. He's looking at me with a worried frown, his eyes flitting over my face, searching for something. "We will have company soon. Whatever you do." Izod pauses and gives me an intent look. "Do not speak. Nothing. Not one word, Clodagh. If you want to see Cork again, you will look at the ground and remain silent." His voice drops low. "No eye contact. No speaking. Do you understand?" He continues to watch me, waiting for me to agree.

Can I trust this weird, silent Fae? "One question." I see the surprise in his gaze, but he nods. "Does Lachlan know who you are and what you did?"

"Yes."

Right so. If Lachlan trusts this Fae, then maybe I can too. I nod and step back, needing some space between us. "Okay. We do this your way."

A ghost of a smile slips across his face before he points to the wall behind us. "Sit there. Keep your eyes on the floor. Pull your magic in. Hide it as much as you can."

I do as he asks, only glancing up when he crouches before me. He reaches around his neck and slips a leather cord over his head. On the end of it dangles a red and black amulet. It flares brightly in the dark, and Izod stares at it for a moment, a crease furrowing across his brow as his eyes flick back to me.

I hear footsteps approaching, and Izod leans forward and slips the cord around my neck. Tugging my top away from my skin, he drops the amulet inside. It falls between my breasts, warm against my skin. He stares at me.

"Remember. Not one word," he says.

Izod stands to face the approaching warriors but I keep my eyes on the stone floor, staring at the sand that refuses to stay outside. It coats the floor, blowing in through the small window. I trace patterns with my fingertip while my ears strain to follow the conversation.

It's a different Fae this time, but I like this Fae even less than the douchebag general. His voice is cold. I cannot see his face, but I imagine the sneer on his lips and the cruelty in his eyes.

Yes, I get all of that from the sound of his voice. I have a vivid imagination. This Fae might be a gentle puppy for all I know. He's not, though; my magic is warning me of that.

For once in your life, Clodagh, do as you're told. Look down. Do not react. Do not speak.

"Who's the girl?" I hear this new Fae ask and feel the heat of his gaze on me. The interest is like a dark tendril weaving across the room to wrap itself around me. I squirm where I'm sitting.

Keep looking down, Clodagh.

I hear Izod step to the right, shielding me from the Fae's view, and the dark tendrils slip away. "She is Princess Clodagh of Soraya. Queen Aisleen's daughter."

He hesitates. It is only the tiniest pause. I might be the only one who hears it.

"She is my wife. We've come home, brother."

Dear Reader,

Thank you for taking the time to read this book. I hope you enjoyed it. If so, please consider leaving a review online. It helps other readers to take a chance on my stories. If you're interested in more information about my upcoming books the best place to do that is on my website www.kathleenwaterfall.com

Kathleen Waterfall

Books by Kathleen Waterfall

The Fae of Emuria Series

1. Into the Looking Glass
2. Into the Clouds
3. Into the Fire
4. Into the Dark
5. Into the Deep

THE DELAURENTIS BROTHERS

1. Always You
2. You, Again
3. You and Me

Milton Keynes UK
Ingram Content Group UK Ltd.
UKHW010631041223
433752UK00001B/41